DANCING IN THE BARON'S SHADOW

FABIENNE JOSAPHAT

The Unnamed Press
Los Angeles, CA

The Unnamed Press
P.O. Box 411272
Los Angeles, CA 90041

Published in North America by The Unnamed Press.

1 3 5 7 9 10 8 6 4 2

Copyright 2016 © Fabienne Josaphat

ISBN: 978-1-939419-57-6

Library of Congress Control Number: 2015959965

This book is distributed by Publishers Group West

Designed & typeset by Jaya Nicely

Cover design by Scott Arany

My dead sleep in this earth; this soil is tainted red

with the blood of generations of men who carry my name;

I am the direct descendant, twice over, of the very man

who founded this nation.

Therefore, I have decided to stay here,

and possibly, to die here.

—Jacques Stephen Alexis (1922–1961)

author, excerpt from his letter to Haitian

president François Duvalier, June 2, 1960

PORT-AU-PRINCE
1965

ONE

Raymond counted his money quickly, licking a greasy thumb to peel apart the gourdes. The dingy bills left an invisible layer of dirt on his hands. Some of the numbers on them were indecipherable, edges and corners smudged by time and friction. The paper's condition aside, there wasn't enough of it.

"Nineteen...twenty."

He laughed ruefully. To be sure, twenty gourdes was not enough. *But we have to make it work,* he told himself, *despite everything.* His fingers rubbed against the portrait of François Duvalier. Even on faded paper, the president's eyes were accusing, spying on him through thick-rimmed glasses, as unrelenting as the man's lifetime term. Raymond shuffled the cash into a miserably thin stack, stuffed it in his back pocket, and turned up the radio. With no idea how long his passenger would be at the brothel, Raymond figured his favorite station, Radio Lakay, would have to keep him company. The cheerful DJ was just finishing the weather forecast. "Here's to a sunny weekend ahead, and don't forget, my good friends, curfew starts at eight p.m. sharp once again, that's right! Staying in effect until further notice."

Music burst from Raymond's scratchy old speakers. *Konpa.* Its rhythms were intended to carry away problems. *Too bad they always come back,* Raymond thought. His eyes swiveled up to the coral-pink building, its yellow shutters and doors open wide to the street. A hand-painted sign in a florid cursive read: "Chez Madame Fils." For just a moment, he let his gaze linger on the pretty women who clung to the balcony, blowing kisses and waving at the men who passed by. They were without doubt the most beautiful hookers in the country, he thought. Used to be, they'd bide their time, only coming out at night when the action picked up, catching the sex tourists' horny eyes with bright floral dresses, but then the sex tourists stopped coming. Now the bored women hung around all day, entertaining one another by shouting insults at the scandalized mothers rushing past. Still, Chez Madame Fils Snack Bar and Disco continued to do a brisk lunch business, and at night, the music got turned up, the rum began to flow, and locals steadily trickled in. Raymond sometimes picked up a sandwich from the snack bar, but he stayed clear of the women. *Come on, man,* he thought, anxious to drive his passenger home and pocket a few more gourdes before curfew.

He adjusted his visor and gazed at the photo tucked into the flap: a small boy with a melon-shaped head Raymond lovingly stroked and a little girl with red ribbons in every tiny braid. Both were flashing giant smiles next to their mother, Yvonne, whose face blossomed like a black hibiscus under a scarf. Enos was the spitting image of his father, his skin always glistening in the blaze of summer. Adeline favored her mother, with bony brown cheekbones and a spear for a tongue. Raymond smiled. Just this morning, as he dropped them at school, she'd tried again to convince him he didn't need to take the time off work to pick them up. "We can walk home," she assured him, squeezing her little brother's hand.

They could. He knew that. But he wanted to give this to his children: the gift of transportation, something he'd never had himself. Raymond had walked several miles to school in bad shoes, on harsh country roads of gravel and stone. Whenever he reminisced about his country days Yvonne, would smile at the children. "See how much your father does for you?" But it was true. Now that he had a life and a family in the city, he wanted to afford his offspring the luxury of a car. Even if "luxury" was this old beat-up Datsun taxi, a red ribbon tied to the rearview mirror to signal that he was still on duty.

He smoothed a dog-ear from the photograph with a blackened fingernail and sighed.

"*Pitit se richès malere!*"

Raymond jumped and turned to peer out the window. Faton had snuck up to the car door, a gap-toothed grin on his boyish face. "It's true what they say." Faton nodded, pointing at the photograph. "Children are the wealth of the poor."

Raymond turned the music down, surprised that he'd been too absorbed in his thoughts to notice the stench of leather and dye that signaled Faton's approach. Ever since Faton quit driving taxis—a trade he'd learned from Raymond—and started a job at the tannery, he carried the odor of decomposed cowhide wherever he went. Raymond covered his mouth and nose in exaggerated disgust.

"Quit busting my balls. You know it's just the lime they use in the plant," Faton said, flashing another gap-toothed smile. "No big deal."

"That's what you think," Raymond complained behind his fingers.

"Hey, we all need to make a living. This"—he tapped the roof of Raymond's old Datsun—"just doesn't cut it. Leather might stink, but it's honest work, and there are perks." Faton lowered his voice to whisper, "Whatever keeps the Devil off my back," before breaking into loud laughter.

Raymond managed a weak smile. He could hear his wife asking: If driving a cab doesn't pay enough for this single guy, what hope is there for us?

"You better stop worrying about bullshit details like the smell if you're seriously thinking about coming to work with me. Five hundred gourdes a month doesn't stink too bad, right? No more scouring the slums for customers, no more waiting at the wharf for tourists or for these losers to get the job done." Faton cast a disdainful eye at Chez Madame Fils.

"I've never said anything about coming to work for you," Raymond said, looking again for his missing customer. But the truth was five hundred gourdes sounded like a dream when he was making twenty gourdes at the end of the day. Raymond hadn't made that much money in a long time. Two years ago, after the Barbot affair had threatened to overthrow Duvalier, nightly curfews were imposed in Port-au-Prince, decimating the taxi business. Especially with competition from the dirt-cheap tap-taps, with all that seating—however horribly cramped—in their covered pickup truck beds.

"You have to survive, man!" Faton pressed.

Raymond nodded. This was what people talked about now. Survival.

"Just say the word when you're ready," Faton said, adjusting the gold chain around his neck and hovering closer. "I'll put in a word with the boss. It's the least I can do."

Faton's thick Afro didn't fit through the Datsun's half-open window, and for this, Raymond was eternally grateful. Still, he wondered whether he stunk too now, and how hard it would be to wash off, especially when water had become a luxury for his family. Faton stepped back, grabbed a plastic pick from his back pocket, and ran it through his hair, checking his reflection in Raymond's back window. Then he gave Raymond an appraising look. "You know, I don't understand you sometimes. Why are you still doing this?"

"I drive taxis. That's what I know." *What in God's name is taking this john so long?* Raymond glared at the brothel. A Jeep caught his eye as it pulled up to the curb three blocks away. He changed the subject: "You grabbing dinner now?"

"Already did." Faton lived a block west of Chez Madame Fils. He was in the habit of eating in the neighborhood after work. When times were better, Raymond sometimes took a break and joined him.

Five men hopped out of the Jeep. Three wore dark blue uniforms. Two, civilian clothes. Faces obscured behind dark sunglasses. Raymond squinted, trying to get a better look. His muscles tightened, and a chill wormed its way up his spine. The men began shouting, swinging their pistols and rifles around nonchalantly. One of them, in a soft hat and a red ascot, cradled something against his chest. Raymond squinted again and caught the outline of a tommy gun, its barrel glinting in the early evening light. The girls on the balcony disappeared, silently pulling the shutters closed behind them.

Faton followed his friend's gaze. The shouting was garbled at this distance, but there was no question who the men were. And with each step they took, pedestrians fled. Raymond saw the distinct arc of a machete blade in one man's hand. He clutched the steering wheel.

"Can't they ever leave us alone?" Faton gasped.

Raymond shook his head, checking the ignition to make sure his keys were still in place. He might have to get out of Cité Simone. If only the damn john would finish his business...

"This is bad," Faton mumbled under his breath. "What the fuck do they want?"

The Milice de Volontaires de la Sécurité Nationale, known as the Tonton Macoute, didn't need a specific reason for anything they did. They were the president's "children." Devil children of the gray-haired man who enjoyed dressing himself up like Baron Samedi—the Vaudou guardian of cemeteries—in a black suit and matching hat. A sinister figurehead for a sinister country.

"M'ale! I'm out of here." Faton took a quick step away from the Datsun, hissing, "I don't like the look of this."

Raymond watched Faton sprint to his van, the words "Tannerie Nationale S.A." etched on both its sides. He clambered in and took off without a glance back. Raymond sank lower in his seat, praying for invisibility. The Macoutes disappeared into a convenience store, a blue building with its name painted in yellow letters: "Epicerie Saint-Georges."

The Datsun's vinyl seat squeaked under his weight as he rolled up his window. Faton's sour smell still hung in the air. From the radio, a familiar jingle filled the car. Nemours Jean-

Baptiste's Super Ensemble crooned a jolly tune. *Our new song spreads joy all over the streets.*

The remains of sunset cast an amber glow inside the Datsun as Raymond shut his radio off. The shop owners rushed about, casting nervous glances over their shoulders before quickening their steps down the street. Small children, playing in stagnant puddles of rain and gutter water, lingered for a few minutes until their parents found them and hauled them off, one by one. The taxi and tap-tap drivers stationed down the street chugged their bottles of cola, tossed their empty paper plates, and vanished. Street vendors picked up their blankets spread with candy and snacks and knickknacks, hoisted them onto their heads, and ran. Raymond clasped his hands around his steering wheel. Damn it! He had to get out of here. Raymond glanced one last time at the brothel, but nothing stirred inside. The john wasn't going to come out. Not now. *Go home, Raymond,* he thought, even as he imagined the look on Yvonne's face when she found out how little he'd made today. *Forget the fare.*

A scream pierced the eerie silence. He listened. Someone was shouting for help, and a familiar dread crawled under Raymond's skin. Then a shot rang out somewhere, probably inside the convenience store.

"Screw this," Raymond muttered. He was reaching for the keys in the ignition when a fist pounded against his window. Once again, he jumped and peered through the glass. Outside, a man, haggard, his eyes stretched wide, beat a wet palm against the glass.

"What the hell do you think you're doing, man? Get away from my car!" Raymond shooed the man like he would a stray animal. "Go on!"

"Help me, brother! Please."

The man's breath fogged the window. Raymond faltered at the sight of those bulging eyes, wide with terror, staring into his. Pleading. This was the face of despair. The man looked over his shoulder, and Raymond saw a woman on the curb in a housedress and slippers. She was rocking a child in her arms, her hair loose under a turban. Raymond shook his head and averted his eyes as he turned the ignition and the old Datsun started up. "I'm off duty, friend, and there's a curfew."

"They're going to kill us."

Raymond noticed the man's shirt had been torn loose at the shoulder. Something wasn't right.

"I—I don't want any trouble," Raymond stammered.

"My wife," the man shouted, pointing at her. "My baby. They are innocent. *Sove nou!*"

Raymond's fingers burned as he squeezed the steering wheel. The hot air was suffocating. From down the narrow street, he heard the Macoutes yelling as they spilled out of the convenience store. They were headed his way, clubbing the men and women who fled in fear, shoving them into the gutters, firing their revolvers in all directions.

The man slapped his palm against Raymond's window once more. The woman squealed. "They're coming. In the name of God, brother!" the man implored.

Raymond's eyes went to the Macoutes. They'd paused to terrorize a woman on the sidewalk, but one of them was staring at his taxi. Suddenly, the man shouted, pointing directly toward Raymond, and the other thugs snapped to attention.

Raymond's hand went to the clutch. He looked again at the window and saw large beads of sweat running down the man's face. Saw the fear in the woman's eyes. Saw the photograph of his own children smiling back at him on the visor.

What kind of man was he?

A cold calm settled inside him, and without another thought, he swung his arm around and unlocked the back door.

"Get in!"

Raymond aimed the car straight for the Macoutes. The men stopped short, uncertain whether to dodge the oncoming vehicle or stand their ground. At the last second, Raymond yanked the wheel right, hurtling the Datsun onto a narrow side street. He floored the gas pedal and the engine roared. He veered left to avoid hitting a woman carrying a large basket of bread on her head. Pedestrians yelped as they leapt out of the way, cursing angrily. Raymond's forehead burned with a sudden fever as he squinted into the rearview mirror. Among a melee of men and women darting for the sidewalk, he caught sight of the Macoutes' Jeep, its silhouette gaining on him in the mirror. The barrel of a rifle glimmered in the dying light. Raymond stomped harder on the gas. In the backseat, the infant burst into tears as Raymond swung the Datsun to the right, tires screeching in protest. Raymond's heart was pounding a tam-tam in his chest. His mouth and throat were parched. *We're all dead.*

Behind him, the Jeep kept pace. A Tonton Macoute's head popped out of a window, and Raymond saw his arms flailing in the wind like skeletal tree branches. The Macoute was resting a rifle against his shoulder, adjusting it, aiming. *Boom!*

Raymond hung a left, hurtling the wrong way down a narrow one-way street. A stray dog jumped onto the sidewalk just in time. Raymond swung down another narrow street. Behind them came a screeching of brakes and rending of metal against stone, followed by a howl. The dog's fate was clear. He took another right, then two quick lefts down the tightest streets in Cité Simone, and then, finally, the little taxi burst out onto Boulevard La Saline. Raymond squinted at his mirror. No Jeep.

The speedometer's needle quivered at sixty, then seventy. The shadows of mango trees and palms traveled over his windshield. He hurtled past coral, salmon, and indigo stucco walls, plantation doors and shutters, swerving in front of a blue Ford, ignoring drivers' furious honks. The Datsun hopscotched from lane to lane, avoiding Vespas and tap-taps, and following the flow of Cadillacs, Nissans, and Oldsmobiles like a fish in water. Finally, the taxi lost itself in Port-au-Prince's dense traffic and crowds, the streets clogged with merchants, business owners, and motorists. Everyone rushing to get home. The smell of diesel and muffler fumes hung thick in the air over Boulevard Harry Truman.

Raymond drove reflexively, brilliantly. In fact, all his adult life, Raymond had seen cars before seeing people. In his mind, life itself was like a fast car. He'd spent most of his waking time inside vehicles, bent over engines, fixing and oiling auto parts.

He shifted gears at the Bicentennaire road, leaving behind the wharf, the cruise ships, the monuments, art galleries, and empty tourist shops.

It was just after seven now, and the peddlers and street vendors had already packed up for the night. The Rue du Magasin de l'Etat was still and silent, save for a few stragglers flirting with the danger of breaking the fast-approaching curfew. Raymond picked up speed again. He wouldn't make it home in time if he didn't get these people out of his car. This was madness. Pure insanity. He had his own family to think of, and if he got caught in the streets past eight o'clock, he might never see his children again.

He leaned back and felt his sweat-soaked skin clinging to his shirt. "We lost them."

The sound of his own voice startled him. He glanced in the rearview mirror—his mysterious passengers sat stiff as statues against the scorching vinyl, the child still crying and the woman patting his back to soothe him.

"Look, I don't know who you are or what you did, but we're coming up on Portail Léogâne," Raymond said, glancing over his shoulder. "That's where you get out."

"Thank you, brother," the man said.

Raymond caught a glimpse of the man's face in the mirror. He was staring up at a slice of sky through the window. The man seemed almost sedated, his frightened eyes shrinking slowly as he took the time to breathe. Their eyes met in the mirror. "Thank you."

Raymond looked away. That voice. Where had he heard it before?

Portail Léogâne sprawled before them, bubbling with curfew's chaos. It was a transportation hub that Raymond was all too familiar with. The trucks and buses sped away from the curb at full speed, zooming past Raymond's Datsun in a blur of hibiscus reds and canary yellows, their frames lacquered with biblical paintings, portraits, and quotes from Scripture. The drivers parked along the sidewalk honked impatiently under a row of palm trees, their horns blaring "La Cucaracha," weaving yet another song into the street's antic brouhaha. Street vendors swarmed through the parked cars, sandal-clad feet stomping against the hot asphalt, headed home with their products tucked away in baskets atop their heads. Others were still brave enough to linger behind, raising oranges and roasted peanut toffees to the windows, desperate for one last sale. *"Bèl zoranj, bèl chadèk!* Beautiful oranges, beautiful grapefruits! Won't you buy a dozen, darling? Good prices for you, *pratik!"*

A mother grabbed her daughter's arm and ran across the street in pursuit of a southbound bus. Raymond honked his horn at a vendor, and the old woman scrambled to move her straw basket as he pulled to the curb. Finally, the Datsun came to a halt.

"We're here," Raymond said quietly over his shoulder. If there were Tonton Macoutes at the station, Raymond was certain he and his passengers would all be apprehended.

A bus loomed over the little cab, and its driver stretched his neck out a window and bellowed, "Move your *bogota*, man! You're blocking me! I need to get out of here!"

Raymond raised his hand to placate the anxious driver as his passengers were scrambling out. At Raymond's window, the man's hands trembled while he dug through his pockets. "God bless you," he muttered.

"Just go," Raymond said. "Get on that bus, get out of town! I don't want your money."

The man peered into his eyes.

"Not a cent," Raymond insisted, holding his palm up. He would not make money off of someone who'd almost lost his life to the Macoutes, no matter how desperate things were. It would be dishonest, even immoral. Somehow, he knew, taking money would upset the balance of things. He just needed to leave, to get away from these people, to make it home by eight o'clock. Thankfully, home was just a few minutes from here.

The more time he spent with these fugitives, the more he was convinced danger would haunt him.

"I owe you—"

"Go!" Raymond repeated. "Get on that bus!"

The woman stopped on the sidewalk, staring back at them. "Milot, let's go!" The man leaned in closer to Raymond at the window, and the bus driver let loose a fresh string of obscenities.

"God bless you for all you've done for us today, brother," the man said. "You saved our lives. If you ever need help, come to the town of Marigot, past Jacmel, and ask for me on the beach. The blue house with red windows. My name is Milot Sauveur."

Raymond frowned. Sauveur. That name was familiar. And that voice? Raymond's face brightened and he leaned closer. "Milot Sauveur? The reporter from Radio Lakay?"

Sauveur nodded. Raymond couldn't believe it. Here was that voice, in the flesh, a voice he'd spent long afternoons listening to in his kitchen while shining his shoes. Here was that voice, whose reports he'd so come to trust. Six weeks ago, when Milot Sauveur had suddenly gone silent, everyone had assumed the worst. Raymond was thrilled to see him in one piece, but what did this mean? He was alive, but for how long? People like Sauveur had only two fates these days: imprisonment or death—the same thing, effectively. Sauveur leaned in and tossed ten gourdes on the dashboard before Raymond could refuse. The bills fluttered around and fell on Raymond's lap.

"I'll never forget this," Sauveur said, squeezing Raymond's arm. Raymond could only nod in response.

Then Sauveur ran toward his wife, grabbed her hand, and shepherded her and the baby onto the bus. There was a brief commotion inside. Raymond could hear passengers sucking their teeth and caught a glimpse of eyes rolling in annoyance as the family stumbled down the aisle. The bus's engine came to life in a cloud of black smoke.

Raymond pulled down his visor and looked again at the photograph of his children. *Go home, Raymond.* His eyes shifted to the rearview. Nothing suspicious. He backed out of his spot, repressing a shudder as he lost himself in the traffic.

Raymond parked his Datsun in the driveway and exhaled. He'd made it home alive, intact, with four minutes to spare. He wanted to run inside and lock the doors. He needed the safety of his home, the two-bedroom apartment they'd been renting for a few years, in the back of an old gingerbread house. Yet he found he could barely move.

He peeled his fingers off the wheel and stared at them, willing the tremors away. His entire body seemed to be vibrating with a mild seizure, and he smelled the sweat festering in his armpits. He closed his eyes and leaned his head back against the headrest. He couldn't extract himself from the car. Not yet. He needed his legs to stop shaking. He couldn't remember the last time he'd confronted death this way, come so close to it. In some ways, he thought, it was surprising. Everyone in Port-au-Prince lived in death's shadow.

Finally, he got out, wobbling. He considered the small white Datsun he'd been driving for years. It was now his accomplice in a crime, regardless of good intentions. He had acted purely out of instinct. And now, heart racing, he faced the likely facts of his situation: they must have his license plate number. A description of his vehicle. He cursed under his breath. The little Datsun was now as incriminating as a murder weapon.

He looked around anxiously to make sure no one was watching. A streetlight cast a white glow over the driveway. Just above the rear bumper, his eye caught a bullet hole in the body of his Datsun. He inserted his finger in it and fought off another chill. He would have to do something about this. His friend Faton knew someone at the vehicle registration office who could get him a new license plate, but bodywork, like everything else, was costly. Raymond scratched the anxiety crawling under his sideburns like a colony of ants.

He glanced at the big gingerbread house. An old rocking chair trembled on the veranda, back and forth. But there was no breeze. The doors and window shutters were lacquered in a glossy, peeling gray that revealed termite bites in the mahogany. The windows opened onto a brightly lit interior with a wooden staircase and a wall of sepia-toned family portraits. Raymond suddenly smelled a familiar waft of tobacco burning in the warm evening air. Now a woman appeared in the rocking chair, her shape becoming more distinct in the dark as she nodded, the embers of her cigarette glittering red like a lonesome *koukouy*, or firefly, suspended in midair.

He steeled himself. Perhaps he could get away with pretending he didn't see her. Perhaps he could walk past the veranda with his head held high, and she would let him go home without saying a word. He scurried up the driveway toward the back. Out of the corner of his eye, he saw a movement and heard a depressing scratch of the throat. Then a voice cut through the night.

"I see you, L'Eveillé!"

He froze, his eyes cutting through the evening light.

"I'll call the police."

TWO

N icolas L'Eveillé stood between his friends Georges Phenicié and Jean Faustin. They were peering over a stack of typewritten pages Nicolas had just freed from the confines of a rubber band.

He could smell the cigarettes and coffee on his friends' breath and could feel the tension as the setting sun threw shadows across the walls of his study. Next to the manuscript was a small black notebook stuffed with newspaper clippings, Nicolas's black Smith-Corona, and a photograph of his wife, Eve, her black hair perfectly curled, holding their newborn.

Jean Faustin, whom Nicolas and his close friends affectionately called Jean-Jean, gingerly slid a newspaper clipping from the notebook. He held it away from the window. In the newsprint photograph, a man disfigured by a scar from his eye down to his chin grinned in the sunlight. Standing next to the man on a balcony was Papa Doc, his smirk and glasses unmistakable. Jean-Jean's age-spotted, bald head tilted back as he let out his habitual, pensive grunt. He was in his seventies and had lived through enough to move away from the window lest anyone see what they'd found. He retreated to an empty space between the bookshelves that lined the walls.

"I don't understand," Georges said. His large belly rolled forward as he leaned over to extinguish his cigarette in an empty espresso cup. He was a handsome, heavyset man who always wore white or beige linen clothing that set off his inky skin. He had large eyes and purple gums that flashed nebulous teeth when he spoke. His rich baritone filled the room.

"I know you said you wanted to write a book, but—when did you have the time to do all this?"

"Took me a few months," Nicolas said. "But never mind that. I called you here because I need your help."

Georges's fearful eyes belied his calm voice. "Help?"

"As you know, I've been collecting notes on Duvalier and Jules Oscar," Nicolas said. "I have the evidence. It's all in the book, but now—"

"Slow down, son. Please." Jean-Jean fell in a chair. He was still holding the photo. He shook his head and lowered his voice as though someone might be listening at the door. "This is very dangerous, Nicolas. Are you prepared for what could happen?"

Nicolas picked up the notebook and approached Jean-Jean. He held it open for the older gentleman to see. He had hoped for help from Jean-Jean, his mentor. Georges was an old friend, yes, but Jean-Jean's sour history with Duvalier had put him in a position of *kamoken anba chal*, a rebel in disguise, someone who actively spoke against Duvalier, if only in whispers, behind closed doors.

The man was like a father to Nicolas. After being accepted to law school in Port-au-Prince, Nicolas had sought an internship at the prestigious Cabinet d'Avocats with Jean Faustin, a judge who himself had started out as an attorney. That first day, Jean-Jean had carefully appraised Nicolas's curriculum vitae, then studied his cheap, worn-out dress shoes and the glimmer of ambition in his eyes, before deciding to take the young man under his wing. And now here they were, in the successful protégé's beautiful library, surrounded by hundreds of books. Jean-Jean leafed through a few pages of the manuscript.

"What exactly do you plan on doing with this?" he asked Nicolas. "You're thirty-five, with a beautiful family. You're far too young to risk losing everything. You must not have thought this through..."

Nicolas's shoulders were broad, and he towered over Jean-Jean, who stared at him with a combination of love and suspicion, like a man waiting for his son to confess to a serious transgression. "I was hoping you could find a way to smuggle it to that friend of yours in France," Nicolas said. "The editor? I have a mountain of research and evidence, things I can't keep locked in my drawer forever. It's only a matter of time before..."

He handed the notebook over to the old man, but Jean-Jean motioned for him to put it away. Nicolas froze. He'd expected shock, yes, but also that Jean Faustin would understand. What he hadn't expected was dismissal. His mentor looked pale.

Nicolas took a deep breath. He was not giving up so easily. "More sugar?" He reached for the cubes on the tray.

Jean-Jean shook his head, waving them away. "You know I can't have that," he grumbled.

In his distraction, Nicolas had forgotten Jean-Jean's diabetes, which required his old friend to give himself insulin injections several times a day. Nicolas backed away and took a seat at his desk facing the two men in their wicker chairs. Their faces drooped—they hadn't been prepared for this when they'd strolled in earlier. The shelf next to them held leather-bound books on civil and penal codes and a black-and-white portrait of the L'Eveillé brothers. Nicolas, dressed all in white, knelt at a pew holding a rosary next to his older brother. Somehow this image gave him strength for what he was going to say next.

"I have proof he ordered the arrest and execution of Dr. Jacques Stephen Alexis. No one will doubt it now. It's just—"

"That's the extent of your plan?" Georges looked at him incredulously. "Export an accusation to France and then sit tight? Like news of this won't come back to hurt you?"

"Have you forgotten where you are?" Jean-Jean bristled. "If you get caught with this, the Baron's spies will take you away."

Nicolas looked down at his shoes, silently pressing his toes against the floor to control his frustration. "Which is precisely why I need it out of my hands."

"And then what?" Jean-Jean asked.

"Are you trying to get us killed too?" Georges hissed. "And what about your family?"

"I realize it's a lot to ask," Nicolas said. "But I can't just throw this out."

"Of course not," Jean-Jean said. "I was thinking a bonfire."

"Help me, Jean! Or I'll find someone who will."

Jean-Jean's voice burned with an anger Nicolas had never heard before. "Like who? That poor idiot who got caught at the airport smuggling in newspapers? Where is he? No one's seen him since. Just for bringing in a few op-eds by foreigners! You are not prepared to handle this—"

"But I am prepared," Nicolas started to argue.

Jean-Jean held up a silencing hand and turned toward Georges, who was now chain-smoking. "Talk some sense into the boy, Georges. What is it your friends at the ministry are calling writers these days? *A danger to the Republic?*"

Georges blew plumes of white smoke into the air. They curled into spirals and crashed against the *art naïf* paintings on the wall.

"He's right, Nicolas," Georges said. "To ask us to help you with this—it isn't just madness; it's callous disregard for everyone's safety. You simply cannot expect us to release this information."

"How can I not release it?" Nicolas said. "Who else will talk about it if not me? Are we supposed to go on pretending that Dr. Alexis just vanished into thin air? It's all here for anyone who could possibly have doubts." He grabbed another clipping from his notebook and held it up. "I have his signature approving the order to be carried out by the warden of Fort Dimanche." He pointed at the photo in Jean-Jean's hand. "It was Jules Sylvain Oscar who ordered his Macoutes to cut—"

"Enough!" Jean-Jean stood up and ran his hand over the thinning gray hair around his bald spot. "I've heard plenty."

He tossed the photograph on Nicolas's lap. The room fell silent.

Nicolas stood up and looked his mentor in the eyes. "You knew Dr. Alexis, didn't you?"

"What difference does it make? And how the hell did you get this information, anyway? Who's your source?"

"I can't get into that right now," Nicolas said.

"Bullshit!" Jean-Jean turned away.

The disappearance of Jacques Stephen Alexis four years ago, upon his return from Moscow and Cuba, had left Haiti bruised and drained. Yet another brilliant intellectual the regime had done away with, fearing the contagion of communism. Of course, it had never been proven.

"You need to slow down, approach this differently, and hope—" Georges paused. He looked uncomfortable, constipated. "Hope like hell this doesn't leak. Who else have you shown this to? Who else have you told?"

"You said you wanted to see him toppled, didn't you?" Nicolas yelled at Georges, who was lighting another cigarette. Georges brought his gold-ringed finger to his lips.

"You said you knew a guy who prints tracts and distributes them in the middle of the night," Nicolas said. "Could he print this book in a compact format? This way it would be easier to—"

"*Ah non!*" Georges shook his head. "Be reasonable!"

"Jean-Jean?" Nicolas turned to the judge, who was staring at him through narrow eyes. "What about the editor you always visit when you travel over the border to visit your sister? I'm sure he'd be interested."

Jean-Jean gazed back in disbelief. Nicolas waited, his heart racing. Finally, Jean-Jean shook his head. "I can't believe you'd entertain that idea. What do you want me to do? Travel with a ticking bomb in my suitcase?"

Nicolas didn't move. He didn't dare. But he held his mentor's stare. "Help me get the book to him while I find my way out of Haiti. The whole world is going to want to read this. I'm not stupid enough to sit here and wait for them to arrest me. I have a plan. But for me to have any chance, the book needs to go out now."

"They'll kill you, you lunatic!" Jean-Jean yelled, and immediately caught himself. He peered out the window, but there were only breadfruit tree branches and rosebushes swaying in the evening breeze.

"I'm going to leave the country," Nicolas reiterated, "and take my family. They won't find us. Jean-Jean, if she'll have us, we could go live with your sister in the Dominican Republic—me and Eve and the baby. We'll hide there until we can figure out how to get to Europe and apply for asylum."

"Are you really serious?" Georges asked. "Is this what Haiti has done to you?"

"It's what Haiti is doing to all of us!" Nicolas snapped. "Come on, Georges! Give me a break. You mean to tell me your passport isn't stamped and ready? You mean to tell me all those phone calls from your kids in Switzerland aren't about figuring out how to get you out of here? Forever?"

Georges's eyebrows met for a moment, but he didn't deny the charge.

Nicolas turned to Jean-Jean. "And you, Jean? Tell me, you old patriot! No one loves his flag more than you, but you're visiting your sister more and more. Before long, you won't bother to come back. Tell me I'm not right."

Jean-Jean tried to answer, but Nicolas cut him off. "I'm not judging you," he said. "I don't want to leave either. I love my home. I love my work. I want to be able to do that work without looking over my shoulder all the time. But I have a daughter now, and a wife who lost her whole family last October in that massacre of rebels."

Nicolas took a deep breath. His friends were silent now, subdued by his outburst. He turned around, pulled out a drawer, and placed the manuscript and his notebook inside before shutting it.

"You know Eve and I had to go into hiding after her father and brothers were killed," he whispered. "I can't take the pressure any longer. When I lecture my students, I can feel myself on the verge of telling them that censorship is wrong, that education should never be compromised. This isn't the Haiti I want my daughter to grow up in."

The older men let an acquiescent silence settle over the room.

Jean-Jean shoved his hands in his pockets. Georges looked at the floor between his shoes.

"It wasn't always like this," Jean-Jean said. "We're better than this." He wrestled himself out of the chair, took a few steps forward, and rested his hand on Nicolas's shoulder. "We've had a rocky political history, but never like this, no. Duvalier's the worst devil of them all."

A dog barked in the distance, as if in rebuke at hearing Papa Doc's name spoken out loud. Georges flinched in his seat.

Jean-Jean squeezed Nicolas's shoulder. His face was sullen. "Walk us out, will you? It's almost curfew."

Outside, the gardens hemorrhaged fragrances of rose and jasmine. Eve had potted every variety of fern and red ginger, dangled orchids from the branches of trees, and placed laurels and frangipanis at the entrance to soak the house in color.

The men stopped in front of Georges's black Citroën. He and Jean-Jean had come together, and now they looked anxiously at their watches.

"Please tell Eve we're sorry to leave in such a hurry," Georges said. "Time is our greatest enemy these days."

Nicolas said nothing. He needed an answer, and his friends were leaving without a promise or even giving him any advice. He watched them climb into the vehicle. Georges started the engine. The rumble interrupted the chirping of *pipirit* birds.

"Let me think about this, Nicolas," Jean-Jean said, scratching his neck in thought. "I will come up with something, God help me!"

Nicolas met his mentor's eyes, his heart swelling with hope. Georges coughed and glanced at the old man.

Jean-Jean lowered his voice. "I mean, I'll see what I can do. But we will need a commitment from you, and a time frame."

Nicolas's eyes sparkled with gratitude. He opened the gate and let the Citroën roll out. Everything was quiet and still, and as Georges drove away, Nicolas watched the sun fall behind the mountains.

THREE

I n times like these, Raymond found himself taking stock of the differences between himself and his brother. Raymond, like any good farm kid, could always dig perfect trenches in the soil, find his way home by the position of the sun, and synchronize the harvest with the moon. Later, he learned how to hotwire cars and siphon out fuel or coolant. Nicolas, on the other hand, was the one who wrote letters for the illiterate villagers and whose teachers wrote him glowing letters of recommendation to medical school in Port-au-Prince. When he didn't get in the Faculté de Médecine, other letters won him a spot in law school and he accepted the privilege. Today, at thirty-eight, Raymond was different from Nicolas in every way. And that was fine by him. He knew that his talents were God's merciful gift. If it had been Nicolas at the wheel earlier today, he would have never been able to find his way out of a convoluted shantytown like Cité Simone, much less lose the Tonton Macoutes. Then again, his brother didn't have to deal with people like Madame Simeus.

"I'll call the police," his landlady threatened again as he hurried toward his little house. "And I'll tell them your rent is past due."

Madame Simeus's voice croaked in the night like an old crow's. Raymond bit his tongue. This encounter was the last thing he needed. He took a closer look to make sure she wasn't sleepwalking again. Alas, no.

She extinguished her cigarette into a potted frangipani and blew plumes of smoke toward the garden. Her gold bracelets clamored around a bony wrist as she pressed the butt into the damp soil and hoisted herself up. When she moved into the light, he saw the bags under her eyes, her thin lips, her small body floating under a large housedress. She stood with her arms akimbo, like vulture wings.

"I'll have it for you." Raymond sighed wearily.

He was used to her threats. Madame Simeus regularly promised to call the police over late rent or his children making too much noise in the yard or when an item went missing in her home. He didn't think she meant it, but he didn't want to push his luck. Although perhaps the police would come and arrest Madame Simeus for wasting their time? He smiled at the idea.

She lived alone and spent most of her time in the garden, escaping the loneliness of her empty home. Her husband and only son had both died of typhoid back in 1960, months before Raymond had moved in. Spending time outside also allowed her to spy on her tenants and her neighbors. It gave her something to do. She knew Raymond's comings and goings, and frequently offered unsolicited opinions.

"With the curfews and all, money's been tight," Raymond added. "Not many people are hailing cabs these days."

"You're three days late," she reminded him.

"I'm good for it, Madame Simeus. You'll have it. Good night, madame."

Raymond hurried toward the back of the house.

"I don't want to have to remind you again!" she shouted after him.

The evening air was heavy, and as he reached his door, he could still smell her tobacco. As much as he disliked her harping, she was right. This was the sixth time he'd been late. He didn't like it, and he couldn't stall her with excuses. She wasn't interested in others' problems. "If you can't pay, you can't stay," she'd say.

When Raymond opened the door, two pairs of small arms threw themselves around his legs. "Papa's home!"

DANCING IN THE BARON'S SHADOW • 23

Raymond let the children hold him for a while and pressed his hands against their small backs. It often struck him how small Enos and Adeline were. He knew they weren't getting enough to eat, and he couldn't get past the guilt he felt when he ran his hands along their backs and felt their bones. But he loved that their smallness was still a kind of innocence in a place where so much experience was painful. He bent over and kissed them on their foreheads. Adeline was six, Enos four, and they wore their smiles like torches, lighting up the dark corners of his heart.

"How was your day? Tell me, my little angels."

He picked Enos up and walked over to the small kitchen table, his other arm wrapped around his daughter's shoulders, the children clinging to their father like vines. As he sat down, the chair wobbled and shifted under his weight. Some nights, he came home with a piece of candy in his pocket, or gum, or *dous kokoye*, sweet coconut. Tonight he had nothing.

On the counter, his wife, Yvonne, had left bowls and basins filled with water they'd fetched from the back of the house. Dishes were piled up, glistening with dinner's rancid oil. On the wall, there was a holographic portrait of Jesus—crucified and resurrected—and a photograph of his wife and children in Sunday church clothes, leaning against Raymond's car. The wall calendar, still turned to January, featured a black-and-white photograph of Duvalier, lips curled in a devious smile, trailed by a gloved First Lady craning her neck like a condor.

Yvonne rushed out of the bedroom. "Where have you been? I was getting worried."

In the dim light, her skin glowed as if lit from the inside, like a *fanal*, those festive paper lanterns. These days, she rarely greeted him happily with the children. Instead, she'd wait for him to come to the kitchen where, wiping empty plates, she'd complain about the price of rice, of shoes, of medicine, about the chronic pain that gnawed at her bones, about the heat that choked them all day and night. Even as they fell asleep, she repeated the familiar questions in the dark: "Must we live here forever? Can't we have just a small, nice *kay* with trees?"

Right now, however, her face displayed genuine concern. Yvonne rested her hand on his head. "It's really late," she said.

"Have the children eaten?" he asked.

"You almost missed curfew!" She pulled away, yanked the kitchen towel from her waistband and threw it on the countertop. "Yes, they've eaten."

She was scared. He recognized this, and still he said, digging through his pockets, "You don't want to know what I've been through today."

He shifted Enos onto his other leg and gave his earnings to Adeline, who handed the money to his wife. Yvonne stared at him for a moment, the way she always did when she couldn't get a good read on her husband.

"Are you all right?" she asked.

He nodded. She reached for his hand. Her palms were sandpaper rough, the result of years of handwashing sheets and towels in hotels with cheap, imported chemical soaps. He looked down and saw how the dyes had stained her nails, how the flesh was worn around the beds. Those hands had never been smooth. The very first time she'd held his face, he'd felt the damage of her life against his cheeks. He recognized the same toughness from his mother's hands.

"Why are your hands shaking?" she asked.

"It's been a long day."

He put Enos down and asked the kids to go prepare him a bath. They grabbed a bucket and ran out, the back door slamming behind them. Yvonne counted the bills quietly.

"That's all?" she whispered. "Thirty gourdes, Raymond. What am I supposed to do with that? That's just enough for the kids' tuition."

"There'll be more tomorrow," he said.

She stuffed the bills into her bra, her eyebrows knitted into a frown. "Enos's doctor bills keep piling up, and we must pay them. Plus Madame Simeus won't stop harassing me about rent. Are you going to solve all this by tomorrow?"

"I said I'll get more money tomorrow," Raymond repeated. "What do you want me to do? I can't work miracles—"

"Maybe you should stop giving away free rides," she said.

This was not how he had envisioned ending the day, but it was how days usually ended. In their arguments, his generosity became an offense to Yvonne, as if having a little humanity was an affront to their family.

"I don't just offer free rides for the hell of it," Raymond said slowly, patiently, clenching his jaw, the desperate faces of Milot Sauveur and his family flashing in his mind.

"There is always someone with an excuse, isn't there? Someone who got mugged, someone who is homeless, someone who's sick. That is not the way to do business, Raymond. Everyone will take advantage of you!"

Raymond closed his eyes. It was so simple for her to tell him how to do his job. She wasn't the one at the wheel, observing the decay out there.

"You forget that's how we met," Raymond said.

Yvonne glared at him. It pained him that they were already fighting. But he couldn't help it. He had to remind her of that fateful day when she'd been left stranded in the rain in downtown Port-au-Prince. She'd have caught a cold if Raymond hadn't come to her rescue.

"That's not fair," she said.

"You don't understand what it's like," he moaned, rubbing nervously at the stubble on his chin. "I almost got killed today."

Yvonne listened as he told her what had happened, staring like he was a ghost. As soon as he was done, he saw her lower lip quiver and he regretted having told her. She had enough to worry about.

"I—I don't know what to say," she stammered.

"There's nothing to say," he replied. "I had to do something. I couldn't let them die on the street like that. Could you?"

She lowered her eyes, but did not answer.

"I'll have to be extra careful the next few days."

"What about us?" she asked. "What about the kids?"

"I just need to get a little work done on the car, replace the license plates, and we'll be fine. They'll never find me."

"How are we going to pay for that?"

"I'll take care of it."

"You can't afford not to work for a few days—"

"I'll take care of it," he repeated. "Could I have something to eat?"

Yvonne jumped up and grabbed a ladle to stir a pot of *bouyon*. The aroma filled the apartment. Raymond began to salivate, and his stomach ached. All he'd eaten today were two hard-boiled eggs, purchased in Cité Simone on the side of the road from a large woman with dirty fingernails and unsightly moles on her face. He watched his wife pour the soup into a bowl, her thin waist and shrinking frame barely visible under her dress. Even her hair was graying early, and these days she kept it hidden under a scarf because she didn't have the luxury of caring for what used to be a spectacular mane of wiry curls. She placed the bowl in front of him. Raymond noticed it was only half full. He ran his spoon through it. No meat. Just a few chunks of plantain and yams.

"I was thinking..." Yvonne swallowed and sat next to him. Outside, they heard the children laugh. She bit her lip. "I was thinking, maybe you could get a loan? Maybe ask Eve and Nicolas?"

Raymond turned to her and she lowered her head, avoiding his eyes. He clenched his jaw again and felt his appetite leave him. "Don't," he said.

"They've got the big house in Turgeau, more money than they need. They're bourgeois, Raymond," Yvonne continued. "Isn't he just a little bit embarrassed that you have nothing? Don't you think he could spare some money for his brother?"

"Stop," Raymond said.

"But it's so unfair—"

"I'm not begging my brother for money!"

Raymond seldom raised his voice. He brought the soup to his lips quickly as if to swallow the anger churning inside. He gulped spoonfuls even though he was no longer hungry. It was impossible to ignore Yvonne. She was there, boiling with need and despair, and he felt it. He understood it. He smelled the permanent odor of laundry soap and ammonia that clung to her skin as she rubbed her temples with impatience.

She sighed. "Well, we're going to be beggars at some point. Might as well beg from your family."

Their eyes finally met. She grabbed hold of his fingers. "Raymond, listen to me," she said slowly. "You've been pushing the same old car downhill since I met you. I just don't see how things can get better for us if you can't even provide for your children. If you won't ask your brother, then maybe I can talk to Eve?"

"Absolutely not!"

She paused. Raymond noticed her nostrils twitching as she pulled her hand away. He continued to eat in silence, hoping she'd drop the subject. But she cleared her throat.

"Well, then I'm going to have to take the kids *lòt bò dlo.*"

Raymond's spoon clattered against the edge of his bowl.

"Not that again!" he howled. "My kids are not getting on a damn raft to Miami. Just last week I heard another story. Twelve families piled inside a rickety tugboat that started to sink. The captain threw them overboard. You really believe those stupid stories people tell you? That money there comes easy? You think you're just going to walk off the boat and start picking money off trees like mangoes?"

Yvonne shook her head. "I'm a hard worker," she said.

"So am I," Raymond replied. "But I'll be damned if my kids end up in the belly of a shark."

He didn't need this. He wanted to take a bath and go to sleep—then the chase, the bullets, this argument could go away for a while.

She finally looked up at him. "They're my children too."

"Then think about what you're saying," Raymond said. "The

Macoutes control the wharfs. If they suspect anything, they'll shoot you on sight."

"It's an option." She still would not look at him. She knew he was right. "It's better than this," she added, and shrugged.

"It's suicide."

A torturous silence fell over them.

"My uncle in Miami has plenty of connections," she said. "He made it fine. He's got a job now and—"

"I'm not having this conversation." Raymond pushed his bowl away and splattered its contents across the table. He stood up.

"I just want something better for us," she mumbled.

He knew she was on the verge of tears, but Yvonne was good at not crying. In front of him, anyways.

"There's no such thing as 'better,'" he said. "Wake up!"

He walked out the back door and left Yvonne sitting at the table.

There was no grass growing behind the house. The ground had been paved to save Madame Simeus the trouble of upkeep. Raymond picked his way over to the edge of the water basin where the kids were waiting, sat down, and fumbled in the dark until he found the faucet he was looking for. The water trickled out in a thin stream.

"Wash your faces, your hands, your mouths," he said as the kids reached toward the faucet with their small fingers. "You need to be nice and clean before bed. Hurry."

The sound of water soothed him, drowning out Yvonne's voice in his mind. Life together used to be good because they'd endured everything in silence, together. But the regular sight of executed men, their bodies displayed as a warning, was enough to rip apart households. The main question, for many, had become: Stay or try to go?

Adeline splashed her brother and the boy laughed. Raymond wanted to chide her for wasting what they didn't have, but for a moment he felt relief to be with his children under the smoky shroud of the night sky. What if he never saw them again? What if he disappeared, and they had nothing left? Maybe Yvonne was right. Not about leaving the country, of course. It was too dangerous. But maybe he should ask Nicolas for help. He felt his face burn with shame at the thought, and he squeezed Adeline's hands together to keep her from wasting water.

He looked up at the diamonds sparkling overhead. "Look." The children followed their father's finger as he pointed upward, and their jaws dropped as they tilted their heads back, their eyes shining with starlight. He released Adeline's hands, now that she was distracted.

"See the biggest one, the shiny one over there?" he whispered. "That's the one the three kings followed when Jesus was born. That's how they knew he was born, and that's the same one I followed every time I got lost in the fields with Uncle Nicolas."

"How do you know it's the same one?" Adeline asked.

He'd told them the story many times, of playing soccer with his brother all afternoon and getting lost as they walked back through the fields. He'd told them how he navigated by the stars while Nicolas cowered against him, terrified of loup-garou—werewolves—roaming the dark. He was also haunted by thoughts of evil spirits, but Raymond had kept his eyes riveted on the guiding star and led his brother to the main road and safely home. He wanted his children to know there was nothing shameful about manual labor—it was good for the soul; it helped him understand the mechanics of the world—and he wanted them to know that their uncle, Nicolas, didn't understand it like he did—that his nice house, his beautiful wife, their beautiful clothes and shiny car didn't mean they were better. Just luckier.

"It's that same one, and it always takes you home," Raymond said.

"That star is old," the girl whispered in the dark.

He chuckled silently and felt her fumble around for her brother. They always managed to make him smile. That's what children do: patch up the wounds their parents spend a lifetime licking.

Raymond relented and let the children play games with the water until, little by little, it ran out. He didn't have the heart to break the spell cast by night and water.

FOUR

Since boyhood, Raymond L'Eveillé had accepted that he wasn't destined to be someone important like his brother. Nicolas was the anointed one and Raymond the worker, the man of humble but practical skills, just another one of the millions of Haitians seeking a modest *lavi miyò*, a better life, in Port-au-Prince. Still, he'd come to suspect that this "better life" everyone chased after was a lie—and it wasn't just him. This realization was spreading through the slums like cholera. In fact, he was pretty sure there was nothing "better" than the life he'd left behind when he moved to the city.

Raymond had grown up in a small farmhouse in the valley of L'Artibonite, north of Port-au-Prince, where his parents had spent their lives harvesting rice. The path was paved for Raymond and Nicolas to take over the farm, but their parents had dreams of giving their sons more and put every cent they could wring out of the little farm toward tuition at the neighborhood Catholic school. Raymond was never good at school. The complexities of mathematical formulas eluded him, and language became his enemy on the classroom's battlefield. He learned to remain quiet instead of raising his hand and risking ridicule for mistaking a feminine pronoun for a masculine one. Pages of text paralyzed him, his tongue tying itself in knots each time he tried to string letters into sentences. The jeers were cruel: *"Anal-*

phabèt se bèt!" If you can't read, you're stupid. Raymond, ashamed, retreated behind his desk, constructing cars out of plastic juice bottles and soda caps.

The friars were efficient at sorting the mediocre students from the best ones. Unlike his brother, Nicolas was eager to please and driven to learn, and he quickly became the friars' favorite. He had a natural intelligence, a remarkable capacity for memorizing tables and retaining conjugations. *"Nicolas est brillant,* especially in French and Haitian literature," the teachers wrote in his report card. "Would make an excellent professor." Raymond's report card rarely had any comments on it. The few he got went something like: "Student seems ill suited for academia."

Creole was comforting to Raymond, whereas Nicolas's elegant French made the headmaster's blue eyes shine with pride. While Nicolas devoured books and aced his tests, Raymond, feeling inadequate, spent his time sitting in the shade of orange trees. Their mother, deeply superstitious like so many peasants, had chalked up his deficiencies to the supernatural, convinced that someone had hexed her eldest. "Someone wants to harm my baby," she said. "I dreamed I found two nickels wrapped in a notebook page inside his pillowcase. Someone's cursed my boy. But I will find out who the culprit is. They will pay."

For a while, Raymond wondered if he might really be cursed. Who would want to harm him? It was true that his family's farm did better than others in the village, but they were still part of the community, and they had their hardships. It didn't make sense to him, and in the end, it didn't matter why he struggled in school—just that he did. His mother brewed him special tea in the mornings, placed leaves between the pages of his books, encouraged him to sleep with lessons under his pillow, discouraged him from accepting gifts from strangers or even friends. Still, his grades never improved. Raymond gave up. Perhaps it was God's will.

As they walked home from school, Nicolas would begin his own brand of teasing. His academic excellence made him feel superior to his embarrassing big brother.

"You're going to end up growing rice all your life, just like Mother and Father," he'd say, trailing behind his brother. "Is that what you want?"

Raymond shrugged his shoulders. "At least I'm not afraid to get my hands dirty," he said. "I can work the field, and I'm pretty good at fixing things. Why does it matter that I can't read?"

"But you'll never be *important*," Nicolas said. "That's why you go to school. To become somebody, to get out of this place. Me? I'll never be a farmer. Never."

He meant it. On *konbit* days, when all the villagers rose before dawn to work together, Raymond had to prod Nicolas from his *natte* and drag him to the rice fields. "Father's going to be mad if you don't hurry up," he'd say.

Nicolas would kick rocks on the way as the sunrise blanketed the rice fields with a soft pink glow; he refused to put his feet in the cold mud while Raymond masterfully wrapped his large brown hands around a bundle of rice. When their father was far in the distance, plowing the ground with his pick, joining in the collective call-and-response song, Nicolas would even pull out a book. He'd find a strong calabash tree root to sit on and forget all about the farmers, the cook who stirred the hot pot for the workers, the cows' tails whipping flies away in the morning air. When he caught Nicolas reading, their father would beat him. "Are you ashamed of farming?" he'd roar as his belt smacked the boy's hips. "You'll get your hands dirty like the rest of us whenever it's required, you ingrate!" Raymond stayed up many nights tending to welts on his brother's body.

When Raymond turned fifteen, he dropped out of school and found a job at a mechanic shop in the nearby city of Saint-Marc. "Let's face it," he told his parents, "I'll never be like Nicolas. Don't waste any more money on that school. If I do good work as an apprentice mechanic, maybe I can open my own shop one day."

Saint-Marc was known for a neighborhood of graceful, old streets that eased up the hills away from the bay and the parks. It was called La Ville des Bicyclettes, aptly named because its residents' preferred mode of transportation was bicycles. Raymond's early work as a mechanic entailed fixing chains and replacing wheels with broken spokes. Over time, he moved on to oiling the engines of trucks that traveled to and from the capital. He learned how to drive, shuttling customers from the shop to wait at a nearby bar. In the evenings, he came home with greasy hands and his pants stained with oil that his mother could never fully wash out. But he came home fulfilled, as if he'd spent the day fixing the entire world with just his wrench. At dinner, his head bowed over his meager bowl of *bouyon*, Nicolas would keep quiet and pretend to study his large history and geography books before scrunching his nose in disdain. "You smell like car grease. What do you do, bathe in the stuff?" Raymond learned to let his brother's snotty remarks roll off his back.

Raymond arrived at Nicolas's house the next day around noon and found Eve in the dining room with their live-in housekeeper, Freda. Freda cooked most of the delicious things in that house, but Eve made some herself, decorating them with sprigs of parsley and orange rinds. "I am a *femme à tout faire*—a woman of all trades," she often joked at the stove. "My mother always said a woman must learn to use all ten of her fingers. Here are mine." And she'd wiggle them in the air.

Today, Raymond watched her hands fly over the utensils. She lifted a serving spoon, topped the rice and beans with a flower-shaped bell pepper, and scooped out a fresh *piman bouk* pepper studded with cloves. She sliced onions into perfect rings to frame the chunks of beef, as if dinner were an arts and crafts project. It was almost offensive to Raymond, this display of luxury, this fussing over aesthetic details, and yet it made his stomach clench with yearning.

"How's everything?" Eve asked distractedly. "We haven't seen you since last week."

Eve was a tall woman, even taller when she wore her wedge sandals around the house. She had a habit of dousing herself in lavender oil and carried a cloud of the scent wherever she went. She'd never been a thin woman; Eve was curvy, with a little meat on her bones. She had beautiful almond-tinted skin and perfectly pressed hair that framed her face like a smoky halo. Raymond was holding Amélie, his niece, in his arms. The baby had just turned one, and she was looking more like her mother all the time, her black hair meticulously combed back on her head. She clung to her uncle's collar. Raymond rubbed the baby's back gently and admired Eve's dedication as she went over a place setting that wasn't up to her standards, switching a silver spoon for a fork here and there. His eyes widened at the sight of lobster, a rarity, bathing in a red Creole sauce. The aroma punched him in the gut and his mouth watered.

"*M'ap knee,*" Raymond said. "Hanging in there."

She looked up and cocked her head to the side. Raymond knew instantly that she was reading worry in his eyes.

"You look tired," she said.

"I'm fine," he said, turning away from her. He didn't want her to see him like this, vulnerable. He kissed the baby's forehead and she giggled, babbling something unintelligible.

"Amélie missed you," Eve said. "Look at her, she's beaming. You're so important to her, you know. When you don't come around, it breaks her heart."

Raymond wondered how much the child was aware of. She was still so young. Amélie always smelled divine from the layers of lotion and talcum powder her mother smothered her in. Raymond had never been able to afford those luxuries for his children. All his money had been spent on food and medicine, especially that dreadful night when Enos nearly died of pneumonia. For a long time, the children walked around barefoot, and their first shoes had been a present from Eve.

"Nicolas will join us soon," she said. "I told him you're here, but he's probably working on that book of his..." Eve shook her head longingly and sighed. "I wish you could talk some sense into him."

Before Raymond could answer, she turned away to pour water into the glass goblets and asked Freda to close the door on her way out. Raymond assumed she was retreating to the help's quarters in the back of the house.

"He won't sleep at night, sometimes, always talking on the phone about his notes," Eve added. "He won't listen to reason either. I tried talking to him but he won't hear it. The telephone is no place to talk about *those things*. You know? After what happened to my family..."

She paused for a brief moment, then continued her work. Raymond knew she was thinking about her father and brothers, who had died with the Jeune Haiti rebels in the southern mountains the year before.

"Trust me, I support him and I want nothing more than to see this regime crumble," she continued. "There isn't a place in hell hot enough for Duvalier to roast in. But why take silly risks, right?" She froze and looked hard at her brother-in-law. "The Baron is cunning, Raymond. You never know who's spying for him. The walls have ears."

She set the water pitcher at the center of the table, and when she turned her head, her body was still turned toward him. To Raymond, Eve was like the Madonna, a woman of unparalleled beauty who carried herself like royalty. His brother was so lucky. Raymond still loved Yvonne, but he had grown weary of her own weariness over time.

Realizing he'd stared at his sister-in-law too long, Raymond's ears burned with shame.

"I'll tell you one thing," Eve continued softly. "I'm preparing myself for the worst."

Raymond stared at her. He wasn't sure what she meant.

"What do you think will happen?" Raymond shook his head. "Everything will be fine, Eve." He knew his brother's ambitions were foolish, but he couldn't imagine they'd really ever take off again like when they went into hiding.

"Won't you talk to him again?" she pleaded. "When I think of what could happen if someone denounced him, it makes my skin crawl. Did you hear what they did to that lawyer downtown?"

Raymond leaned against the kitchen counter, shaking his head. Eve grabbed a newspaper from behind the fruit basket and handed it to him. Raymond unrolled it with his free hand, trying to ignore the smell of bananas and pineapple. He was hungry.

The grainy front-page photograph gripped him in the gut. He was looking at the charred skeleton of a man, the melted remains of a rubber tire clinging to his bones. There was nothing left of the corpse but blackened gristle and two rows of stark white teeth.

"How can you do that to a human being?" she asked, her hand on her hip. She shook her head. "He was a good man, never harmed anyone. Nicolas knew him."

Her voice wavered, and Raymond realized she was fighting back tears. "Someone denounced him. They said he was plotting against the regime—" She blinked. "I haven't slept since reading this."

"I already tried talking to him," Raymond said, dropping the newspaper back on the counter. "You know that. He won't listen to you, so what makes you think he would listen to me, a taxi driver from *anba lavil*?"

Nicolas walked into the kitchen, and they fell silent. Eve stepped away from Raymond. Raymond wondered how much his brother had overheard.

The brothers shook hands with awkward formality, muttered quiet greetings to each other. The resemblance was there, even with their difference in height. Nicolas was younger than Raymond, but he was taller, leaner, while Raymond's shoulders were broader, his arms and calves more muscular. But the brothers' jaws and foreheads were of the same squareness, their noses the same width, their skin the same chocolate brown.

Nicolas pulled Amélie away from her uncle. "Come to Papa."

"Leave him with Raymond," Eve started. "She hasn't seen him in a while."

"She just took a bath," Nicolas said, finding his way to his chair.

Raymond glanced at Eve, but she avoided his eyes and pretended to wave at Amélie. His brother likewise kept his eyes glued on the baby. Nicolas sat down in his usual place at the head of the table. The insult stung, but Raymond bit his lip. The last time they'd gotten into it, Raymond had stayed away for a month—and it would have been much longer if Eve hadn't intervened. As they both got older, Raymond found his bitterness deepening, impatient with a life lived in the shadow of his brother's ego.

Raymond had come here to borrow a bit of money from Nicolas to repaint his car, but the thought of asking his brother for help still pained him. He'd mulled it over all morning as he brushed his teeth and drank his tea. He was going to ask because he had no other choice. He didn't mention anything to Yvonne, just in case.

For the first time, he started to regret not having taken a job with Faton at the tannery. Perhaps that's what he should do. Accept the inevitable, that he needed to provide more for his family at any cost, to get a job working for someone, for a company. Accept the stench of decomposing cowhide and lime and dye that seeped through the skin. He'd have to accept the consequences of that stench as well: the icy distance from his wife and children, whose warm embrace he depended on; Amélie, whom he'd never again be allowed to hold; his sister-in-law, who would back away when he entered the kitchen; and Nicolas, who would surely keep him farther away.

Raymond found his place at the table, next to Eve. Who was he fooling? This charade of not believing in anything better, this resignation to a *vie de misère*, it was a lie. Raymond was intensely aware of this as Eve filled his goblet with passion fruit juice and her gold ring caught the ceiling light. He wanted this, all of it, the luxuries in life: the brushing of the soft tablecloth against his legs, the slam of full cupboards doors, and the humming of an electric refrigerator.

As they ate without saying much, he listened to the ambient noise around him. Utensils scraped differently against ornate porcelain plates than against his cheap aluminum back home.

As Raymond reached for a serving spoon, he realized that the apparent inconvenience of having to stand up and reach around the glass candlesticks and crystal water pitcher would always be an extraordinary privilege for someone like him.

Raymond lifted his eyes and saw Eve watching him. Next to her, his brother ate without a word, but with the subtle pout of a man savoring lobster with distinction, knife and fork poised, methodical. Raymond himself chose to forgo the knife, stabbing at his food and simply pressing down on the crustacean's shell until it gave.

The baby sat on her mother's lap and Eve attempted to feed her a mouthful of rice. She squinted at Raymond. "Aren't you hungry?"

He'd been picking at his food, his appetite dulled with the first cold blow from his brother. "I'll take some of it home, if you don't mind," he answered. "For the kids. Yvonne struggles terribly with the cost of food these days."

"It is outrageous," Eve said, and nodded. "How can they expect the *malheureux* to afford a single cup of rice with this inflation? I'll fix you a plate for them, of course. How are the kids, anyway? Do they have what they need for school?"

Eve bounced the baby on her knee and Raymond nodded politely. "They're fine," he said.

"Good, because I told Yvonne last time I saw her that my friend owns a shoe store downtown. All she has to do is tell the staff that I sent her and they'll give her a great discount."

"The man says they're fine!" Nicolas's voice cut through the room and Eve lowered her eyes once more.

"Leave him alone and mind your own business," Nicolas added.

Eve waited for him to begin eating again and glanced at Raymond. "Are you sure you're feeling all right?"

"Yes," Raymond answered. "I'm just a little preoccupied. I have a little problem with my car. I'm going to have to get it fixed up."

Raymond watched his brother spear a large chunk of beef with his fork and chew it slowly, saw the veins in his temples dance.

Finally, he cleared his throat softly, still staring at his plate.

"What's wrong with it?" Nicolas asked.

"The car?" Raymond said. "Could be the transmission."

"Could be?"

"I can fix it myself, but I'm going to need to buy the part," Raymond said. "Could run me about five hundred."

"Five hundred?"

Nicolas finally looked up and stopped chewing. It was Raymond who avoided eye contact this time. Asking for money was bad enough, but lying wasn't something that came easily to him. He decided to tell the truth.

"Also, I need to get it repainted. I ran into some trouble with the Tonton Macoutes yesterday."

Nicolas nearly dropped his knife and fork, and Eve froze. Even the baby stopped fidgeting. Raymond had never seen his brother like this, his black eyes staring at him so fixedly. He'd seen him afraid before, like when he panicked when they got lost together in the fields, or when their father passed away, or when Eve was in labor. But never quite like this.

"What are you saying?" Nicolas said.

"This family asked me for help yesterday evening," he said. "They were banging on my window. The Macoutes were after them, so I had to do something."

Amélie banged a spoon on the edge of her mother's plate, jolting the tense adults.

"Turns out it was Milot Sauveur and his family," Raymond added, as if this fact would somehow alleviate the gravity of the situation. He looked at them, but Eve and Nicolas were still staring back like a pair of stunned birds.

"Come on, you know—Milot Sauveur?" he repeated. "The journalist from Radio Lakay who went missing?"

Raymond fought the urge to get up and walk out. He hoped his brother might still be reasonable and come through for him. He'd been on edge all morning, looking over his shoulder, praying he wouldn't be pulled over. He had removed the red ribbon from his rearview mirror so he wouldn't be pegged as a taxi driver, but the problem with that, of course, was that no one hailed him for a ride. The whole thing was a disaster.

"They had a baby," Raymond said. "What was I supposed to do?"

"What *did* you do?" Nicolas asked, his voice hollow.

"I told them to get in and the Macoutes chased me around Cité Simone," Raymond said. "They thought they could catch me, but they didn't know who they were dealing with. I know every dark alley in Port-au-Prince, so I stepped on the gas and..."

Eve groaned softly, dropping her head as if she'd been struck.

"Did they get your license plate?" Nicolas asked, his voice burning.

"I don't think so," Raymond said. He squeezed the handle of his fork.

"You don't think so?" Nicolas echoed, nodding repeatedly as he made his point. "What if they did? What if they find you? They could show up any minute. Are you a complete idiot? You're endangering us just by being here."

"They didn't see it, okay?" Raymond dropped his fork.

The table wavered slightly between them. The goblets of fruit juice and ice water sweltered in unison. Raymond took in the raw cotton of Nicolas's shirt, the stiffness of his collar, the perfectly trimmed Afro, and the elegant sideburns. In the corner of his eye, there were the red nails of this woman he sometimes longed for, the trophy child, the glass and the gold.

"Relax," Raymond continued. "I know what I'm doing. I always do. You should know that."

"This isn't child's play," Nicolas spat.

"Do I look like a child to you?" Raymond replied.

"You're going on and on about knowing your back alleys like it's something to be proud of," Nicolas said.

"I'm not ashamed of what I do," Raymond responded calmly.

Eve gulped some cold water as the brothers stared each other down. Raymond felt his jaw twitch. There was so much he wanted to say to Nicolas, but what was the use? This was his house, after all. Raymond was only a guest who had come to beg. *The whole thing was a bad idea in the first place.* He didn't want to fight, but he also didn't want to put up with this kind of condescension from his brother.

"You don't see how what you did was wrong?" Nicolas said.

"I saved their lives! Since when is that wrong?"

"Very noble, but what's wrong is when you jeopardize the lives of others trying to be some kind of hero."

"I'm sorry you don't approve of my choices," Raymond said. "Maybe you're right. I should have left him and his wife and their baby, younger than Amélie... I should have left them to be slaughtered in the street."

Nicolas rested his elbows on the table and leaned in closer. "I don't think you're hearing me—"

"I'm hearing you," Raymond retorted. "It's you who's not hearing me. You can't, because we're speaking different languages." He pushed his plate away. He regretted the way the utensils clattered aggressively, but his heart was racing with the familiar rush of anger that overpowered him whenever he tried talking to Nicolas.

"You are not a *kamoken* rebel," Nicolas said. "You're just a taxi driver."

Raymond bristled. "So you keep reminding me. Ever since we were kids. Do you think you could make it through just one day without giving me shit about how I make a living?"

"Please," Eve said, clearing her throat. "Let's not get into all this now."

Raymond pushed on. "I'm just a cabbie. I'm poor. Why does that offend you so much? I do honest work, always have, while you sat around like a prince, like labor was beneath you. Do you seriously think you're better than everyone else? You and your snobby friends sitting in your study, drinking whiskey, smoking, running your mouth about politics, like you have any idea what it's like out there."

Nicolas raised a menacing finger in the air. "If you don't like my friends, then don't come to my house." His eyes bulged out of their sockets.

"I won't then!" Raymond pushed his chair back.

Eve reached out to grab him by the arm, surely to insist that he didn't have to leave, that Nicolas never meant what he said, that he was just overly sensitive. She couldn't stand the way her husband treated his brother. She had grown up in a loving family before she married Nicolas, and she believed in the bond between siblings because she herself once had brothers. It was one of the things Raymond liked about her.

"Raymond," she pleaded.

"Let him leave, Eve," Nicolas said.

Raymond didn't wait for her to finish her sentence. He started down the hallway, but then spun around and walked back to the dining room. He didn't know why. It was the same instinct that made him drive Milot Sauveur out of Cité Simone.

Nicolas and Eve were still sitting there. Nicolas was chewing furiously on a toothpick, nearly stabbing his gums. Eve held her head low in her hands like she was suffering from a violent migraine. When she saw him return, she implored Raymond with her eyes.

"You know the real difference between you and me, Nicolas?" Raymond asked. "You're an ass."

Eve began to protest, but he continued, unfazed.

"No, please. Let me speak my piece or I'll choke on it tonight. Nicolas needs to hear this." He paused and looked right at his brother at the head of the table. "Everything I do, I do for my family. I slave away out there, I sweat. Sometimes I only eat once a day. The other day, I had to syphon gas out of a car just to get my car going. My meals, my money, my blood, it's all to keep my family alive. I always think of them first. But you, Nicolas, you don't think about anyone but yourself."

Nicolas stared back, quivering with rage. Raymond sighed. Suddenly, all of this just seemed exhausting.

"You're selfish," he said, dropping his voice. "Look at all you have, and you're risking losing it all."

"You're angry because of what I have?" Nicolas roared. "How typical."

"I'm angry because you don't cherish it!" Raymond's mouth filled with spit. "Any man who plays with fire like you do, dancing with the Devil, is bound to burn." He looked at his brother knowingly. "And what will your family have left except your ashes?"

Nicolas slammed the table with the palm of his hand and Amélie's face twisted with fear. Eve jumped up as the baby began to cry. Her husband's eyes glimmered like fiery lumps of coal.

Raymond chuckled, but his laugh was tired, empty. He shook his head.

"You stupid, stubborn little man."

"Get out!"

"Nicolas!" Eve seized her husband's arm. She looked to Raymond, but he had already walked away.

FIVE

Raymond knew he wasn't going to get much sleep that night. He lay frozen on the mattress next to Yvonne, listening to her rhythmic breathing and the creak of bedsprings each time she shifted. He stared at the dark ceiling and let starlight bathe his half-naked body, the sheets rolled down to his waist. He was used to the city heat. When Yvonne opened her eyes and found him wide-awake, she barely lifted her head off the pillow.

"You should sleep," she said.

There was concern in her voice. Also exhaustion. She needed sleep too, probably even more than he did. When the sun rose, she'd rush out of the house to her job laundering clothes, a job they both knew was more physically taxing than Raymond's.

"Don't worry about me," he whispered. "I'll be tired soon. You go back to sleep."

She lay there, staring at him, until her eyes closed. He felt grateful. He didn't want to talk to her, didn't want to explain himself, and by now, she was used to him returning home from his brother's house silent, stewing, rehashing threadbare arguments in his mind.

"God will provide for us," she muttered as she drifted off. "Don't give up hope."

What does God know of our suffering, he wondered, *or our hope?* Hope was a luxury, nowadays. Haitians liked to believe that *l'espoir fait vivre*—where there is hope, there is life—and that you could survive on hope alone, but there was a breaking point.

And Raymond had to admit that he could not survive as a taxi driver. Sometimes he wished he had stayed in the village, kept their parents' house, and farmed the land. But the exodus of villagers to Port-au-Prince had swept him up. He needed to make a life for himself and his family, and there wasn't much money in fixing up cars in Saint-Marc, nor in rice harvests. Breakneck inflation kept the working class on the edge of starvation while the bourgeois like his brother were starting to import luxury goods. There was nothing left for farmers to do. Yvonne could barely afford rice these days, much less meat. In the darkness, he shook his head, eyes still wide open.

What does God feel about all this? Raymond felt as if God had stopped listening, up there, wherever *there* was, but quickly regretted his blasphemy. Losing faith was not an option. After all, God had enabled him to be alive so far, and given him such blessings: a beautiful family with a devoted wife, gems for children. He turned to look at her sleeping face.

He silently thanked God for that day in the city when they'd met, and that he hadn't had the heart to let her stand there in the rain. She'd just finished her shift at the Karibe Hotel. Her dress was soaked, and she had to get to her next job in Martissant. He flirted with her the whole way, because he liked the way her red dress clung to her small body, wet with rain, and how she never looked him in the eye when he joked with her, but instead looked away with an amused smile.

"What's your name?" he asked. "Mine is Raymond. Raymond L'Eveillé."

She laughed. "You're chatty, aren't you? And fresh too." He pressed until she gave in and told him her name. He was there to pick her up again that night, surprising her as she walked through the hotel gates after another long shift.

"Let me give you a ride home," he said to her.

"You just give out free rides, huh? You're just generous that way?"

Lying next to her in the darkness, Raymond shuddered. Where had all their flirtation and joy gone? A few days after they met, he'd driven her to the Champ de Mars and bought her a *fresco*. They made love in his car. A few weeks later, he told her he wanted to marry her and she said yes.

"What are you thinking of?" Yvonne asked. So she wasn't asleep.

He stared at the ceiling. The starlight outside his window spilled over his tired face and he held himself as still as he could, hoping she would leave him alone. She reached out in the dark and touched his bare chest. Her palm was hard but warm, and although he'd grown accustomed to the sweltering heat in the room, he felt flames where her fingers grazed him. She felt for his heartbeat.

"It'll be okay, Raymond," she said.

Raymond closed his eyes and felt his body sink deeper into the mattress, against the springs, and prayed for sleep to take him even as he felt disgusted by her words. Nothing was going to be okay and she knew it. Still, Yvonne curled up against him. Her breath melted into his ear, and he felt something inside unfurl. She leaned in, seeking his lips in the dark, but all he could do was squeeze her arm in response.

"What's that sound?"

Yvonne stopped and listened, her head cocked against his shoulder. Raymond thought he heard a whimper. No, it was a voice. A woman's voice, calling in the night. "I'm ready!" Yvonne's hands ran across his chest, but as soon as she leaned in again to kiss him, the sound of soft knocks jolted them. She grabbed Raymond's arm.

"Don't—"

"I have to," he said. "You stay in bed. I'll go help her."

Raymond scrambled in the dark to put his clothes on. In the kitchen, he called out as the knocks persisted. "You have to wake up, Madame Simeus! This is a dream; you're not awake."

He opened the door to find his landlady standing there, her coarse silver hair combed back into a chignon, mumbling incoherent words. She had smeared peach lipstick around her mouth and donned a pearlescent gown he'd never seen on her before. Her eyes were open, vacant, but deeply asleep.

"Will you take me to the dance?" she asked.

Raymond stifled a smile. He saw her legs uncovered where the dress stopped at the knee, her ankles scrawny, her feet in fuzzy white slippers. Madame Simeus, always so proud and indignant.

"Come, I'll walk you back to bed."

"I'm waiting for my date."

"Right."

He grabbed her arm and guided her back into her house as he'd done many nights before, thankful for the interruption, his eyes searching the darkness around them.

Nicolas was also awake, staring at his notebook, holed up in the darkness of his study, and hoping that if he couldn't sleep, at least he could work. The manuscript was tucked away in its usual spot, and as usual it seemed to blaze and crackle like a glowing fire in the room. Maybe that was why he felt slightly feverish.

Eve had finally fallen asleep after starting to fold clothes and precious little things. They were slowly preparing to leave for the Dominican Republic. Amélie was at her side in her crib. Nicolas, on the other hand, hadn't been able to sleep since he'd started working on the book.

In the glow of the lamp, Nicolas peered over his notes. He bit his nails at the thought of Jean-Jean reprimanding him for writing the book, for unearthing such sensitive information in the first place.

And yet he couldn't ignore the anarchic nudge within to challenge all of this, to change the world around him when everyone else was being coerced and corrupted. Sometimes the sleeping anarchist in him would just wake up in the middle of a lecture. His students would sit there in shock as the words poured out of him. When they began to gasp or grow awkwardly still, he'd know to rein it in quickly. He hated that look of resignation on their faces. Resignation sickened him.

Molière! he thought sadly. *Where are you?* Molière, his former pupil, who had been the opposite of resigned when he reached out to Nicolas. "I'm now an archivist in the prisons of Port-au-Prince," he'd said with a quiet smile. "I remember what you taught me about justice." And Molière presented Nicolas with what would become the backbone of his book. "You said there were many ways to start a revolution, Maître. Remember? Well, here. I thought you'd want to know about the disappearance of a certain Dr. Alexis."

Three days now of trying to reach his young source and still no word. Nicolas tried not to panic when the last phone call led him to a relative who announced sadly on the other line: "Molière is gone. He has disappeared."

He heard a pop outside the window. Nicolas jumped and peered through two louvers. Something had hit the shutters, something thrown. A stone, possibly. His eyes adjusted gradually, and he could make out the branches of almond trees swaying eerily over the hood of his car. A distant streetlight cast a bright glow on the sidewalk. Nicolas pushed the louvers wide open and looked at the fragile stems of garden roses that held their weight against the quiet breeze and the sleeping anoles.

Nothing moved in the night. He must be getting paranoid. Probably just blind bats dropping *cachiman* fruits on the house midflight. Then, just as he started to close the shutters, a shadow streaked through the garden. It headed for the gate. Nicolas's blood ran cold. He opened the shutters wide again. Yes. A silhouette was stepping over the bougainvillea bushes. A man.

"Hey!" Nicolas shouted.

The intruder reached the wall surrounding the property. The gate was padlocked, and he tried to hoist himself over the edge. Nicolas fumbled around under his desk. His fingers found the release and the hidden drawer popped open, revealing a space where he kept his notebook and a blue pouch. He unwrapped the fabric with trembling hands and emerged from under his desk with the Colt .45. The thing seemed to grow heavier each time he held it, especially when he cleaned it under Eve's reproachful eye.

As he left his study and rushed past the bedroom door, Eve's head popped out, her eyes panicked. "I heard something. What is it? Why aren't you in bed—"

"Get back in the room and stay inside!" Nicolas pushed past her as she gasped at the gun he held, running to the front door, bumping into the console table and rattling lamps and framed family photographs.

With a grunt, he unbolted the door and ran to the veranda. The warm midnight air coiled around his knees and ankles. He stood there in nothing but his robe and a pair of leather slippers. He caught his breath and stopped for a moment, looking. Was the man still here? There he was, pulling himself over another part of the wall. Nicolas raised his gun to eye level. "Stop! I'll shoot!"

The silhouette fell over the other side of the wall, landing with a thud.

"*La police!*" Nicolas yelled. "Police! *Au voleur!* Thief!"

Heart pounding, he shouted with all the air left in his lungs. He had to alert the neighborhood! He had to scare off the intruder.

A car door slammed, and an engine sped off furiously into the night. The dogs of the neighboring homes howled and barked in concert. Windows lit up, silhouettes ushered behind curtains, residents carefully avoiding exposure. Nicolas looked around to be sure that there was no one else stalking the house. His hand was still wrapped around the handle of the Colt, his finger resting against the trigger guard, as he'd been taught to do.

As dawn lit up Turgeau, the police came to inspect the garden. Nicolas was annoyed when they said the crime had already been committed, so they wouldn't come out till curfew was over.

"I don't think the intruder or his accomplices would stick around for you to come inspect my garden," he said. "I've already looked. No one is here!"

Eve tried to placate him, and he kept quiet, allowing them to look for evidence. Maybe the intruder had dropped something. Maybe he was trying to break in. Who knew?

The neighbors asked questions Nicolas was unable to answer. Nothing was stolen, nothing was missing, no door was broken, no harm was done, and there was no conclusive report to be written. His next-door neighbor, Monsieur Pierre-Louis, a retired airline pilot, called him over to the fence that separated their two houses.

"Neighbor, is everything all right?" he asked. "You know we should look out for each other. If you need anything, let me know."

Nicolas nodded thankfully. Yet, as the officers left and the neighbors shook their heads in sympathy, Nicolas was filled with a fear and unease he knew would haunt him for days. Who was the true suspect here? When he invited the police into his home, when they took their time wandering the grounds, staring into the windows of his study, were they really searching for clues about the intruder or were they curious about something else? Nicolas shook his head in regret. He shouldn't have caused a scene, shouldn't have called the police. If he wanted to get his family safely out of Haiti, he would have to be smarter than that.

SIX

The couple that hailed him on the Bicentennaire wharf was laden with souvenir bags brimming with wooden sculptures and hats.

"Holiday Inn, please!" the man declared, squeezing his frame into the small backseat.

In the rearview mirror, Raymond caught a glimpse of their milky arms and necks, now red from sunburn.

"Holiday Inn, Champ de Mars!" Raymond confirmed as he stepped on the gas.

"Yes, and *doucement*," the man pronounced with awkward inflection. "Take your time, we like to look out the window. Understand? Drive slow? Please?"

"The scenic route then," Raymond said.

They were American, a rare breed these days, and a blessing. Americans weren't visiting as much, and the hotels were barely scraping by. Raymond recognized the language, of course, and he understood it some, but he didn't speak much. His favorite tourists were the Scots, though he had no idea where Scotland was located. He liked the lilting brand of English they spoke. It was endearing and friendly, what little he understood. The French were easier for Raymond to understand, and he could answer in short, broken French phrases. With Americans, Raymond felt at ease. They appreciated a good time, at the disco or the brothels, and most days he was happy to drive slowly for them. But today, driving extra slow probably wasn't wise. Nor was speeding. He'd gone out this morning with his heart in his throat, checking his mirrors for incoming Macoutes, his head scrunched down between his shoulders. The facts were simple and conflicted: in order to avoid the possibility of being recognized and arrested, he needed to not drive the cab until he could change the plates and possibility repaint it. But unless he drove the cab, he'd never be able to afford to do those things. As usual, Raymond didn't really have much of a choice.

At least the Americans were a welcome surprise. The only time Raymond felt like he had any inkling of power was when he had foreigners in his car. Foreigners found Haiti special and intriguing. They peppered him with questions about poverty and politics, thrilled by their own boldness. Raymond knew corners of the city the tour guides didn't dare visit, and he made sure his passengers got an eyeful of the real Haiti. So what if it was just an exotic diversion, a spectacle of wealth, poverty, beauty, decay, and chaos that they put into their scrapbook of world travel? So what if he let their imaginations run wild as he drove them through slums and alleyways? Why not razzle-dazzle them if it was a way to share forbidden knowledge with the outside world?

The tourists he drove now wanted to see the sapphire sea unfurl as they left the cruise port behind. But he wanted them to see Haiti as a living entity, not a tropical getaway. When he'd arrived in the city twelve years ago, Raymond sensed that his talent for navigation would save his life and quickly turned from fixing cars to driving them. He'd watched from behind his windshield as Port-au-Prince morphed from a quiet, peaceful, prosperous city into a buzzing beehive, and now he knew the city as well as a professional guide. In better days, when Magloire was still president and the tourists still came, he would marshal his limited English to teach them all about this small, complicated world. And earn extra tips for his family, he thought,

Yvonne's thin face in his mind's eye. But today, with these Americans, Raymond didn't have it in him. He still trembled when he thought of the Macoutes, how he'd almost left his children fatherless, his wife destitute.

Raymond picked up a little speed. He needed to make as much money as he could before curfew. Plus, driving too slowly might call the attention he so feared. Still, he didn't drive as fast as he wanted to, knowing that his passengers needed time to ogle exotic paintings and leather sandals and masks for sale, strung along fences around the parks. They pointed at monuments of mermaids and civic fountains, and when Raymond passed the casinos, the man pulled out a camera and snapped photos while his wife clutched her shopping bags on her lap.

"*Très joli,*" she said to Raymond, mimicking her husband's bad French good-naturedly.

As they sat in traffic near the parliament, she smiled under her large hat when Raymond pointed at pyramid-shaped structures rising from the ground. He smiled back. Raymond always used the same smile with the women tourists. It was both innocent and flirtatious—carefully calibrated to flatter without causing offense to either the woman or her male companion.

"Musée du Panthéon National," Raymond announced.

"Ah, museum?" the husband asked.

Raymond nodded and braked gently, allowing them time to take a closer look and snap a photo. A sea of children in blue school uniforms flooded the steps, trailed by a handful of teachers, also in uniform. Raymond hoped that one day his kids would get to see the national treasures that the children of the rich took for granted. Right now, they were too young to make much of the museum. He still had to help them butter their bread and hold their hands when crossing the street. Suddenly, he was shaken with regret at not chauffeuring them to school this morning. Instead of letting them crawl in the old, peeling backseat of his car, Yvonne had insisted that she'd walk them over before work. "You have enough troubles as it is," she'd whispered, glancing at the

Datsun with a peculiar avoidance in her eyes. "You need to stay home and focus on getting your car fixed up."

Raymond had kissed the children good-bye and then paced his kitchen for an hour before deciding that he had no choice but to work.

Two pedestrians hailed Raymond's taxi and he let them in, grateful for the extra fare. One squeezed in next to the tourists, and the other sat in front next to Raymond.

The Datsun passed the Palais National.

"Faculté de Droit. Law school. My brother teaches there."

"I'm sorry?" the American man asked, incredulous. "He's a lawyer?"

"A lawyer?" The wife's eyes bulged disbelievingly. The other passengers grinned at her surprise.

"Yes," Raymond confirmed without elaboration. "A law professor."

The couple rode in silence for a little ways, digesting this news. The other passengers signaled their stop and paid Raymond before hopping out.

"That's so interesting," the wife said.

In the corner of his eye, Raymond saw a blur, a dark shadow moving across his windshield. He braked just in time, his tires screeching against the curb. The black Jeep drove past slowly and he caught a glimpse of men in uniform, their eyes hidden behind sunglasses, their faces devoid of emotion, the barrels of their guns pointed always at the world. Raymond swallowed hard. He hadn't seen the Macoutes. In fact, he'd nearly plowed into them.

The Americans gasped. "There they are," the man whispered knowingly. "Papa Doc's enforcers. The Tonton Macoutes."

"Oh my goodness!"

The Macoutes scanned Raymond, their expressions glacial in the sunlight. Raymond nodded and waved in apology, seeing the submissive gesture reflected off their sunglasses.

"Is it true they put rubber tires around you?" the husband asked. "Burn you alive?"

"Stop it, Bill," the wife scolded.

Raymond took a deep breath and cruised slowly across the intersection.

"I don't know," he said.

He had to maintain his composure. He couldn't let fear take control of him. The husband started in with questions that made him increasingly nervous—not all Americans were innocent, he knew—and in his voice, Raymond thought he detected a note of amusement. His wife simply averted her eyes and waved her fan. Just as they pulled up to the hotel, the husband asked if laws still mattered much in Haiti, and Raymond responded by announcing the fare loudly. The tourists paid him and jumped out. All around them, cars were honking, and buses loaded and unloaded right there in the middle of traffic. Raymond pocketed his money and sped away, his heart racing.

Sweat pooled on Nicolas's forehead and in his sideburns, and he pulled out a handkerchief to wipe his brow. Overhead, the ceiling fans spun quietly, barely dissipating the tropical heat. His mother always said, *"Santi bon koute chè."* *It takes a lot of money to look like a million bucks.* Nicolas L'Eveillé stubbornly weathered the heat of his classroom in a fine suit, and the female students admired his refined taste in pinstripes, charcoal grays, and navy blues, his rich mauve ties and gold cuff links. The male students studied his shoes and tried to memorize the style, the fit, the color, the stitching, the leather Eve had the maid polish each morning.

But nerves exacerbated his sweating this morning. He didn't know how the students would receive his lecture.

"Turn your books to page two hundred and sixty, where we begin our lecture on the penal code."

Some students scribbled furiously as he began, but others eyed each other quizzically. A hand shot up in the air.

"Maître? What about the lecture on human rights? The one from last week?"

Nicolas maintained his composure, but beneath his stoic appearance, he was crumbling. "We have to catch up with the curriculum. As I was saying, the law penalizes people who may or may not be criminals, but those people will one day be your clients regardless. You will have to represent them." Nicolas turned to the blackboard and scribbled the name of a case study in large letters. It would be foolhardy to venture into anything as incendiary as human rights right now.

At two o'clock, the students still hadn't shut their notebooks. Nicolas scrutinized the auditorium, scanning for a face or two who would protest his new lesson, but found none. Nicolas had a reputation for being an eloquent and passionate orator. Students and professors alike referred to him as "Maître." Unlike most professors at the Faculté de Droit, Nicolas was not dictating or regurgitating doctrine. He had ideas. Loud ones. Borderline dangerous ones. Lately, straggling students on their way out of other classes would huddle by the windows and doors of his lecture hall, eavesdropping through the open louvers. They'd whispered to each other. "Maître L'Eveillé is crazy," they'd say. "He makes sense, but he's crazy."

Nicolas's greatest fear was that his students—that the entire next generation—would transform Haiti into a nation of obedient sheep. Sometimes he couldn't resist pushing the bounds of his lectures in an attempt to shake them from their complacency.

"Before long, they'll probably rewrite the history books," he'd complained to Jean-Jean once. "I know it's risky, but it's my duty to teach my students something about their country before it's too late."

But now, with his family's life on the line, he had to show more restraint.

He glanced at his watch. "Next week we'll pick up where we left off."

Nicolas himself exited with the clamoring students, swallowed up by the swarm. He'd gotten used to this strange intimacy, the whirlwind of young people's hair pomade, cologne, and rapid chatter. He could see the unruly hairs on the napes of necks, the sweat-stained collars, the modest jewelry.

The crowd spilled into the courtyard. Nicolas inhaled the fresh air and made his way beneath a canopy of bougainvillea. He'd first sat in this courtyard years before, a fresh-faced student trying to escape his loneliness with a book. Today, he followed the cobblestone paths past a monument he didn't dare look at: a bronze bust of Papa Doc. Nicolas heard someone call after him.

"Maître! Wait!"

He turned around and saw a young man racing to catch up. He was limping, his face contorted in a grimace. Nicolas wasn't sure he recognized him, but with at least eighty students in each class, that wasn't unusual.

"I really was hoping you would finish last week's lecture on censorship and human rights. It was very interesting."

The young man waddled alongside Nicolas, huffing. He was short and stout, with a large chest and square shoulders. In one hand, he carried a black notebook and a legal pad, and in the other, a tape recorder. Nicolas felt for his keys and kept walking toward the campus gates.

"For instance, what did you mean the other day when you said we were being censored?" the student asked.

"What did you think I meant?" he asked, taking quick steps toward the parking area.

"I'm not sure," the young man said. "Were you referring to the government's crackdown on communism? Because that's what it sounded like."

"I never said that." Nicolas glared at the student.

They arrived at the sidewalk. Behind them, the university's white walls loomed under a blue sky. A string of cars parked along the curb made it difficult for Nicolas to spot his own vehicle. Students rushed past them, weaving through traffic and hailing tap-taps and taxis, which serenaded them with honks and street music.

"Because communism is a disease," the student said. "That's what His Excellency says. We are to eradicate it from our midst. Don't you agree?"

Nicolas spotted his car. He stopped just inches away from it and turned to face the young man, the hairs on his neck bristling. He saw the tiny beads of sweat glued to the student's forehead.

"What is your name?" Nicolas asked.

"Philippe Joseph, Maître."

"Tell me, Joseph. What is it you're after?" Nicolas asked, wanting to dive into the Peugeot. "You want me to talk about communism? You want me to lose my job? Is that it?"

The young man faltered. "I'm sorry, Maître—"

"I never once said a thing about communism," Nicolas said. "That's something I know nothing about. So what do you want exactly? You want to teach the class for me? Is that it?"

"Well, no—" Joseph answered.

"Do you know you can get yourself in trouble that way, talking about communism?"

Joseph fidgeted. "I'm just interested in your lecture, Maître."

"Right, so why don't we address the core of the curriculum? You seem much too intelligent to be concerned with trivialities."

"But—"

"Next class, we'll talk about misdemeanors and punishments. I'll bring in a mock case, and you get to take first crack. Show me what you're made of. How does that sound?"

Joseph grinned, his face beaming in the sunlight. "*Au revoir,* Maître."

Nicolas left the young man standing there as he got in his car. Through the din, he recognized a particular car horn, blaring repeatedly as it got closer. He looked over his shoulder and saw a white Datsun fly past the university. An arm popped out the window, and a large hand waved. Raymond. Nicolas waved back, and then Raymond was gone again.

Behind the wheel of his own car, he thought about what Raymond had done, how he'd risked his life without thinking of the consequences. His brother knew how to push his buttons, but they had to find a way back to each other again. After these scuffles, Raymond always pretended nothing had happened, and

Nicolas would generally offer a stiff grin and try for a while to be more tolerant of his older brother. Sometimes, though, he'd drag out the tension until Raymond gave up and avoided their house for weeks. He hated to admit it, even to himself, but Nicolas relished torturing his brother that way. Eventually, when he got tired of his own passive aggression, he'd find an excuse for them to speak again. He'd invite Raymond to come over and watch a football game, or he'd stop by Raymond's place with books for the kids or to teach Enos how to kick a ball like Pelé. He'd always stay in the alley, though, refusing to enter the tiny apartment.

"Won't you come in?" Yvonne would ask. "I'll make coffee."

"Oh, thanks, but I don't have time," Nicolas would say. "I'm just saying hello."

He didn't want to look at the broken faucets or inhale the permanent stench of onions and decaying wood. He didn't want to bring to his lips a cup he suspected hadn't been properly washed or sit on a wobbly chair. So Nicolas stayed outside and Raymond bit his tongue.

When he pulled in that afternoon, Raymond found Madame Simeus in front of the house, mumbling as she watered her plants. She regularly patrolled her front yard, plucking dead leaves from hibiscus bushes, straightening croton branches, and sometimes talking to herself. Today, she was wearing an oversized plaid dress and kept pulling bits of string from her pockets. Her gray hair was set in rollers, and she held a cigarette clamped between her lips as she tied expert knots around bundles of branches and stems.

Raymond approached her with a sigh. He noticed a solemn droopiness to her face as she muttered to herself. He couldn't make out what she was saying, but her tone was oddly grave. Had someone died? Was she sleepwalking again?

He greeted her and expected the habitual, acerbic "Where's my rent?" Instead, she lowered her eyes.

Raymond preempted her, producing the neatly folded money

from his pocket. She took the bills quietly, counted them, and shook her head.

"I told her it wasn't proper, but she wouldn't listen."

Raymond shook his head, confused. "I'm sorry?"

"I don't want to get involved," she continued. "What goes on between you and your wife is none of my business, but..." She shook her head.

"What are you saying?"

Madame Simeus blinked. "Your wife. I saw her pack her bags and get in a taxi with the kids. Someone else's taxi, of course."

Raymond took off running toward the apartment. It wasn't possible. They'd just discussed leaving and he'd made it clear that he wouldn't stand for it. The kids had to stay home. Raymond fumbled with his keys, grabbed the handle too hard, and finally managed to push the door open.

"Yvonne! Yvonne! Where are you?"

The kitchen was perfectly clean, no dishes soaking in the sink; a five-gallon container of water sat half full in a corner. Raymond ran to the bedroom and saw the children's cots empty, the blankets folded. The small, scuffed shoes had disappeared. Their boxes and suitcases had vanished. The armoire door was open, but the hangers hung bare except for Raymond's. The children's books were still there, surely too heavy to take.

Raymond's stomach convulsed. "Enos? Adeline?" He knew they were gone, and saying their names would not conjure them back.

His and Yvonne's bed was neatly made, her clothes and shoes missing. Raymond felt his chest cave in, and he grabbed his head with both hands. Gone. Raymond struggled to breathe. An invisible fire tore through him as he careened out of the house, crushing a small toy car he'd made for Enos out of a juice box and bottle caps.

In the garden, Madame Simeus was standing in the same spot, dumbfounded. She was shaking her head in sympathy.

"Where are they?" he shouted.

She shrugged, and for a moment he thought he recognized genuine fear on her face. She tried to speak, but the words didn't come.

"Where?" he said again.

"I don't know," she said.

"What did she say?"

Madame Simeus stepped back. He'd never been aggressive like this before.

"That's all I know. Shall I call the police? What kind of woman—"

Raymond's eyes widened. Of course. The uncle. How could he not have seen it coming? Of course this is how she would have done it. The only way she could have.

Raymond jumped into his car, leaving Madame Simeus in her garden, perplexed. As he backed out, the taxi's wheels sloppily spinning against the grass, she began running toward him, the skin sagging from her forearms as she waved frantically.

"You're ruining my garden!"

He sped away, his bumper grazing the open gate.

"My gate! Slow down. *M'ap rele la police!*"

The Datsun roared, tires screeching, around the corner of Rue Capois.

SEVEN

By the time Raymond made it to the Plage Publique de Carrefour Dufort, the sun was bowing out behind a curtain of flames. This, he supposed, was where the boat would have come. Yvonne had mentioned once or twice that Dufort was the place. Raymond sprinted through a dense forest of palm trees, sinking into small crescent puddles that the high tide had left near the shoreline. His toes caught the root of a palm tree, and he broke the fall with his hands.

Then he saw the ocean sprawling far into the horizon and frothing gently against the shore. Raymond felt furry cattails brush against his legs as he raced toward the water, avoiding the green coconuts littering the sand. He passed a group of fishermen pushing their canoes between clusters of tree trunks. Inside the hulls, they'd dumped large, heavy fishnets filled with crabs and silver-scaled snappers.

"Yvonne!"

He knew it was hopeless. There were only fishermen and a few teenage boys on the beach now. Yet some part of him believed she was somewhere nearby, that she'd changed her mind. Maybe she'd hear his voice on the wind, turn around, and wave back at him. He didn't see any boats on the water. They were long gone.

Raymond felt something crack inside him. His shoulders dropped.

He spotted a young man sitting on a hollow tree trunk with a geography book and asked him if he'd seen a woman with two little kids. He held up his precious photograph in the fading light. Ribbons in Adeline's hair, blue shorts on Enos, a floral scarf around Yvonne's head. The young man shook his head.

"The boy is very small," Raymond said, gesturing with his hand. "Like this. No?"

The boy might very well have been there, the young man explained, seeing as the ferryman had come today. Whenever he pulled up his little tugboat, the hundreds of men, women, and children massed on the beach would fight their way aboard, begging for the privilege to pay the ferryman's colossal fee. The boy might have been there, but the young man couldn't remember seeing anyone who stood out. There were just so many of them.

How had Yvonne gotten the money? Raymond wondered. She must have been saving up for a very long time.

Raymond appealed to the fishermen, but they hadn't paid any more attention than the young man. He finally came across an old man who said he'd seen a mother with two children boarding a boat around noon. That would mean they really were long gone, probably past the isle of La Gonâve by now, in a boat overflowing with refugees.

"She didn't tell you she was leaving?" the old man asked. "So much danger in this *kanntè* business. These boats are not safe. Too many people."

Night soon cloaked the shore in an inky blue. Raymond kept walking. His body was exhausted, but his eyes still frantic, searching the horizon. There was nothing but a fine line slicing through sky and sea—no trace of a sailboat, ship, or raft.

How could he not have seen it coming? He should have paid attention to what she'd been telling him for so long about her plans to take the children to live with her uncle in Miami. She had given up trying to get him to come with them. He wanted to punch himself for not having listened. Had he really believed she would stay by his side when he couldn't feed his children? Raymond dropped to the ground and sat another hour, his head on his knees, until he lost all feeling in his legs. He took no notice of the drunks and vagrants traipsing around by the shadowy coconut palms. Exhaustion and pain throbbed in his bones, but there was another pain running even deeper, a great darkness he knew would plague him forever. He remained seated awhile longer, until the stars shimmied overhead and a breeze began to blow in off the ocean.

Raymond found a vendor selling *clairin* and bought a little bottle of the sweet spirit with the remaining change in his pocket. He wasn't a heavy drinker, so the alcohol swam up to his head on the first sip. He plunged through the darkness in the direction of his car, balling his fists, his nails digging into his own flesh. He wanted to hate Yvonne for what she'd done.

As Raymond neared his car, he felt his knees go weak, envisioning it before him: an overflowing boat, the turbulent waves, interception by the Macoutes, the possibility of getting shot, of capsizing, of being chased by the American coast guard, of being eaten by sharks. He plopped into the seat of his car and leaned against the headrest. Defeat was settling in, bone crushing. Under the soles of his muddy shoes, he felt the grittiness of sand.

Raymond removed the red ribbon from his mirror and tossed it on the floor. He lowered his windows. With no chance at making it home before curfew, it seemed best to stay here. He closed his eyes, praying for sleep. But behind his eyelids was the image of Yvonne on the day of their small church wedding. She'd seemed to him like the Virgin Mary herself, in a dress of intricate lace and flowers a local seamstress had stitched.

They had traveled to her hometown on the island of La Gonâve. They'd found a pretty blue church on a hill. That day, she wore a veil that hid her face. He lifted it to find that she'd smeared her cheeks with too much rouge, and that the hot comb she'd used to straighten her hair had burned her hairline. She'd doused herself with so much perfume that his head spun when he leaned in to kiss her cheek.

"I had to cover up the ammonia smell," she whispered, lowering her eyes.

Raymond smiled, moved by her desire to be beautiful for him on their special day. He knew her job as a laundress would ruin her looks, but he loved her regardless.

If she hadn't left, she'd be in bed, breathing next to him. He would turn and move his face closer to hers, feel the heat of her body. And he would listen in the night, shutting out the scurrying and scratching of mice against the wooden floors to pick out the sound of his children's soft snores nearby.

Opening his eyes in the dark car, he brought the bottle to his lips and gulped the rest of the alcohol, giving himself over to absurd fantasies about their return. Remorse burned his throat.

At dawn, right when curfew lifted, Raymond drove home like a zombie, lips tight at the corners. He swerved off the road once to avoid an oncoming pair of headlights. When he opened the door to his apartment, the silence shattered his heart all over again. He couldn't stop looking for the torn laces and damaged soles of his children's shoes, the dirty socks rolled inside like little cotton fists. Now there was nothing.

He fell onto Adeline's cot, curled up with his head nestled in the hollow of his arm. He stayed there all day. The silence was in his head, biting at him under his scalp like lice. When night fell again, he tore at his hair to get it out, but it was no use. The silence ate him alive.

A day after the intruder in his yard, there was a loud banging on the front door. Nicolas jolted out of bed and listened.

The knocks persisted. Eve sat up, startled.

"What is it?"

Before Nicolas could answer, a voice rose in the night, shouting something he couldn't quite understand. His heart quivered in his chest. He opened the bedroom door halfway.

"Who is it?" he called down the hall. He could hear the tremolo in his own voice. "It's the middle of the night!"

"MVSN! Open up!"

Eve cursed. She jumped up and grabbed the baby from the crib. Nicolas froze. Impossible! His body sagged against the doorway, and he clasped the knob to keep himself upright.

"Open up, or we blast this door open!" the voice shouted.

Nicolas had rehearsed this moment in his mind many times. Now it was truly happening. The strange phone calls, the shadows in the yard, and now here they were. He turned to his wife.

"Take the baby. Get out of the house. Now!"

"You're not coming?"

Her voice was uneven, and in the faint light, he could see that she was white as a sheet. Her chest rose and fell as she tried to breathe through the terror.

"Go! Find Raymond. He'll help you."

The banging on the door rattled the furniture around them. Amélie started to fuss. Clutching the baby, she headed toward the kitchen. Nicolas waited a few moments longer, heard the kitchen door close and the latch click. *Let her make it safely,* he thought. He hoped she would follow their plan. They'd talked about it, of course, like so many Haitians had: She would sneak out the back, escape to the alley. She would find a place to hide. She would jump the fence if she had to. She would go to their neighbor's and find a way to contact Raymond.

Nicolas pushed his way to the beleaguered front door as if through water. He turned the lock and was immediately flung back. Men dressed in blue, with red ascots around their necks, stormed into the foyer and the living room. They held their machine guns up and scanned the room while one of them shouted orders in Creole. Nicolas was grabbed by the collar, his face pulled toward the barrel of a handgun.

"What is this?" Nicolas cried out.

He was surprised to find the courage to speak into the mouth of a gun. Somehow, he hadn't expected such sudden violence.

Hostility, yes. But not this. He blinked at his own reflection in the Macoute's aviators and saw there a naive and coddled fool. It wasn't the Macoute he hated in that moment, but himself.

"Go!" the Macoute ordered, and the other men dispersed into Nicolas's home.

The Macoute kept one hand on Nicolas's pajama collar while the other adjusted his grip on the weapon. He seemed ready to fire, and Nicolas clenched his jaw as the man turned to him. Perhaps it was for the best that the glasses hid his assailant's eyes. Whatever evil leered beneath was probably worse. The glasses were a crucial element of the Macoutes' uniform, fueling the rumors that they were not men but devils, evil spirits, loup-garou.

"Are you Nicolas L'Eveillé?" the Macoute barked.

Nicolas nodded, breathless. The Tonton Macoutes were ravaging his home, tossing cushions, tables, and chairs across the room. They seemed possessed with anger. A vase shattered; a picture frame slammed against the terrazzo floor. He heard more commotion behind them. They were in his study. Nicolas thought of the secret compartment, the drawer in which he kept his gun and his notebook. It was shocking how foolish real fear made you feel. How stupid.

Nicolas noticed his assailant's bushy mustache. His upper lip quivered with rage when he spoke. Nicolas recognized spite when he saw it. What had he ever done to this man?

"Am I under arrest?" Nicolas asked, dropping his voice to the only octave of calm he could summon. "What is this about?"

In the background, men moved briskly, methodically ransacking the living room. He heard other sounds coming from the study: a heavy piece of furniture scraping over the floor, drawers sliding open, the rustle of paper. He prayed they stayed inside. He prayed Eve was gone, safe from the wrath he'd brought upon them. He wanted to leap across the room and destroy these men. But what could he do? For all of his revolutionary fervor, he'd never hit a person in his life.

"You are under arrest for high treason," the man replied, and laughed.

"Treason?" Nicolas echoed. He felt something crawl into the lining of his stomach, a wave of sickness churning in his guts. "I don't know what you mean."

"Oh, you don't know?" the Macoute said.

He lowered his gun and shoved the barrel deep into Nicolas's belly. Nicolas held his breath. He wasn't thinking of the bullet. A bullet was quick. If he had to die, then he wouldn't suffer much, he hoped. He was thinking of Eve and Amélie. He couldn't stand to think of what might be done to them.

"Are you mocking me?" the Macoute said. His breath reeked of *clairin*.

How much alcohol had this man consumed? Nicolas's mind raced. How could he stall the Macoutes to give his family more time?

"W-why would I mock you?" Nicolas stammered. "Why are you charging me with treason? I haven't done anything."

The man laughed again. "I am charging you with nothing. I only follow orders."

"Found something!"

One of the men came out of his study holding the green folder. He handed it to the mustached gunman, who passed off Nicolas to several others.

His book, his manuscript, with all of those names right there in black ink: Jacques Stephen Alexis, Jules Sylvain Oscar, Juan Bosch, François Duvalier. *These names will kill me,* he thought, heart racing as the Macoute scanned the pages with a plump finger.

"What's this?"

Nicolas did not answer. He couldn't even if he wanted to, his jaw was clenched so tightly. He heard a scream from the back of the house and his blood curdled. He jerked in the men's grasp, but the head Macoute didn't lift his eyes from the document. Finally he stopped on a certain line. He squinted incredulously as he brought the page closer to his face.

"Are you aware of what you've written?" He looked directly at Nicolas. "You wrote this?"

Nicolas said nothing.

"This is a plot, a plot to conspire against His Excellency. What do you know about Jacques Stephen Alexis? Where did you get this information?"

"I don't know what you're talking about," Nicolas blurted out. The words collided in his head. Had he ever, in the luxurious comfort of his study, imagined actually denying this?

Nicolas didn't anticipate the blow to the face, and he kept his eyes closed as the man struck him again. Pain came next, rocketing through his jaw, but he almost welcomed it.

"Traitor!" the man spat. "You are an enemy to the Republic of Haiti. Our source was right."

"No...no traitor," Nicolas grunted, gritting his teeth. He'd never been hit before. His lips were numb with pain, but he tried to think on his feet. "I have friends at the Ministry of Fi—"

"Shut up! You seem to think you're in a position to argue. One more peep and I will blow your brains out. Then I'll collect them and bring them to His Excellency myself." He stared hard at Nicolas, clearly eager to deliver on his promise. "You are coming with us to Casernes Dessalines, and there you will await your transfer to Fort Dimanche!"

The Macoute turned to the others. "Anything else?" he asked.

Nicolas bit his lip.

"There's no one else here," one of the Macoutes replied. "We found an empty crib, no child. No wife. A packed bag. There's a maid out back. She claims she doesn't know anything, but we'll see about that."

Nicolas gasped. Poor Freda! And yet it seemed like Eve had gotten away. For now.

The Macoute's mustache twitched again. "So noted. The wife's escape is proof of her guilt as well. Let's go."

The men filed out of the house. A cool wind blew in from the garden through the open door, and Nicolas smelled the familiar fragrance of his roses and jasmine blossoms. They'd never smelled so sweet. Two pairs of hands dragged Nicolas outside. He resisted their grip, then felt the hard butt of a rifle against his cheek. Another punch to the jaw darkened his consciousness for a moment. He came to quickly, his mouth filled with blood.

Monsieur Pierre-Louis's dog leapt against the fence, barking furiously. The other dogs on the street swiftly joined in and a concerto of howls rose in the night. Nicolas thought he saw a light at Monsieur Pierre-Louis's window. Maybe Eve and Amélie had found their way in next door.

He felt a tightening around his head. A hood. Flashing before his eyes in the sudden darkness, he saw his garden, the pink-and-white rose petals crawling along the stucco, and he felt his daughter's small hand clutching his finger, the softness of Eve's raven hair. He was thrown into a truck and felt himself pulled under.

Raymond only opened his eyes when he accepted the knocking on the door would not stop. He lay there waiting, praying that Madame Simeus would leave. He could hear her raspy voice insulting him through the door.

His head was pounding. He'd found a half bottle of rum that Yvonne had snuck home from her Friday night job, and he'd downed it in one sitting, hoping to escape his agony. Raymond had never been a drinker. In fact, Nicolas always teased him about it, saying he had the alcohol tolerance of a five-year-old girl.

"L'Eveillé! Open up!"

Raymond was soaked in sweat. What day was it? He tried to remember, and it came back, slowly, the memory of having remained in bed all day without going to work. The memory of that evening on the beach, of the night in his car when he'd come to understand the depth of his abandonment. He rolled over and moaned, his head throbbing against the pillow. Slowly, he stumbled out of bed.

He limped barefoot in the dark. He lit a kerosene lamp on the kitchen table and stepped over the shoes he'd kicked off at the entrance. When he opened the door, dawn blinded him. A black silhouette stood before him. He squinted, bringing it into focus. Madame Simeus stood with a hand on her hip, her face scrunched into a scowl.

"It's six o'clock in the morning!" she snarled.

His eyes burned in their sockets. "Wake up, Madame Simeus!" he roared. "You're sleepwalking again."

"I beg your pardon?" Madame Simeus grumbled indignantly. "You have a phone call. We've discussed this before: phone calls are between eight and six. Have you no respect for others?"

"I don't understand," he mumbled.

"Someone is on the phone for you!" she snapped. "It's the third time she's called this morning! And it's not your wife, L'Eveillé. Is this why Yvonne left you? You're a *coureur de jupes*? A womanizer?"

She stuck her neck out, sniffing the air before grimacing. She reminded Raymond of a turtle. "Eh! And you've been drinking?"

"I don't have a girlfriend," Raymond slurred.

He fought back the urge to vomit. He needed water desperately. He had no idea who was calling him. If it wasn't Yvonne, then who? Since he couldn't afford a phone of his own, he'd given Madame Simeus's phone number to the children's school and to Nicolas and Eve in case of emergency. Had something happened?

Raymond backed away from the light. He grabbed a pair of pants, gulped some water, and tried to keep his balance as he stumbled out into the yard. Madame Simeus walked ahead of him, muttering under her breath. Raymond followed close behind, shading his eyes from the light. The thick, sweet smell of the gardenia blossoms made his stomach churn.

Once in the house, Madame Simeus led him to the telephone in its small vestibule. A faint smell of coffee floated in the air, together with the salted herring and cornmeal she always had at breakfast. Raymond's face flushed with embarrassment. He'd always been an early riser. Right now, he should be getting ready for work. But he'd been too weak to get out of bed since Yvonne had left.

"Is this going to happen again?" Madame Simeus asked, pointing at the receiver. "If it does, you're out of here, no excuses."

"Thank you, Madame Simeus," Raymond spat before picking up the receiver.

"And tell the hussy to stop calling."

"I'll let you know when I'm done," Raymond said.

He watched her walk down the dark hallway, pausing briefly to adjust an old photograph of her deceased husband on the wall. Suddenly, he felt sorry for the sad, old woman. He was like her now: left here all alone. Raymond pressed the phone against his ear.

"Who is this?" he asked.

"It really happened, Raymond."

"Eve?"

Raymond supported himself against the wall. It was Eve's voice, but he had never heard her like this. The poise was gone, replaced by urgency, desperation.

"They took him."

"Eve? What are you saying?"

"They took Nicolas, Raymond!" she screamed into the phone. "They came into the house, and they took him! Do you understand? The Tonton Macoutes arrested him, and they took his manuscript. They found it. Oh God—" She broke into wails at the other end of the line.

Raymond was suddenly awake.

"They took Nicolas?"

"Are you listening to anything I'm saying? Raymond, I need you."

Raymond heard her speak, but it was like a dream. His head felt like it was full of cotton. He tried to shake off the exhaustion and self-pity and rum.

"Eve, slow down!" Raymond was convinced he was going to be sick right here in Madame Simeus's vestibule. He took a deep breath.

"There's no time. You wake up right now. Get dressed. You have to get him back for me. Do you hear me? You have to help us!"

EIGHT

Raymond's car slipped through the gates of his brother's house at seven. The padlock had been severed—the Macoutes must have used bolt cutters to let themselves in. The sun had already risen, and the Turgeau neighborhood rang with the bells of shoeshine boys canvassing the streets. He parked next to Nicolas's car.

The neighbor's yellow mutt ran to the fence to bark at him, and Raymond jumped back, startled. He wondered what the dog had seen, and if it had been barking when they came to take his brother away. Did Nicolas know they were coming for him?

Raymond found the front door slightly ajar. The strike plate was loose, indicating an attempt to break the door down. Raymond ran his fingers along the acacia frame before pushing the door open. The chaos inside left him breathless. He took in the shattered glass, torn lampshades, overturned chairs, dangling paintings, and, there, the rocking chair he used to sit in with Amélie—a gaping hole in the center of its ornate caning. Raymond's heart broke.

"Eve?" he called as he entered the living room, stepping over books and papers.

The house was unrecognizable. Nicolas and Eve had been so proud when they first bought it. Raymond had helped them move in the furniture Eve had commissioned from the friars of Saint-François de Sales, fixed the cabinet doors, and painted Amélie's crib. He knew this house as well as they did, almost as if he'd built it with his own two hands. He had the blueprint etched in his mind, and he fantasized about using this house as a model for the one that he would own one day, that he would build for his family. A house with three bedrooms, a kitchen with running water, tables carved out of mahogany or oak, and a backyard where his kids could play without having to answer to a grumpy landlord. Nicolas's house was all he'd ever wanted for himself. Raymond felt as if it were his own home that had been violated.

"Eve? Where are you?"

"I'm in here."

He followed her voice as she repeated, "I'm in here, in here," like a chiding parrot. He didn't know what to expect when he walked in Nicolas's office, but hoped she wasn't hurt. He found Eve sitting in a corner, holding Amélie against her chest. The child was sound asleep in her small white shirt and pants. The room was dim, so Raymond pulled back the curtains. The sunlight spilled in, blinding Eve. Raymond saw her rocking back and forth, eyes swollen, skin pale in the bright daylight. No bruises. No blood. He wondered if he should look away because she wasn't properly dressed, but in this moment, he had to ignore the shape of her bare breasts under the nightgown, her bare shoulder where the child's brown head rested.

"Are you all right?" he whispered as he approached her.

He stepped over an antique clock whose time had stopped, the glass cracked, the hands frozen at four o'clock.

He saw trails of dried tears on Eve's face, and her eyelashes were still wet from crying.

"No one would come," she muttered.

Raymond rested his hands on her shoulders and kissed her forehead. She let him, didn't push him away. His knees trembled and nearly buckled as he righted a chair and sat down next to her. Raymond put his arm around Eve and pulled her closer.

Amélie awoke, opened her eyes, and smiled when she saw her uncle. She reached for him and Raymond sat the baby on his lap.

She was warm and smelled like talcum powder, and he buried his face in her curls. She too had been crying, he could tell. "No one would come," Eve repeated. She turned to face him. Her hair was still in large pink curlers. Her lips reminded Raymond of faded rose petals. "I've been up all night with the neighbors," she said. "Monsieur Pierre-Louis from next door saw me jump the fence, so he took us in. He hid us in his maid's room."

Raymond felt her body move away, as if she were suddenly waking up. She shifted in her seat.

"I wanted to stay with Nicolas," she continued. "But he wouldn't allow it. He made me leave. And Amélie, I had to think of her."

Raymond listened but didn't speak. He let her describe how she'd first run to Freda outside, how the maid had held the baby while she jumped the fence. She'd often played out the scenario in her head and had planned to take the bag that she'd prepared for emergencies. But when the moment came, she'd forgotten, too crippled with fear.

After the Macoutes left and everything seemed quiet, Monsieur Pierre-Louis had warned her not to return to the house, warned her that they might come back, but she had to go see for herself. She wanted to make sure Nicolas wasn't there, that he wasn't dead. Freda had spent the night awake in terror.

"The Macoutes sent men to interrogate her," Eve said. "They didn't arrest her, but she was afraid for her life. She told them she had no idea where I was. They beat her..."

Raymond's eyes lingered on Nicolas's empty desk chair. He pictured men handcuffing his brother and hitting him. It was difficult to stomach. Nicolas was too dignified a man to be treated this way! His brother's absence, the fact that Duvalier's henchmen had really and truly abducted Nicolas—the meaning of it all started to sink in.

"Freda said she heard them take him away, my Nicolas," Eve added, her voice breaking. "She said they were taking him to Casernes Dessalines. My poor Nicolas..."

She paused, unable to suppress a shudder. "I called everyone we know," she said. "I called Jean, Georges, and neither one would come. They were too afraid. They said there was a curfew." She turned her large, wet brown eyes toward him, her thin eyebrows arched in desperation. "I'm never going to see him again, am I?"

Raymond lowered his gaze.

Amélie rested her face against Raymond's chest and he sighed. He missed Adeline and Enos. He held her closer as if to compensate for their absence. Amélie was round and chubby, her skin almost as delicate as a spiderweb. She was different from his own children, who were frail like small twigs and black like the night; his children, who smelled like the lemongrass leaves they stirred at night in their tea when there was nothing to eat for dinner. He felt overcome with a wave of grief. He thought of telling Eve about their departure, but he was afraid both of them might collapse under the weight of so much loss.

Raymond handed the baby over to her mother and stood up to peer out the window. No one was out there, but he was still uneasy. Monsieur Pierre-Louis was right. Returning to the house hadn't been a good idea.

Something crunched under his shoe. He picked up the picture frame and stared at the black-and-white photograph. Two little boys stood side by side in shorts, long-sleeved shirts, and ties. The taller boy had an arm around the younger one. Raymond's heart sank. He'd forgotten this picture existed, but remembered the day it was taken. It was from Nicolas's First Communion—a rosary dangled from the boy's hands. Raymond searched the young faces and found that he was the only one smiling. In the photo, his little brother was frowning. That was Nicolas. Always so serious.

"Raymond?" Eve said. "Will I ever see him again?"

She'd started to tear up again.

The words rolled out of his mouth as he put the picture frame down.

"Don't worry," Raymond said. "We'll find him."

NINE

Jean Faustin's office was located on Rue Pavée, at the center of downtown Port-au-Prince, a few miles from Nicolas's home. Raymond almost missed it, its narrow steel door wedged inconspicuously between a third-generation Lebanese fabric store and a sandwich shop where Nicolas once said he used to buy lunch for his mentor.

The entrance was further obscured by the mass of street vendors on the sidewalk. Raymond and Eve had to fight their way through spreads of peanuts, coconut brittles, and avocados. The door was locked, and they waited a few steps away for Jean-Jean.

The old man turned up just a few minutes later and paused a moment to bicker with the vendors. Raymond heard him plead with them that the clutter was bad for his business.

"My clients won't come to consult me in the thick of an outdoor market," he complained. But the vendors paid him no mind.

One woman laughed at him outright. "Everyone needs to make a living," she said. "The streets belong to all of us."

Jean-Jean finally relented and pulled out his keys. He fumbled with them, holding them up to the light. Raymond had heard his brother say that the judge's vision, affected by diabetes, had started to fail him, making it increasingly difficult to locate small objects or read street names. He didn't notice Eve and Raymond standing there. Raymond kept his hand on Eve's back, steering her through the crowd as she held the baby.

Jean-Jean was hunched over the latch, his face close to the bolt as he manipulated the key. He was dressed in a navy suit and held a tattered briefcase, which he carried everywhere he went.

"Jean-Jean," Eve called. She shifted Amélie from one arm to the other. The little girl sucked on a pacifier and kicked her legs, her eyes damp with uncertain tears. "It's me."

Jean-Jean turned around, startled. The color drained from his face, and his mouth trembled.

"Eve? What are you doing here?" he asked. His eyes darted left and right to make sure no one else was lying in wait. "You can't come here."

"I didn't know where else to go," Eve said. "You said on the phone that you couldn't come because of the curfew, so we came to you."

Raymond stepped in closer and looked at him. It took a moment for Jean-Jean to recognize rough, disheveled Raymond as Nicolas's brother.

"Can you help us?" Raymond asked. "Nicolas was arrested this morning. They found his book."

Jean-Jean averted his eyes, but Raymond had already seen the sheepishness in them. He knew that look. He'd seen it many times in his cab when passengers scratched their heads because their wallet had suddenly gone missing, or mumbled that they were short on cash. Disappointment seeped into Raymond's bones. This was the man Nicolas spoke so highly of?

"I warned him about making waves," Jean-Jean said. "I told him."

He shook his head, shrugged his shoulders. He still wouldn't look Raymond in the eyes, and Raymond swallowed his budding disgust.

"I'm sorry," he continued. "I wish I could help."

"But you're a judge," Eve said, moving in closer. "You can do something. They'll listen to you if you intervene on his behalf. Nicolas always said you were the first person I should contact if something ever happened to him."

"I can't take that risk." Jean-Jean glanced over his shoulder.

Raymond recognized fear when he saw it. The man was afraid.

Trucks and cars zoomed down the street, honking incessantly for slower drivers and pedestrians to move out of their way. Uniformed schoolchildren had flooded the streets, buying porridge and bread on their way to class. A man with wavy gray hair and fair skin came out of the fabric store and stood at the threshold, sipping a demitasse of coffee. He glanced at Jean-Jean and nodded politely. The top two buttons on his shirt were open, revealing a Star of David caught in the wiry black hair of his chest.

"So you're going to let him die?" Raymond spat.

His head was stuffy. He hadn't eaten. Eve had dressed in a hurry, throwing on a blouse and skirt; they hadn't thought about food. He needed water or coffee—something in his stomach. He couldn't manage to hide his anger and disgust with Jean-Jean's cowardice.

The man at the fabric store cleared his throat.

"Ça va, Maître Faustin?" he asked. "Everything all right?"

Jean-Jean turned around and nodded politely.

"Good morning, Mr. Levy. Yes, everything is fine! Don't worry. These are friends of mine."

Mr. Levy caressed his bushy mustache with his small, stubby hand. A gold ring glittered as he raised his cup to his lips. He looked dubious. Raymond could smell brilliantine.

"Are you sure?" Mr. Levy insisted.

"We're discussing private business," Raymond said.

He didn't like the way Mr. Levy looked at him. Raymond could see the contempt in the storeowner's eyes as he assessed Raymond's dirty pants and scuffed shoes. Raymond turned back to Jean-Jean and shook his head.

"You're supposed to be Nicolas's friend," he said.

"And I am, but that doesn't mean I can compromise my own safety just because you show up here like this, at my place of business, unannounced!"

The judge was now waving his arms as he spoke. He was agitated. Nervous.

"Jean, it's us you're talking to," Eve said. "Please. Can't you do anything for us? For Nicolas?"

He looked over his shoulder again, scanning the crowd, and

lowered his voice as he turned back, choking on his words. "I'm being followed. Most likely they will arrest me too. I will lose my job. I will lose everything."

Raymond stared at him. "My brother will lose his life," he said. "I guess he was wrong about you."

Jean-Jean thought for a moment, then shook his head slowly. "I'm very sorry. I can't help. I can't do anything."

Eve cocked her head to the side. "And what about Amélie?" she asked. "What am I supposed to tell her?"

Jean-Jean's eyes flared with anger. "I asked Nicolas the same thing, Eve. What about his family? Your life? He said he had a plan for you if things went bad. Well, I'll tell you now, things are bad. If you have a plan, then I recommend you take immediate steps to follow it, and hope it's not too late to save yourself and your daughter."

Raymond studied Jean-Jean one more time and concluded by the way his shoulders drooped that it was no use. He was too afraid. The judge still couldn't look them in the eyes, just stared down at his shoes.

"I'm going to work now," he muttered, turning the key in the lock.

Jean-Jean slammed the metal door behind him. He climbed the steps up to his office and left Eve and Raymond standing on the sidewalk. Eve shook her head in dismay. Mr. Levy was still staring at them. The air between Raymond and Eve grew cold.

Raymond parked in Georges Phenicié's driveway and took a deep, appreciative breath, inhaling the smell of the leather seats in Eve's navy-blue Renault. Raymond had never been in a new car before, not one like this. And he'd certainly never ridden in Eve's. His children had once, and they made it sound like their aunt had taken them for a ride in a plane. He pulled the key out of the ignition and glanced over at Eve. She hadn't said a word during the drive from Jean's office.

"It's a nice car," he said. "But I don't think we should drive it again."

She nodded. "And I don't think Georges will help us."

Raymond's hands clutched the soft wheel of the Renault.
"Are you all right?" she asked.

He nodded. "I'm fine."

"Have you been drinking?" she asked.

Raymond sighed, realizing that he still reeked of alcohol. He hadn't had time to wash up before leaving the house. He longed for a decent pillow and a strong cup of coffee, but so far the adrenaline had kept him on his feet.

"I didn't know you drank," she said.

Amélie had fallen asleep in Eve's arms, her head rolling from one side to the other.

"I'm fine," Raymond repeated, pushing himself out of the car. "Let's go."

He'd never been to Georges's house or any home this grandiose. It was a newer two-story gingerbread in the hills of Bel Air, one of the few parts of the city he barely knew. It was the sort of neighborhood designed for old money, and everyone owned their own vehicles. He'd been there only a couple of times to drop off the help outside the gates. Georges's house was stark white with balconies and parapets hidden behind vines and stems of wild orchid blooms cascading over walls. Around them, hidden in the branches of breadfruit trees, doves broke into high-pitched symphonies. The house was minutes away from downtown, but it stood in sharp contrast to the city's chaos. Raymond watched Eve stroll up the walk like it was no big deal.

"This way," she said.

She'd here before. She said she'd sat at the dinner table with Georges and his wife before she'd died of a heart attack. Raymond was seeing another side of his wealthy brother's life: friends who were even wealthier. This was no time to think about material things, but still, Raymond fought a gnawing discomfort as he followed Eve. He felt impossibly out of place. His pants, his shoes, his callused hands—they belonged in the slums of Cité Simone, not here in Bel Air.

Eve knocked three times at the front door, her knuckles banging the carvings of flowers in the oak grain. Amélie woke up, fussing a bit before burying her face in her mother's shoulder again. Raymond wiped sweat from his forehead with the back of his hand. The midday heat had begun to eat away at the city, to eat away at him. They waited, but no one came to the door. This time, Raymond pounded on the door.

"*Honneur?*"

He called out the common, rural salutation, "honor," and soon they heard footsteps approaching. The door swung open, and a young woman's round face appeared. She had a red scarf wrapped around her head. Her skin was of smooth, lustrous ebony, and her small nose twitched when she saw Raymond standing there.

"We're here to see Monsieur Georges," Eve said, leaning closer to Raymond. "It's urgent. Tell him it's Madame Nicolas L'Eveillé."

The servant hesitated as she eyed them both. She recognized Eve and greeted her politely, nodding her head.

"Monsieur Georges is not here," she said, almost singing her answer in Creole.

Raymond recognized a northern accent.

"He left early this morning."

"Left?" Eve echoed, her eyes wild with panic. "I don't understand. To go where? For work?"

The servant shrugged. "I don't know, madame. He didn't say." She dipped her head to express humility just as Raymond's eyes found the black Citroën parked in the driveway. He'd seen it before at Nicolas's. Georges's car. Raymond knew a man like him wouldn't walk and he wouldn't take a taxi.

Something snapped inside him, and Raymond pushed against the door and forced the woman back. "*Pardon,*" he said over her protests. He stormed into the house, and Eve followed him into the foyer, stunned.

"Georges Phenicié? It's Raymond L'Eveillé, Nicolas's brother!"

His voice reverberated against the high ceilings of the house. Eve followed him down a narrow hallway. Raymond walked into a large kitchen, but no one was there. The table was set, the place setting nicely arranged on a hand-embroidered tablecloth, and a fruit holder at the center of the table held scarlet pomegranates and bright, round oranges. On the kitchen counter, Raymond noticed a glass pitcher, the ice still melting in its belly.

"Sir, please," the maid begged, following them both. "You can't just barge in. Monsieur Georges is not here."

She tried to position herself between Raymond and the kitchen, but he walked around her. When she extended her arms and insisted they leave a message, he pushed her aside.

"*Ti chérie*, please, stay out of this!" he said.

Raymond went into the dining room, the living room, and saw nothing but empty couches and chairs, embroidered pillows and chandeliers. Exotic bouquets of eucalyptus and peacock feathers fanned out from ornate crystal vases. No one.

"I don't believe this," Eve muttered.

"Georges Phenicié!" Raymond screamed once more. He glanced at Eve and lowered his voice. "He's got to be here somewhere."

The maid gasped and covered her mouth to stifle her indignation when Raymond ran up the stairs toward the bedrooms, holding on to the railing. Raymond heard her mumble something about calling the police. Eve followed him, out of breath and slowed down by the child in her arms. Amélie had started to cry again, disturbed by Raymond's shouting.

Upstairs, the hallways led to an empty balcony overlooking the city and several bedrooms, all of them empty. Then they arrived at the master suite. *The bed could fit four people,* Raymond thought. The sheets were bright white, bleached and starched, and the curtains had been pulled open to let light shine into the vast space. Raymond was disoriented until he heard a rattling sound.

He stopped in his tracks. "Did you hear that?" he whispered.

Eve froze. They listened, their eyes glued on the armoire that the noise had come from. There it was again. The mirrored door moved.

Raymond walked toward the armoire and pulled the doors open. A shadow shifted between the suits and soon resolved into the silhouette of a man hiding behind ties and double-

breasted jackets. Raymond recognized his two-piece linen ensemble. He called his name and noticed the whites of Georges
Phenicié's eyes as he looked up, sheepish, like a child caught
stealing wedding cake.

"You're hiding from us," Raymond said bitterly. It was pathetic—
this big, imposing, important man cowering in a closet. "Is that
really necessary?"

Georges climbed out of the armoire and ran his fleshy hands
down his pants to smooth the wrinkles. He saw Eve struggling to
soothe the child in her arms and his eyes darted away.

"I'm on my way to the airport," Georges mumbled. "I'm just
packing clothes. I hope you are too, Eve, though I imagine you
have a more stealthy plan for escape than the airport."

Eve shook her head. "I can't abandon him, Georges."

Georges stared at her in disbelief.

"Earlier," she pressed him, "you wouldn't even listen to me on
the phone."

A vein bulged on his forehead.

"The telephone is not a good idea," Georges spat, slamming a
drawer shut. "By now, given your husband's work, I presume you
know about phone tapping—"

"We need your help," Raymond snapped. "Can you do something? They found some of his writing and—"

"I have nothing to do with this," Georges said. "We were clear
with Nicolas that this project was unwise, that he was risking his
life. And now look at us."

Georges walked around the bed. He dragged a suitcase from the
corner and stuffed a few gourdes in his pocket.

"Georges," Eve cried out, "you must know someone at the Ministry of—"

"What do you think is happening here? Do you think that your
husband can write this book and not face the consequences?"

"You can help us, I know you can. Please, appeal on his behalf?"

"I am only the secretary," Georges said, pulling out a passport.
He leafed through it before tucking it back in his pocket. "And if I
am lucky, I will be a refugee by this evening."

Raymond noticed his hands shaking.

"What you need is a judge. Talk to Jean-Jean," Georges added, a little desperately.

"He won't help us," Raymond said. "Both of you are turning your backs on Nicolas, on his family. But when he was passing out cigars and sweet cakes, you were first in line, weren't you?"

Georges turned to look at Eve and then Raymond. His breathing had grown shallow. He stepped closer to Raymond, just a few inches away from his face.

"How dare you insinuate such things?" Georges growled. "Nicolas was my friend."

"Is he still?" Eve asked, a dangerous fire in her eyes.

Georges sighed, looked down at his gray shoes.

"No, Eve." He shook his head. "How can he be? He may be your husband, but he is as good as dead. And look at us. He has forced us to run."

"After all Nicolas has done for you? My God, Georges, he got you out of trouble when that girl's family accused you. Have you already forgotten? It was Nicolas who defended you, who consoled your wife—"

"That never happened!" Georges's eyes widened. "I never touched that girl."

"He fought for you in court," Eve said, brandishing Amélie. "When your wife died and people said horrible things about you, Nicolas stood up for you—"

"Damn it, Eve, this isn't personal," Georges shouted. "I need to leave now and hope like hell that they don't stop me at the airport. I don't know what you want me to do."

"Can you bribe someone?" Raymond asked.

"All my money's tied up abroad right now," he said, shaking his head in protest. "I have kids in college overseas. Once I am free, I will advocate for Nicolas's freedom every day. I will fight for him."

Georges lowered his eyes and squeezed them shut. When he opened them, he produced his wallet and pulled out some bills. He counted them, one by one, and handed them to Raymond instead of Eve. Raymond took the money without a word.

"That's all I can do, one hundred," Georges said.

Raymond's eyes widened. One hundred gourdes was more than he'd ever had in his wallet at once. The amount could pay his children's tuition for four months.

"Take that money to Casernes Dessalines, ask to see Adjudant Joseph. He never says no to money."

Without another word, Georges grabbed his suitcase and walked out. He didn't look back. Raymond stared at the crisp bills in his hands, nothing like the used, crumpled ones he tried to smooth out in his taxi at the end of each day.

Through an open window, the birds sounded loud, almost angry, as the engine of Georges Phenicié's Citroën roared to life. Raymond suddenly felt all the anger and indignation toward Nicolas's friends leave his body. In its place was pity. His brother had caused all of this, and there was nothing these sad, old men could do.

Raymond couldn't figure out what it was about Adjudant Joseph that made him uneasy. Although he looked young and strong, he nonetheless struck Raymond as a man who did very little real work in his life.

When they walked in, Adjudant Joseph was sitting back in his chair, laughing on the telephone with his feet up on his desk. He and Eve stood together before him awkwardly, wondering whether to sit or stand. The officer made no sign of acknowledgment, just continued his conversation as if he were alone.

"Don't worry, my friend," Adjudant Joseph said, his eyes wandering over the view out his window. "I've got you covered. Bill me by head count, I'm good for it."

Raymond considered his perfectly manicured nails, his starched collar, and his freshly shined boots.

"You know me, I like things quiet. No one needs to worry about it."

Finally, Adjudant Joseph caught a glimpse of Eve. He undressed her with his eyes, tracking the contours of her figure, lingering on her chest and her hips. Eve switched her daughter to her other hip as if to remind him of the other realities attached to her body.

After ten more minutes of cryptic conversation, he hung up and rested his hands on the desk, fingers interlaced.

"How can I help you?"

Raymond swallowed with difficulty. Before he could open his mouth, Eve spoke up.

"Adjudant, please, I'm here to beg for any information you may have on my husband. He was taken in the middle of the night from his home in Turgeau. They said they were bringing him here. We deserve to know on what grounds he is being held."

"Grounds?"

"Yes," Eve said. "Please, he's innocent. What has he done? He hasn't harmed anyone."

"Madame, if he was arrested, surely there must have been a reason," the officer said, his eyes flirtatious, his tone coy, as if this were a pickup line in a nightclub.

"His name is Nicolas L'Eveillé," Raymond cut in. "He's my brother. A good man, a father."

Adjudant Joseph looked over in irritation and noticed Raymond, it seemed, for the first time. He shook his head in contempt. "I don't recall..."

"If you look at your files, you'll see," Raymond said, digging through his pockets. "He was probably brought here this morning, early, at dawn. Adjudant, please, we were told you are powerful, that you can help us. You're a good man, that's what Georges Phenicié said. He said you call the shots around here."

Raymond pulled out the roll of gourdes that Georges had given him. He'd added his own cash to the pile on the drive over. His dirty bills stuck together, and he hid them under Georges's crisp new ones. He knew the officer was watching him. His hands trembled slightly as he folded up the money into a wad and held it out.

"Will you help us?" Raymond asked.

Adjudant Joseph stared at the money for a moment, then glanced at the door. He reached for the bills and took them, counting the money before stuffing it in his pocket. He then opened a drawer and pulled out a folder. He flipped through papers. For a moment, all was still except for the sound his fingers made as he skimmed through files. Raymond glanced over at Eve, but she didn't look at him. Biting her lip, she reached for the gold medallion around her neck, a heart with an embossed portrait of the Virgin Mary, and held it against her lips.

"L'Eveillé, yes!" Adjudant Joseph ran his finger over the black lettering. Raymond could see an official stamp on the header, the familiar effigy of palm trees and bayonets, and a signature scribbled at the bottom of the page. "Ah, yes, I remember now. He was brought here on very serious charges. Treason."

"Treason?" Eve shook her head. Her black curls bounced with the movement. She cradled Amélie with both arms. "My husband is no traitor. He's a good man, a citizen, a professor, and he's well respected. He didn't commit any crime."

"Adjudant, we will be forever in your debt if you help us," Raymond said. "I can chauffeur you any time you want, anywhere you like. You name it. I'm your man. No one knows Port-au-Prince like I do. I'm a good cabbie."

Adjudant Joseph silenced Raymond with a crude gesture. Eve fell into the chair behind her.

"Can I see him?" Eve ventured. "I just want to hear his voice."

Adjudant Joseph grabbed his phone again and dialed a number. Raymond's lips moved in silent prayer, but every word was hollow in his heart. Prayer meant nothing since he'd lost his family.

Adjudant Joseph waited on the line. His eye wandered lazily back to Eve, who was still seated, exhausted. Raymond reached for her hand. *We've made a mistake,* he thought. *We've walked into the lion's den, stupidly claiming attachment to a prisoner who's been arrested for treason.* And yet beyond this office there were cells and locked doors, and Nicolas might be behind one of them. Raymond hoped to at least see him, speak to him, try to come up with a plan before he was transferred to Fort Dimanche. Raymond knew he must do everything in his power to free his younger brother.

"Yes, Nicolas L'Eveillé, case number 203786. Scheduled for Fort Dimanche. Has the truck left yet?"

Raymond saw Eve sit up, her hand over her mouth to stifle a cry. Adjudant Joseph listened, nodded, and grunted, *"Oui, merci,"* before hanging up. He stared at Eve and Raymond.

"He's already been transferred to Fort Dimanche," he said. "Nothing I can do."

"No," Eve moaned in her chair before dropping her head in despair.

Raymond stepped closer to the desk, cautious to not touch anything. "There must be something you can do?"

The officer was watching Eve wipe tears from her eyes. Raymond noticed a sly smile forming on his lips. Amélie, unhappy with her mother's tears, began to wail.

"You know? It's such a funny coincidence!" the *adjudant* said, brightening suddenly. "I was once a student of your husband's!" He nodded eagerly at Eve, whose eyes widened in fear.

Raymond glared in disgust at how the man was playing them. His anger was nearly blinding, and he imagined smashing his fist repeatedly into his face.

"Yes!" Adjudant Joseph went on. "And would you believe that my brother Philippe is, or I should say was, attending a lecture course by Maître L'Eveillé this very term! So you see, it turns out we have a lot in common."

Raymond and Eve gaped at the young man.

"Perhaps," he drawled, shifting in his chair, "there is another way. Perhaps, if madame would care to add something extra to the package, I might be able to do something after all. Perhaps I could arrange a private visit to Fort Dimanche."

Eve stared in horror. Raymond trembled in anger. He spun on his heel, grabbed the child from Eve, and gestured for her to stand up.

"Pardon?" Eve began, her eyes widening. "Do you not understand that I'm here for my husband? I'm a married woman. How dare you!"

Raymond took her by the wrist, pulled her up gently, and moved them both quickly toward the door.

"My husband is not a criminal!" she shouted.

"Merci, mon adjudant," Raymond mumbled, nodding with false gratitude. "You've been most kind. Thank you."

As quickly as they'd received the gourdes, they were gone. And for nothing. Raymond guided Eve through the dark hallway by the wrist, carrying Amélie in the other arm. He sped down the stairs so she wouldn't hear the tormented moans and grunts of prisoners shackled inside the cells. Eve was mumbling something, but he dragged her toward the car. He opened the back door to let her in, but she planted her feet in the ground, stubborn, grief stricken, sobbing.

"Eve, get in the car! We have to go."

She let her head drop and cried softly. Raymond tucked the child inside the car and squinted back toward the building. Someone was standing at the window in Adjudant Joseph's office, staring right at them. Raymond felt a pang in his stomach, as he had in his taxi just days ago when he rescued that reporter in Cité Simone. There was danger all around them. Coming here had been a grave mistake. The Macoutes hadn't found Eve that night of the arrest, and now for her and Raymond to walk right into the prison was madness. They might take them away any minute now, the baby included.

"Eve, we can't stay here," Raymond repeated. "We need to go. Now."

"I can't. I won't leave him, Raymond."

The heat, the despair, the fear—all of it had begun to take a toll, and she was coming undone. "I can't abandon my husband," she said. "Everyone else has."

"We can't help him like this," Raymond said. "Get in the car, now! I don't trust this *adjudant*."

Raymond pressed his hand against her back, but she pushed his hand away.

"I'm not leaving," she said. "I am not leaving him."

"He's not here!" Raymond shouted, seizing her wrist.

He squeezed harder, feeling her bones under his grip. She gasped and stared at him in pain and shock.

"You can stand here all day and night crying if you want, and he still won't be returned to you. He's been transferred. You can't help him now. Not like this."

"Everyone's forsaken him." Eve pushed at the tears on her cheeks with the backs of her hands. "Everyone."

"I haven't," Raymond said. "He's my brother. I didn't betray him, I never will. I will find him." He squeezed her wrist more gently this time, and her sobs subsided.

"I will find him," he repeated. "Trust me. But right now, I need you to get in the car, please. We have to get out of here before they come for us. For Amélie, Eve."

Eve fell into the Renault like a broken bamboo stalk. The baby's babble cut through the silence of the car as her mother picked her up and sat her on her lap. Raymond shut the door, and when he got behind the wheel, he looked toward the entrance of the Casernes. Two men were standing in the doorway, staring at them. A third man stepped in between them: Adjudant Joseph. He said something to the men. Raymond scrambled for the ignition.

He hit the gas and swerved away from the curb, missing the car parked in front of him by an inch. Raymond stuck his arm out the window, pressing for drivers to let him through.

"We need to ditch this car," he muttered.

Somewhere around Chemin des Dalles, with the shadows of the afternoon encroaching, Eve accepted that Nicolas was gone. Stopped in front of a street vendor on a crowded street, Raymond got back in the Renault with two colas and a fruit juice and found Eve regarding him sharply while she nursed Amélie.

"Nicolas won't get out of Fort Dimanche, Raymond," she stated flatly. "Not with the charges they have against him. Not with the book."

She had rolled her window down to purchase a bunch of *ti malice*. The fruit sellers, sensing a customer of means, were swarming around the car, but Eve didn't seem to mind as she bought the tiny bananas. Raymond pulled away before they were completely surrounded, not knowing where exactly he was headed.

"She's so hungry," Eve said, wiping the baby's face with a handkerchief. "You must be too. Here. Eat something." She handed Raymond a peeled banana.

Raymond took it and thanked her. He ate two as he drove, washing them down with the soda. They tasted so good that he had to stop himself from eating more.

"Raymond?" Eve adjusted the baby on her breast. "Yvonne is going to worry. We need to call her. I'm putting you and your family at risk now too."

Raymond drove, his eyes glued to the winding road up the mountain. "I'm not sure you understand. We need to warn her. She and the kids should go to the country for a while. You too—"

"Yvonne left me."

There was a moment of silence. It pained him to say it, but he had to get it over with. There was no family left to worry about him or for him to endanger. No home to return to. He told her about the empty house, the bare hangers in the armoire, the deserted beach.

"Oh," Eve moaned. "Oh, Raymond. My poor Raymond."

When he glanced in the rearview mirror, he saw that she was crying quietly once more, her face buried in Amélie's curls.

"Please don't cry," he said. "It's all right. Yvonne did what she felt was right for the children. I can't blame her: I could not provide for my family. And now, I must admit, I'm relieved they are gone. Because you're right, we're all in trouble now."

"But it's not fair, Raymond," Eve said, peering at him in the mirror, her eyes like black roses against her face. "None of it is fair. I'm so sorry. I feel so selfish, asking you to help—"

"Stop, please!" Raymond snapped.

Eve's voice cut off and she watched him, startled.

"It's done," he said. "Let's not talk about it. Is there any more fruit?"

Eve blinked, her lashes still wet. She dug into an orange with her red fingernails and peeled off the stubborn skin. Raymond pulled over and ate the orange quickly, sweat pouring from his brow. All around them, vendors called to the pretty lady in the back of the fancy car, begging for business.

Eve ignored them, looking at her baby instead. Sated and happy, Amélie grinned at her, and she grinned back.

"Amélie and I are leaving, Raymond," she said suddenly. "Jean-Jean was right. There is nothing I can do for Nicolas now, but there is a plan in place for our escape, a phone number I can call. It is hidden at the house. We'll have to go back."

"I'll go back on my own," he said. "It'll be safer. Just tell me where it is."

She shook her head. "I have to go myself."

Raymond tried to dissuade her, but she was silent. It was as if someone entirely different had taken control of Eve's body. Even Amélie was quieter, different—following her mother's lead in all things.

"Take only what you need, nothing more."

Raymond pulled the curtains to the side just an inch. Nothing seemed out of the ordinary outside. They had placed the call to the person Eve said would help them escape. A suspicious elderly voice—sex indeterminate—had taken her number and promised to call in ten minutes. A couple of cars drove by outside the gate, but no one stopped. Raymond wasn't sure what to look for. A vehicle stationed outside the house? A truck? A group of men in uniform or in civilian clothes? Raymond had parked three blocks away and they'd snuck in through the alley, taken all the necessary precautions, but what if somebody came? Then what would they do?

"Hurry," he said.

He was in Nicolas's office. On the other side of the hall, Eve was opening and shutting drawers, making sure she wasn't forgetting anything. Their bag was already packed with diapers and a can of powdered milk. She grabbed her jewelry, gold chains and bracelets she could use as currency. She hid them in tissues and stuffed them among other things. Raymond watched her take a black and white photograph of Nicolas and himself, small boys dressed in white on First Communion day. She threw it in the bag.

"Your passports," he said. "Grab Nicolas's too. Hurry."

They had checked the back of the house and found Freda gone along with her belongings. The mattress in her room was speckled with blood. The poor woman had probably fled in terror. Raymond would have done the same.

Amélie was on the bed, crawling toward the bag, chewing on a piece of bread. She cooed and reached for a hairbrush. Eve trudged into Nicolas's office. The mess hadn't been touched, and she stepped over books thrown carelessly on the floor as though they were stones in a field. She knelt before Nicolas's desk.

"What are you doing?" Raymond asked.

Eve was looking for something, her hand wandering beneath the drawer.

"We have to get out of here, Eve!" he pleaded.

She found what she was looking for, and when she stood up, she smiled at him with relief. He peered at the metal box she set down next to the typewriter. Eve fiddled with the clasp, and they both heard a click. She lifted the lid. Inside laid a small, worn notebook with a black leather cover. Newspaper clippings fluttered between pages.

"No," he said.

She stared back at him, her chin held up in defiance. A strand of dark hair stuck to her wet forehead.

"You can't do this," Raymond said, shaking his head.

"I have to," she said, running her finger over the notebook. "This is all that's left of his work. If I can take it with me, then I'm not abandoning him, not totally."

"It's too dangerous," Raymond said. "We can't take the chance of being caught with this."

Eve held the notebook against her chest. She clenched her jaw. "I won't leave it behind," she said. "I won't. You can do what you want."

Who was this woman? For a brief moment, he felt duped, as if he'd never really known her. In the background, Amélie was still cooing in the bedroom.

"I can't take this risk," he said.

"I'm taking it, Raymond! I just need to know that all this wasn't for nothing. I'll do whatever I can for Nicolas, to make the world see what's happening to our country. That's what he would have wanted. I need you to understand that."

Raymond rubbed his forehead to ease the pain.

"I *have* to," she insisted.

Right now, nothing was more important than them leaving, going into hiding somewhere. He'd heard the rumors about families that the Macoutes came back for, taking them away to their deaths. Raymond threw his arms up in resignation. There was no time to argue. Eve placed the notebook back in the box. At the bottom, Raymond noticed something wrapped in blue fabric. He was going to ask her what it was, but she cut him off.

"Damn it, when are they going to call?"

As if in answer, the phone jangled and Eve's hand leapt toward the receiver.

"Hello?" she said, and listened attentively for a few seconds. "I understand."

"Our arrangement is no longer valid," she said to Raymond, her eyes wide. "We are too hot to handle right now. We have to sit tight and call back in two weeks. They'll see what they can do then."

Raymond met her eyes, his face ashen. "We have to get out of here, now!"

TEN

Nicolas only came to when the truck drew to a complete stop and the engine turned off. It was too dark for him to see the other prisoners. He tried to move and get his blood circulating. His urine-soaked pants stuck to his skin and the smell filled the air. He wanted to apologize, but he was too embarrassed to speak. And then it occurred to him that the others also stank of piss, and worse.

The truck doors opened, the light blinding. An order came to stand and he saw the bodies of other men struggling to get up. He saw the fear on their helpless faces. One man was still in his underwear and slippers.

The guards kept their gun barrels pointed at them, and Nicolas had one shoved in his face as he exited the truck. He felt his tongue sticking to the roof of his mouth. Water. He needed to drink something. He tried licking his lips, but everything, even his tongue, was dry. He needed to change his clothes, to clean himself up. When he stepped out, he knew exactly where he was: Fort Dimanche.

The pestilence surrounding the fortress was unmistakable. Fort Dimanche was built on swampland, just off the bay of Port-au-Prince, near Chancerelle. A smell of sea salt and decay pervaded the air, rumored to stem from the marshes that had become the prison's execution fields. The Haitian American Sugar Company plant was nearby, and it was said that the roar of processing turbines concealed the screams of tortured prisoners.

The bordering slums of La Saline and Cité Simone, as well as the outdoor market of Croix des Bossales, added to the stench.

Nicolas thought it uncanny that men and women were brutalized and silenced here under the orders of a man who called himself a *noiriste*, a believer in Black Consciousness, right across from the very place where people were once sold into slavery. How much had actually changed when Duvalier was now the disease eating away at Haiti from the inside?

Armed guards surrounded the prisoners, toting their rifles with nonchalance. Many of them were young, barely twenty-five, dressed in the standard Macoute uniform, their eyes hidden behind dark glasses. Nicolas didn't recognize any of them. Some others wore civilian clothes and paced back and forth, hands glued to their pistols. The prisoners didn't speak, but Nicolas heard someone whisper a prayer. They all kept their eyes glued on the massive, mustard-colored edifice rising before them.

Nicolas had never seen Fort Dimanche up close. He took in every dark angle of the prison, every crack in its aging walls. A ray of sunlight blinded him as it reflected off the grimy windows behind steel bars. *Maybe some of the cells have windows,* he thought. What terrified him was the possibility of perpetual darkness, not seeing the sun or the sky for the rest of his short life.

Under the midday sun, Fort Dimanche glowed yellow like a pus-filled wound in the vastness of the land. The walls surrounding the property were flanked with barbed wire, left over from the American occupation in the 1930s. Fort Dimanche had been many things in the past, having served as barracks, a military base for the American marines, a training camp, a shooting range, and even an armory. It took Duvalier's sadistic rule to convert it into a prison death camp.

The metal door swung open and three men walked out of the fortress. Two of them wore slacks and carried rifles. They flanked a third man who was shorter, his hands clasped behind his back. He was dressed in a sharp, crisp khaki uniform with gold chevron insignia on his broad shoulders. Nicolas's eyes followed the glimmer of a small gold medal on his lapel. Black and red. This man was more imposing and intimidating than the others, despite his height.

The three men stopped in formation and stared at the prisoners. The man in uniform began to speak, and Nicolas noticed the scar running from his right eyebrow to chin. His heart skipped a beat. He'd seen that scar in photographs. He'd written about this man who was now shouting orders at him between dramatic pauses.

"Prisonniers, en garde!" the man bellowed.

The prisoners adjusted their stance, awkwardly shifting their weight from one foot to the other. They glanced at each other, uncertain. They weren't soldiers. They had no idea how to obey those orders. The scar-faced man laughed at this and began to pace down the line, detailing each prisoner's presentation and features. Nicolas stood motionless between two other men, his wrists raw with pain.

The officer stopped in front of Nicolas but seemed to take no special note of him.

"My name is Jules Sylvain Oscar," he said. "I am the warden here. *Bienvenue à Fort Dimanche.*"

And then Jules Sylvain Oscar smiled directly at Nicolas, eyes twinkling.

Nicolas spent the next two days alone inside a cell so tiny he could touch the walls by stretching out both hands. They called it a *tibout,* or small piece. Every few hours, guards came and treated him to a *bastonnade,* their clubs raining blows on his body coiled on the hot cement. The first time they came, he could only think to ask them how they could stand to be torturers. "This," they said, laughing, "this isn't torture." After that, Nicolas didn't say anything, accepted the beatings. He wondered if he would die here like this, weak with pain and hunger.

On the third day, the men pulled him out of the *tibout* and dragged him down a hallway by the arms. His torso was stained with blood and bile, and they didn't want to get any of it on their clothes. One of them complained that cell number six was too far to bother with.

"They should just let us waste the sons of bitches," he said.

Nicolas couldn't see through the swelling in his right eye. The blood had started to coagulate there, leaving a sticky film coating his eyelashes. His heels scraped along the cold floor. Nicolas didn't know in which of the ten cells he would land. Not that it mattered. He was going to die. He was sure of it. He didn't know how he hadn't died in that first cell.

Along the hallway, Nicolas heard voices, screaming and moaning.

"Please," someone lamented. "*Yon ti dlo*, a drink of water..."

They finally stopped in front of a narrow metal door. Nicolas heard the chiming of keys. A third voice was there, another man. Nicolas tried to see through the blood and thought he spotted a guard in a striped shirt standing against a wall with a pistol. Nicolas's head fell back as he collapsed to his knees.

"Stand up!" the guard ordered.

Nicolas heard them shout, but he couldn't respond. His legs were too weak. His head was spinning too fast, and everything throbbed. Soon, Nicolas, bloody and lacerated, was propped up like Christ on the cross, his arms extended. He felt a cool wind rush against his bare legs. He felt naked in his soiled underwear, but had no strength left for shame.

The guard next to him shouted, "Prisoners, step away from the door!"

Nicolas had never prayed for death before, but as the guard toyed with his keys and unlocked the door, he wished again for God to strike him down on the spot. He'd never suffered this much before, and when hands shoved him into a dark cell, he expected to meet an icy cement floor, to break his jaw or crack another rib. Instead, he landed onto a curious ensemble of limbs that broke his fall. Hands—hard, soft, callused, rough—brushing against his skin as they pulled him left and right, as if kneading and molding dough. He heard murmurs, whispers, and smelled a myriad of foul odors.

"Toss him there!" someone ordered. "This is my corner."

"Eh! *Kenbe li*, catch him!"

Nicolas's head landed on a mat. He kept his eyes shut, his mouth closed. The air was thick with heat and stench, and the fiery ground sent pain rippling through his body. He cried out with his mouth open. No sound came out. He needed help. A doctor. Medicine. Painkillers. Air.

The mat was a single, unpadded layer of woven straw, and it stuck to the open wounds on his back when he tried to roll over. He'd slept on mats as a child, sharing a room with his brother. His mother bought the *nattes* herself from an artisan who wove them by hand. But those were comfortable.

He tried to speak and, instead, found himself gasping for air, trying to breathe in this oven. A wave of nausea swelled in his stomach. He turned on his side so he wouldn't choke if he threw up and promptly lost consciousness.

He dreamed of the countryside, of his parents and his brother and the fields. He dreamed of the children too, Amélie and Enos and Adeline, running and playing in the surf. He dreamed of the smell of the sand and his wife's skin. All around them on the beach, it was sunny, but gray clouds mounted on the horizon. They came and retrieved him as he was still dreaming, before he could run down to the shore and pick up his daughter, and he was almost grateful to have been pulled from the cell without having to meet its other inhabitants. Assuming he was going to be shot, he grasped for the memory of his dream. His lips moved, but no prayers came.

At first he thought the stench in the black hall was urine, but then he realized the odor was emanating from the walls of the prison itself. It was the smell of something rotten and decomposed, flesh that had been left to decay.

Fort Dimanche was a narrow two-story building, and Nicolas counted five cell doors on both sides of the hallway. A bright lightbulb flickered overhead, casting stark shadows over the heads and shoulders of prisoners. They disappeared into another corridor, and Nicolas felt as if he were being swallowed whole into the mouth of a monster. Without warning, something sharp poked him in the rib. A Macoute was pressing the barrel of his rifle into his side.

"This way!"

Another guard grabbed Nicolas by the arm, leading him up an unsteady staircase. Nicolas's heart raced. The fear was real, alive in his flesh. Nicolas managed to look back toward the cells, but he saw nothing but inky darkness. He heard a thunderous whack behind a locked door. A feeble howl rose in the air. Then another whack, followed by a groan, and then...silence. Nicolas thought of his father, and his mother, and the friars at Frères de Saint-Marc Institution and the words they'd taught him to pray. *Our Father, who art in heaven...*How did the rest go?

The men finally stopped before a closed door. Nicolas saw a warm light shining beneath it. One of the men knocked. Nicolas closed his eyes again and tried to quiet the voices fluttering in his mind like wild, frightened birds.

A voice shouted from inside. *"Entrez!"*

One guard opened the door and the other shoved Nicolas inside. Nicolas stumbled forward toward the light.

The room glowed orange from a lamp atop a metal desk where papers and folders were piled in stacks, forming a small barrier around the officer sitting at the desk. He kept his head down, signing and stamping documents one after the other. His movements were mechanical, and Nicolas could hear the grating of the ballpoint pen against the grain of the paper. The man kept his head down, but when he finally angled his face in the light, Nicolas recognized the stitched welt across his brown skin, the droopy eyelid over a scarred eye.

There was the man he'd researched, written about, sought to destroy with proof of his crimes, a man as repulsive as the leader he served. Oscar was personally responsible for horrors: selling

Haitian citizens over the border to the Dominican Republic for forced labor, trafficking cadavers to medical schools and young girls to pimps abroad. And then his name had come up in connection with Alexis. All of it was in the book Nicolas had written—which, of course, the warden now had.

"Sir, this is the prisoner, L'Eveillé."

Nicolas's eyes swept over the desk and noticed an envelope stuffed with green American dollars. He stared at the bills and wondered why there was such a large amount of money just sitting there. Next to it, Nicolas recognized Duvalier's *Catechism of the Revolution*. Children were made to memorize it in school.

"Make him sit," the warden said, putting his pen down.

Oscar grabbed the envelope and ran a red tongue across the fold while the Macoutes pushed Nicolas down onto a wooden seat. The guards unknotted the rope around his wrists and, just as he sighed in relief, grabbed his hands and bound them again around the back of the chair. He felt his flesh burn as the rope bit even deeper into his skin.

Behind the warden, there were shelves of books Nicolas sensed had never been read, the spines dusty, the lettering smudged and erased. There were also two framed plaques recognizing Jules Oscar for services rendered to the Republic of Haiti. Above the warden's chair loomed a large, framed portrait of François Duvalier, his steely eyes smirking. The president's skeletal gray hand and aging face were a testament to rumors about his declining health. He looked like a ghost, like the remains of a man, shrunken and solemn. Nicolas clenched his teeth at the sight. Even in a photograph, Duvalier's eyes seemed to see everything.

The warden reached down below his desk. When he came back up, he held a brown leather briefcase with a gold lock. He carefully stored the envelope of money inside and placed the briefcase back under his desk. Finally, their eyes met. Nicolas told himself to remain calm and composed. The men who had brought him in retreated into dark corners of the room, and

Nicolas was relieved not to have them breathing angrily down his neck, machete and pistol inches away.

"Nicolas L'Eveillé." Oscar smiled. "It seems you are interested in me."

His voice echoed in the cavernous room where the walls, crumbling and chipped, were stained with mildew. He gave a little laugh. Nicolas stared at the warden and tried to swallow, his dry throat sharp and painful.

"I know some things about you too, you know?" Oscar said, still smiling.

Nicolas tried to picture him without the scar, but it was impossible. There was a silent rage to his face, a cold, deep-seated spite.

"Attorney at law, worked out of Jean Faustin's practice back in...1953? Now you run your own show, I see. A bigmouthed professor. Getting off on impressing the youth with your intellect. How many books would you say you've read?"

The warden looked him over from head to toe with disdain. Nicolas drew a deep breath. He smelled the warden's spicy cologne. Oscar's plump fingers rested on the desk, and Nicolas noticed the scabs on his knuckles. A gold ring on his index finger flashed in the light.

A sharp howl came from close by. Nicolas couldn't stop himself from looking around, his eyes wide with terror.

"You hear that?" The warden was now grim. "That's the sound of cooperation."

Nicolas realized that everything was calculated here. The tiled floor increased the resonance of guards' boots in the hallways. The torture chambers were kept close so prisoners could hear one another howl. All of it was designed to instill terror in every prisoner in Fort Dimanche all the time. It was a product of Duvalier's sick, complex mind, and it was effective. He stared at the warden's mouth. He wished for the ability to punch this man precisely there, to knock out a few of those mocking gold fillings.

Oscar grabbed a folder from the stack next to him and thumbed through a ream of typed pages.

"You're a very interesting man, Nicolas L'Eveillé," Oscar said. "Very intelligent, very educated. You've been told why you're here."

Nicolas gritted his teeth but said nothing. The law, which he had taught for so many years, scrolled its statutes in the back of his mind, all of it meaningless. *What lies have you been teaching?* asked a horror-stricken voice inside him. The warden scanned the documents slowly, quietly. Nicolas realized it was his manuscript.

"You seem to know me well," Oscar continued. "You've been taking notes on my comings and goings, my personal transactions. Did you personally know the communist traitor Jacques Stephen Alexis?"

"No, sir," Nicolas muttered.

Oscar stared back, his face blank.

"You're plotting to overthrow this government," the warden stated simply, as though describing a physical characteristic.

Before Nicolas could protest, the warden grabbed another sheet of paper from the folder and pushed it across the desk.

"Do you recognize this? This signature here? Do you know who that is?"

Nicolas leaned in. He let his eyes skim the paper, and the words that jumped at him were primarily legal in nature, mostly jargon. Then he saw the words "high treason" and the names, typed in all caps: "GEORGES PHENICIÉ, JEAN CICERON FAUSTIN, NICOLAS L'EVEILLÉ." His blood froze in his veins. At the bottom of the page, the warden pointed at a signed name that was now vaguely familiar: Philippe Joseph.

"Now who could that be?" Oscar asked.

Nicolas couldn't find the words. Everything he wanted to say seemed pointless in the face of this absurd reversal of fortune. All of this was happening too fast, and for what?

"Thankfully, your ex-student is a true patriot," the warden added. "His allegiance is to our father, Duvalier! Philippe Joseph had the good sense to denounce you."

Nicolas had lost all feeling in his legs and wrists. The name Joseph still drummed in his head. The officer at Casernes Dessalines, the one who processed him. His name was Joseph, wasn't it?

"He told us you were a *kamoken*," the warden said, putting the form back in the folder. "He was right. We have found the black-and-white evidence, *noir sur blanc*. His Excellency has already heard of this. There is a penalty against all traitors."

"How does my writing make me a traitor?"

Oscar slammed an open hand on the table. The lamp vacillated, the desk shook, and the orange bulb flickered.

"You will not speak unless I tell you to, do you understand me?"

Nicolas stared into the warden's eyes. There was nothing to see there, except hatred.

"I am in charge. Not you. You are an enemy of the state," Oscar bellowed, slamming the desk again. "From now on, you will be treated as such, you piece of shit. Writing propaganda against the republic is betraying Duvalier."

Nicolas held still, trying desperately to calm his rapid heartbeat.

"And you were packing your bags, ready to flee. That's because you know you're guilty. You're a rat, a traitor, a coward!"

The warden pushed his chair back and stood up. Quickly, but expertly, he smoothed his uniform with both hands. Nicolas got a good look at his broad head and bull-like shoulders. There was no question he was a strong man. Nicolas thought he would destroy his desk and chair with every touch.

"People like you disgust me!" Oscar spat on the ground. "Who do you think you are, challenging me like I'm some sort of imbecilic pawn? I despise you elitist bourgeois, getting fat in your luxurious dining rooms and feeling indignant that you're not in charge. You have no idea what life is truly like. You look down on everyone, and you think that gives you the right to spy on me?"

He walked toward the door, rolling his sleeves up to the elbows. Nicolas tried to breathe, but he couldn't. He tried to turn around, but he was bound too tightly. Tears of frustration welled in the corners of his eyes.

"You are a threat to this nation, and this government has no tolerance for it. There is no place for your behavior in our society." Nicolas saw the warden remove his watch, fold its leather band, and slide it inside his pocket. There was a brief silence in which the warden seemed to compose himself.

"Of course, sometimes some people need to be reminded of that," Oscar continued. "So we help them, you see. We correct their behavior."

Nicolas knew begging wouldn't help, but still, he stammered, "I—I have a wife and child. Please, you must listen to reason."

The warden approached quickly from behind and gripped his shoulder with a large, icy hand.

"You have no family now," he said, squeezing Nicolas's clavicle. "You are nobody. There is no reason for nobody."

The warden stepped away. Nicolas's head pivoted, trying to track Oscar as he walked toward a wooden armoire in the corner of the room. He opened the door and reached inside, and when he turned around, the hair on Nicolas's body bristled.

"I am innocent," he said. "You can't do this. Please, for the love of God—"

"God?" Nicolas heard him snicker. "In this room, God is dead, Maître."

The warden brandished a black club, its varnished shaft catching the light. He motioned for the Macoutes.

"*Flanke l' sou djak!*"

Nicolas's cry died in his throat. The men kicked the chair forward and his head hit the edge of the desk. He gasped for air, his skull buzzing. They untied him. Hands grabbed his wrists and squeezed as they secured a metal rod behind his knees and at the top of his forearms. His chest and ribs burned in pain.

"Please," Nicolas implored. "Please, don't—"

He wondered if his pounding heart would stop dead, like a broken clock. *It would be better,* he thought. *Please God,* he prayed.

Please. Nicolas turned his head and made eye contact with the warden. Oscar's eyes were dead. He was caressing the club with his fingers, admiring the finish before smacking it against the palm of his hand.

"When I'm through with you," the warden said, "you'll be singing Duvalier's praises."

The warden approached and Nicolas, undone, vomited on the floor. Yellow bile splattered on the desk and on the warden's shoes. Nicolas kept his head down, embarrassed and paralyzed with fear. *Joseph.* Yes, he knew a Joseph, a student, that limping young man who'd recorded him in class and followed him to his car. He whimpered a stupid prayer as the warden's hands tore off his underwear.

He was naked when the warden's teeth sank in his flesh. He gasped with both pain and shock and let out a scream. The warden was on top of him, and there was blackness, a sickness, a wave of rage against his own helplessness. When the club penetrated him, his entire being convulsed. He tried to scream again, but a sudden silence deafened him. He went limp.

When Oscar finally pulled away, he wiped the club against Nicolas's skin and exhaled. Nicolas gritted his teeth, but more pain was coming. The club came down like a machete hacking away at cane stalks in the fields. The blows fell on his bones as if to crush them one by one, as if he were being tossed between the jagged wheels of a sugarcane mill. The agony rippled across his neck and head. There was nothing left to do now but to hope for death.

Raymond knew Eve had fallen asleep after they'd passed Portail Léogâne and merged onto Route du Sud, southbound. Glancing back, he saw her head resting against the window, her forehead smudging the glass. Amélie was asleep on her chest, rocked by the motion of the car. Raymond was desperate himself for rest, but didn't think of stopping. His head still hurt, but the air got cooler the farther he drove into the southern mountains. His hunger pangs had subsided, but his stomach was now gurgling uncontrollably.

Raymond weaved in and out of traffic, ignoring the irritated drivers honking their horns after him. No one seemed to be tailing them. Perhaps they were safe. He wedged his Datsun between two large public transportation trucks painted in bright reds and yellows. Men and women sat in the open backs, hanging on to straps like smoked herring in the blazing sun. Some men clung to odd parts of the vehicle to avoid falling off onto the road.

It was the same kind of truck Raymond had taken to get to Port-au-Prince the first time. Nicolas had been the first to leave l'Artibonite, and he'd caught a ride with a friend who owned a car, but Raymond had no friends with such resources. So he'd climbed up among sacks of charcoal, just like these people, hitching a ride to the capital. The passengers seemed unaffected by the rough conditions, their faces burning with hope for a new beginning. Raymond hadn't contacted Nicolas until he'd already found a place to stay and a job. He knew he'd have to distance himself from Nicolas and prove to himself that the trip to the capital had been worth it.

The tap-tap behind Raymond stepped on the gas and went around him, blasting evangelical hymns as it sped down the Route du Sud. The farmers huddled on the rooftop of that car were traveling with goats, and through his window, Raymond heard their screams, like human children in agony. The sound made Raymond's skin crawl. He wished he could roll his windows up to drown it out, but he had no air-conditioning and was relying on the pure southern air to keep them cool.

Raymond smelled the ocean, and out the window where Eve rested her head, he saw palm trees and a slice of azure shimmering in the sunlight. He knew this beach. This was where he'd gone looking for Yvonne and the children. Raymond looked straight ahead and kept driving. He couldn't think of them now. It would do him no good.

His limbs felt numb as he sped down the road, and his eyelids were heavy with sleep. Raymond was exhausted, but he had no choice. He struggled to stay awake as he drove through green mountains, past open fields of sugarcane, rice paddies, and plantain trees in full bloom, their purple buds dangling over the fertile earth, pregnant with fruit. The hills that bordered the road soon parted to reveal Lake Miragoâne, a good sign of progress. He kept driving, hopeful. The village of Marigot, where they were headed, wasn't too much farther.

He pulled over at a gas station to refuel after a three-hour drive. They were in a small town near Jacmel. The attendant pumped his gas without a word. Raymond surveyed the area, watchful for police. He asked the attendant how much longer he needed to drive, and the young man shrugged.

"Where you going exactly?"

"Bainet," Raymond lied, naming a city past his intended destination.

"Another hour or so, maybe."

So Marigot was just minutes away.

As they arrived in Jacmel, the ocean unfolded before them. Eve rolled her window down to smell the salt air as the wind tossed the waves against cliffs and boulders. They passed the beach of Ti Mouyaj, and in the distance, Raymond saw a finger of land extending into the sapphire sea: Marigot.

A few minutes later, Raymond slowed down. He called over two shirtless boys who were selling freshly caught snapper by the side of the road. They held up their prize with pride and grinned, hoping Raymond was stopping to make a purchase. The fish scales caught the daylight like a prism.

"Bèl pwason?" the boys cried out. "Buy some fresh fish?"

"Where is the turnoff for Marigot?" Raymond asked.

Just a mile later, Raymond pulled into the small, sleepy community of Marigot. Yellow and red banners flapped in the afternoon breeze, and everywhere they looked, ribbons and signs clung to tree branches. A large banner floated overhead, announcing in painted letters, *"Fête Patronale de Marie Madeleine Pérédo à Marigot."* Raymond drove carefully, noting the stares of passersby. They'd arrived during the annual festival for the town's patron saint. The residents were still hoisting signs announcing the names of their local sponsors: mayors, doctors, and justices of the peace. Raymond knew most of those local leaders must hold a MVSN Macoute card. Duvalier's influence was everywhere and often felt through Macoutes appointed as *chefs de section*, or deputies, and local police throughout Haiti.

He turned down a narrow path that had not been paved. The sign at the entrance was hand painted, a red arrow indicating *"Plage."* The gravel crunched under the car's wheels as they drove deeper into a small forest of palm trees bearing clusters of green coconuts. Through the palm fronds came glimpses of turquoise ocean. On both sides of the road, they passed women and children riding mules and pulling donkeys, balancing baskets of mangoes and avocados and cobs of golden corn on their heads, each one eyeing the car with curiosity.

Eve rolled her window down. "This is so beautiful," she murmured. She turned to Raymond. "Is this where we're going?"

Raymond didn't answer, and when he approached the sea, he saw it: a blue adobe beach house with a thatched roof and red shutters like open eyes. Eve whispered something Raymond couldn't make out.

"Where are we?" she asked again.

A group of small, barefoot children ran out to see the Datsun. Some of them sprinted away to the shore, where small, painted canoes were beached on the sand. Others hid behind coconut palms. Raymond parked under a giant West Indian almond tree, and the rest of the children crowded around the vehicle. There were no other cars around. Raymond noticed a bicycle leaning against a tree behind the hut.

"Raymond?" Eve repeated. "What is this place?"

"Stay here," he said.

Raymond exited the car and looked around. He didn't step forward so as not to frighten the children. Instead, he leaned against the vehicle.

"Bonsoir, timoun," he said, greeting them politely. *"Honneur.* Are you alone here?"

The children shook their heads. Their ages ranged from eight to twelve, and they were shirtless, like most of the fishermen and children whose livelihood depended on the ocean. Their skin was gray from constant sun and sea exposure.

"I'm looking for Milot Sauveur. Is this where he lives?"

Raymond braced himself. He had taken a chance by coming here and now he was nervous that it had been a mistake. If he couldn't find the journalist, if he couldn't get help from him, then he wasn't sure what their next step would be. He was running out of adrenaline and out of ideas. His mind started to race when the kids exchanged cautious looks.

Then an adult male voice startled Raymond. "Who's asking?"

Raymond's eyes searched for the speaker. He stepped away from the car door and his shoes landed not on gravel, but on soft sand.

"My name is Raymond L'Eveillé. I'm a taxi driver from Port-au-Prince. I helped Milot Sauveur out of Cité Simone."

Something moved on the porch. A silhouette rose from a rocking chair, came forward, and stopped on the steps. He was a man of average height, and when a lone ray of amber sunlight caught his face, Raymond registered an unkempt beard, bushy hair, and dark eyes that scanned his face with curiosity. Was this the same man he'd rescued from the Macoutes? Raymond stepped closer.

"He said if I needed help with anything, to come here and ask for him."

He thought he saw a glimmer in the man's eyes, and suddenly a bright smile flashed through the thickness of his beard.

"Brother!" the man shouted. "It's you! I remember you!"

He ran down the steps toward Raymond, and instead of shaking the hand he was presented, he grabbed him by the shoulders and hugged him, holding him close like an old friend returned from a long voyage.

"My brother! Welcome."

Raymond looked through the window of Milot Sauveur's kitchen. The shutters opened onto a square of undulating waves, and the breeze fondled green palm fronds. The sun was bowing low, and the horizon blushed in gradient shades of twilight. This world was far removed from the incessant hum of Port-au-Prince. Here on the shore, there were no cars. There was no honking, no screaming, no *rat-tat-tat-tat* of gunshots piercing the air at curfew. Raymond thought of the city noise that rocked him to sleep at night, of the chant of coffee vendors that woke him like a call to prayer at dawn. Here, on this beach, Haiti's heart beat to the slow rhythm of waves.

Raymond saw Eve down by the shore, pacing. She held her palms pressed together in prayer. She'd left Amélie asleep on a cot next to Sauveur's infant son while Claudette, Sauveur's wife, kept an eye on the children as she brewed tea on the veranda. She was using a three-legged *recho* stove and fanning the flames with an aluminum lid. The coals glowed red under the pot, and when she switched the tea for a hearty stew, she fanned the smoke away from her face.

Raymond watched his sister-in-law as she plopped down in the sand and faced the ocean. He could only see her silhouette against the sunset.

"She might be angry with me," Raymond muttered. "I can't tell. When her escape plan fell through, I just started to drive. You were the only person I could think of..."

Sauveur sat across from him at the kitchen table. He was rolling cigarettes in the light of a small *gridap* lamp, using his fingers to measure the tobacco before folding the paper around it. In the next room, scrambled radio voices were announcing news in Spanish from the Dominican Republic.

Sauveur looked out the window and saw Eve.

"Don't be stupid." He shook his head. "Women don't get in cars and travel miles with people they're angry with. You will be safe here for a while. Don't worry."

Raymond took a closer look at the man whose life he'd recently saved. Sauveur looked nothing like he'd expected, but each time he spoke, his voice put Raymond at ease. On the radio, Sauveur always began the news with his trademark line: "You're listening to Radio Lakay, *vwa pèp la*, the voice of the people." Radio Lakay was now on and off the air, struggling to keep its reporters who, like Sauveur, were under constant threat of being arrested—abducted—in the dead of night.

Raymond had always pictured Sauveur as a heavyset man because of his deep, throaty voice. But Sauveur was small framed, probably in his thirties, with a little nose and high cheekbones, his teeth yellowed by nicotine. Sauveur coughed, straining to detach phlegm from his lungs, and then licked the flap of his new cigarette and sealed it. The aroma of tobacco was embedded in his brown skin, his discolored nails, and the linen of his embroidered *gwayabèl* shirt.

"They'll never let my brother out of that prison," Raymond said. "The last time we saw each other, we squabbled over the risks he was taking. He got so mad, you would have thought I was Duvalier by the time I left their house."

Sauveur offered him a cigarette. Raymond shook his head. Sauveur tucked the rolled cigarette behind his left ear.

"These days, we're all pitted against each other. It's what fear does to us. My Claudette, for instance." Sauveur threw a tender glance toward his wife. Dusk cast a solemn glow on his face.

"Tonton Macoutes came to the hospital where she worked," he said. "A journalist from Radio Caraïbes was recovering from a severe beating. The Macoutes came to finish the job and shot him in the mouth right before her eyes."

Sauveur paused and shook his head. Raymond could tell the horror was still swimming there.

"She panicked and ran home. Didn't even take a taxi. She was still scrubbing the blood off her uniform when I came home that day. That's what got me into trouble, see? I reported the story on the radio that same evening, and the next thing I knew, they were calling the station looking for me. We fought about that for a while. She was angry I reported the story. I was angry she brought it home!"

Sauveur's eyes caught the flicker of the flame between them. "Thank God for you, my brother. We'd have died that day without your help."

Outside, Claudette was transferring the stew into a large enamel bowl. Sauveur licked the edge of another rolling paper and spun the cigarette between his fingers. Raymond saw his eyes gleaming in the fading light.

"Now we're here," Sauveur said. "I'm in the middle of starting a newspaper along with three other local journalists."

"A newspaper?"

"Sure. A rebel newspaper. The best kind!"

Raymond had caught a glimpse of a room with a pair of headsets, a radio speaker, and a couple of handheld transceivers he'd only seen used by the police and the Macoutes.

He motioned toward the garbled sounds of the radio. "Isn't that—"

"Yes, quite dangerous," Sauveur said. "There is a good Samaritan helping me stay incognito here. He also brings me news from abroad, and I keep the locals informed of rebel insurgents in the mountains, at the border, or even overseas. The latest is that the Haitian rebels in Santo Domingo are allying themselves with the Constitutionalists to fight the war with them."

"But it's not our war," Raymond said.

"It is if we want the Dominican Republic to continue offering us safe refuge from Duvalier," Sauveur exclaimed, his excitement growing. "Plus, the *kamoken* could use the training and the weapons. Once things get back to normal over the Dominican border, they will return with arms and the know-how to overthrow Papa Doc."

Sauveur said those final words with a passion Raymond found disconcerting. Here was a man who truly loved the danger and chaos of his profession. Here was a man who meant business. His position against the regime was clear, and although it jeopardized his safety, he was in it for the long haul. He remembered the fear in Sauveur's eyes that fateful day, and he had imagined the close brush with death would force Sauveur to back down. He had been wrong.

"I do my part by letting the local community know about the rebels so they can get what they need: food, weapons, training."

Sauveur inspected a cigarette in the light of the naked flame between them, then tucked this one behind his right ear. It made sense for a man who chain-smoked all day. He was already rolling another, and this one he lit with the same flame. The end of the cigarette burned red, and Sauveur puffed plumes of fragrant white smoke as he sucked assiduously. He then leaned back in his seat, pushing against the back of his chair until it rested against the wall.

"I am the voice of the people, a messenger. Duvalier is the criminal. He is the one who eliminates those who stand in his way."

He paused. The smell of tobacco was comforting—the first moment of normalcy Raymond had experienced in a while. He never wanted to leave this kitchen, the wooden surface of the table, the basket of plastic fruits between them, or the clay jug with a ladle in the corner, cooling the drinking water inside.

"You said if I needed help I could come find you," Raymond interrupted.

Sauveur nodded.

"I need to get my sister-in-law out of the country. That's first."

Sauveur squinted. Raymond expected him to say something, but he did not. A garbled merengue came through the radio speakers in the background.

"Everyone's deserted us," Raymond said. "All the so-called friends of his, they're gone. No one will help. We tried pleading with Adjudant Joseph at Casernes Dessalines, but he wouldn't help either. It's clear Eve's not safe. I'm afraid they'll come after her and the baby."

"Did they say why they were arresting him?" Sauveur asked.

"Treason," Raymond snapped.

He realized he'd raised his voice. He took a deep breath and leaned in closer, regaining his composure. Sauveur did not flinch, his gaze steady.

"He's just stubborn," Raymond continued. "That's all. Worse than a mule. He wrote a book, and—"

"A book?" Sauveur asked. "What kind of book?"

He moved forward and sat up in his chair, as if this information had suddenly raised the stakes. He was fully attentive, staring into Raymond's eyes. Raymond told him what he'd heard from Eve and Nicolas in passing, the notes his brother kept hidden, the manuscript he'd just finished that mentioned the writer Alexis.

"They found the book while they were searching his house."

Sauveur's eyes suddenly caught fire. "Really? Who betrayed him?"

"What difference does it make?" Raymond asked. "They charged him with treason and they threw him in Fort Dimanche. Simple as that."

"You realize, this sort of thing makes your brother an enemy of the state, the worst kind. How do you know he's still alive?"

"I need to believe he is!" Raymond said. "I was hoping you could help me figure out a plan to get him out."

Sauveur pushed his chair back and sucked his teeth, thinking. The sweet smell of lemongrass and vervain leaves lingered in the air. The tea had steeped enough, the stew was warm, and Raymond was desperate for food. Outside, Claudette was moving the pots away and dousing the fire with water. The tobacco, the salt, the ocean, and the tea leaves overwhelmed his senses. He felt light-headed and rubbed his forehead to regain focus.

"The first thing you need to do is get your sister-in-law and your niece out of Haiti," Sauveur said. "It's not safe for her here, but if she manages to get across the border to the Dominican Republic, she'll have a chance."

Raymond took a deep breath and glanced out the window again. Eve was walking back toward the house. She moved with unassuming grace, her feet tossing up little clouds of sand and dispersing it into the wind.

"Can you help us do that?" Raymond asked.

Sauveur drew on his cigarette. "Does she know someone

there? Because she'll need a place to stay safe. With all the chaos over there now—"

"She knows Jean Faustin's sister," Raymond said. "It's not ideal. Her brother was less than cooperative when we asked him for help. But it's what we have for now."

"I'll send one of the neighborhood boys out tonight to contact the boat captain I know. We'll have to plan and smuggle her out quietly."

"By boat?" Raymond asked.

His vision was blurry, and he blinked to make sure he was still awake. Hunger and fatigue were taking over, and his head was splitting with pain again.

"I know it's very dangerous," Sauveur said. "The Macoutes are patrolling the waters. But crossing the border by land is near impossible now. The borders are closed, and there are patrols on both sides. At sea, there's a better chance if the captain can sneak you in through the border town of Anse-à-Pitre."

Raymond thought of Yvonne, Adeline, and Enos on a boat, at sea. They'd left from the bay of Port-au-Prince, headed for the States. Had they made it? He would find out as soon as he'd seen this journey through with Eve and figured out what to do about Nicolas. For now, there was nothing he could do but hope, and in some ways he clung to the hope and dreaded the truth. Finding out whether they'd made it or not would be the most terrifying part of this entire ordeal.

Raymond sighed and looked at Sauveur. "How much will we need?"

"Oh, my friend!" Sauveur raised his hand to stop him. "Please. There will be no talk of money. You saved my life, and now it's my turn to return the favor."

Raymond felt as if God was finally listening. "And my brother?"

"That—" Sauveur paused and thought for a long moment.

"I have to try everything in my power," Raymond said. "I can't let him die."

"I will make some calls," the rebel journalist said quietly.

Raymond's eyes grew wide. He almost wanted to grin, but his body was too tired.

"First, we need to confirm his status in the prison," Sauveur said. "Then we'll have to talk about what to do."

The women came in, carrying food and children with them. "Let's eat first. You need it. *Sak vid pa kanpe*. An empty sack will not stand upright."

They all sat together, sharing a loaf of bread, pouring hot tea in enamel cups. Raymond watched rogue lemongrass leaves swirl in his cup. When he brought it to his lips, he closed his eyes and felt the warm, sweet liquid revive his entire being.

Claudette filled Raymond's bowl to the brim with stew. He was grateful for her kindness, and he waited for his host to eat first. Sauveur held his son on his lap and poured hot tea in a saucer for him. Eve sat across the table from him, feeding her daughter more bread. They silently reveled in the aroma of fish and onions and peppers. Raymond ate quickly, shoveling spoonfuls into his mouth. He could not remember his last proper meal.

When he was done, he watched Eve stir more sugar and tea leaves in her cup. Their eyes met over the babble of drooling babies and the clatter of spoons against the chipped rims of saucers. For the first time since their lives had been brutally interrupted, she offered him half a smile, a crescent moon against her tired face.

ELEVEN

Nicolas opened his eyes and saw Boss lower his head. The old man—a lifelong mason and handyman before his arrest—watched, unperturbed, as a cockroach crawled between his legs. He let the roach brush against his black toenails. When they'd brought Nicolas to the cell, Boss was the only one who had acknowledged him, whispered to him, nursed him as best he could. Nicolas felt broken in half, and Boss hadn't moved from his side while the other cellmates had slept.

Nicolas watched the bug until Boss looked up and caught his gaze again.

"Maître, you don't look good. We need to clean your wounds before they get infected."

The old man stood up and looked over his shoulder. His thin hands reached inside his old, worn briefs and pulled out a wrinkled member barely visible inside a shrub of gray pubic hair. Nicolas raised his hand to stop the man.

"No."

"It's the only way," Boss said.

Another prisoner muttered something behind them in the dark. Nicolas couldn't see who it was. Shocked, he tried to sit up in protest.

"In here," Boss said, "if you don't want to die of gangrene or fever, you have to use urine to clean your wounds, Maître."

"I...I need a doctor," Nicolas muttered. He curled into a ball, his body pressed against the wall. Nicolas's famed logic, what people called his *bon ange*, his guardian angel, had taken flight. He wanted to smash his head against the wall. All of it seemed like a long, vivid, tortuous nightmare from which he couldn't wake up.

"Doctor?" Boss chuckled. He looked over his shoulder.

Others, Nicolas realized, were awake and paying attention. There was a general sentiment of amusement, but no one seemed to have the strength to laugh.

"There is no doctor to help you," Boss said, his hand still wrapped around his penis. "I don't think you understand. There is no medicine in Fort Dimanche. The closest thing you get to a doctor here is a torturer. Trust me, Maître L'Eveillé. There's no healing for the already dead. No salvation."

Nicolas stared at the old man. He flexed his jaw and squeezed his eyes shut, a violent sob rending his chest. He then turned his head away and Boss sighed out loud. When the warm, foul liquid splashed over his face and chest, he groaned. They should have killed him in that interrogation room. Boss's words tolled in his head as Boss, and then another prisoner, and another emptied their bladders over his raw wounds.

There's no healing for the already dead, Nicolas repeated to himself. *No salvation.*

Nicolas woke up screaming from a nightmare in which he could feel the warden's teeth sink into his flesh, the monster's face obscured in darkness. When he opened his eyes, there was a violent pounding on the door. Where was he?

He was in the cell. It came back to him now, slowly. The banging reverberated across the room. Nicolas couldn't see anything through the darkness at first, and he had no idea what time it was, what day, or how long he'd been asleep. A constellation of bumps had formed on his back and his legs where the bedbugs had feasted on his bruised skin.

"You were dreaming?"

Nicolas thought he recognized Boss's voice. He groaned once for yes.

"You were crying in your sleep," Boss said. "Don't worry. It's normal. You'll dream about your lectures, and you'll dream about your wife. You'll dream about your little girl, and you'll dream about that notorious book of yours. But after a while, the dreams will go away. All of them. And you will have relief."

Nicolas's heart was pounding. Suddenly, the old man seemed crazy, demented.

"How do you know these things about me?" Nicolas demanded.

"You talked a lot the other night," Boss stated gently. "After they brought you back."

Boss turned to scratch something on the wall with a small piece of metal. It was a broken handle from an old *kin*.

"Today is May twenty-eighth," he said. "I tell myself the date every day. It's important. Now sit up. The guards are here."

Nicolas tried his best to sit up. Some of the men sprang to their feet. Before Nicolas could turn to Boss, light from the hallway spilled into the cell and revealed a guard standing at the door holding a club.

"No sudden movements," he shouted.

Another silhouette stood against the light. Nicolas couldn't see who it was, but he made out aluminum plates being pushed into the cell and smelled rancid cooking oil. Someone else was there in shorts, a T-shirt, and sandals. A kid like any other you might see on the boulevards, carrying a cauldron by the handle and serving them a watery, oily cornmeal with beans and bread. The guard held the door open as the plates glided in.

Nicolas watched in horror as the prisoners leapt forward, fighting to grab a plate. They attacked the meal with their fingers.

"It's hot! Watch out," they cried, shifting the plates from one hand to another, sucking on their fingers and blowing on their food. The cornmeal, still steaming, scalded their skin, but they had no utensils and no other choice but to dig in with their bare hands.

Some ate their bread; others broke it and stuffed it under their mats. Nicolas watched them suck the meal caking their crusty fingers. He heard the smacking of lips, and he grimaced in disgust. He wasn't touching his plate. He'd lost his appetite long ago, and the sight of the oil separating on the surface of his food turned his stomach again. It was the kind of food Nicolas would never dream of feeding a dog. He thought of Eve, who had always scolded their servant, Freda, for using too much oil in their food, and he was moved by the memory of her hand as she meticulously drained the oil from their meal at the dinner table, shaking her head in exasperation.

Nicolas looked away from the spectacle, but there in front of him was Boss, scraping his plate with his roll of stale bread. The corners of his lips and his beard were speckled with grit.

"Are we all animals?" Nicolas whispered, unable to mask his repulsion. He covered his mouth with the back of his hand to control his urge to vomit.

Boss continued to chew, unfazed.

"You eat too, Maître," he grunted, his mouth full. "You need it. You need strength."

Nicolas glanced at his plate sitting by the mat. The glob of cornmeal smelled toxic, and the bread was spotted with green mold.

"If you don't want yours, I'll have it," another man said, blowing on his hot cornmeal before stuffing his mouth with it. Nicolas noticed how his ribs nearly poked through his skin. He looked to be around twenty.

"Eat it quickly," Boss said. "It could be all you get for the day."

Nicolas grabbed the bread and struggled to open his mouth. He felt sick, but he knew Boss was right. He had to eat something if he wanted to live. He hadn't expected to be alive this long. He brought a piece of bread to his lips, his joints aching from the warden's beating. Chewing was excruciating, and the heat from the cornmeal made him realize he was missing several teeth. Down the hall, the guard was banging on other doors.

"Plates! Now!" the guard shouted.

Nicolas chewed faster on the bread. With his fingers, he peeled off the moldy crust. Boss leaned in and grabbed Nicolas's plate, and like the other prisoners had started to do, he flung it at the wall behind them. The cornmeal clung to the chipping surface for a moment before dripping. Nicolas didn't have time to protest. The steps in the hallway were approaching. Then the banging came again. Nicolas jumped back. That noise, the sound of guards banging on metal doors, had begun to leave its invisible scars on his psyche.

"Plates!"

Nicolas watched the prisoners slam their meal on the wall and lick their plates clean. The guards were coming back to collect the dishes from them. They'd barely been given five minutes to eat. Outrage crawled up his throat. When the nightstick banged the door once more, he groaned as if feeling the blows and the violation all over again.

The door opened, and the men extended their plates forward.

The guard hovered over the cook, glaring at the prisoners. The cook now held a bucket, and with a rusty aluminum ladle, he poured a single serving of water onto each dirty plate. The men gulped greedily, too starved and dehydrated to protest. Two prisoners punched the bottom of their plates in with all their might. Once, twice, three times. Nicolas covered his ears. *Punch. Punch. Punch.* The sound was sickening. They were trying to turn their plates into bowls to hold the water. They drank avidly, the water picking up remains of food and dripping past the corners of their mouths, washing down their chin. Nicolas sat on his mat, shaking his head.

"You!" The guard with the nightstick pointed at him. "Didn't you hear me? Hand over your plate!"

Nicolas couldn't move. He sat there, staring at a man he didn't know but loathed, as he loathed every cruel, monstrous hand that had tossed him into this dungeon.

Boss grabbed the plate from the ground and slid it forward.

"Don't make trouble," he whispered. "You're going to get us killed."

"Shut your *djòl!*" the guard shouted.

With his boot, he kicked Nicolas's plate out into the hallway. The men all held out their plates and pleaded.

"More water! Please. More water, we beg you!"

"Turn in your goddamn plates before I break your skulls with my *cocomakak!*" the guard roared, waving his club in the air.

Nicolas watched the men slide their plates out of the cell with reluctance. In spite of everything that had happened, some ember of his former pride flared up and his blood boiled. How could these men allow themselves to be diminished like this? They were like children: obedient, submissive, cowardly. It was debasing and he couldn't bear to watch it. But what else could they do in the face of barbarism?

The guard pointed his club at Nicolas, who remained still, clenched his jaw, and bit down hard to swallow his rage.

"No water for you," the guard spat. "I hope you learned your lesson."

The guard shut the door and locked it, leaving them to grope around in the darkness. Nicolas felt another sting on his mat, and he twitched, shifting to sit on the cement.

"Don't be a smart-ass," Boss whispered, crouching in his corner. "If you defy them, they'll beat all of us in here, no questions asked. You hear me? Don't be stupid."

Nicolas collapsed onto his back in the dark, his throat parched.

"And what happened to you, Boss, outside, that you're in here now?"

Nicolas wanted an answer, but Boss had moved away from him, and for the first time, he did not seem inclined to chat.

The room they were in was about thirteen by fourteen feet, with cracked walls plagued with bloodstains and mildew. Above them, a white lightbulb was screwed into a socket, but there was no light. Nicolas peered at an opening in the wall, a small rectangle of a window. But through it, he couldn't see the sky or any real light. Instead, he saw boots and passing shadows of men pacing outside in the yard, back and forth. Guards.

Nicolas felt sick. He stood up abruptly, and the men around him jumped back in surprise, pressing their bodies against the wall. Nicolas rushed to vomit into the *kin*, a bucket that was already overflowing with feces and urine. Flies swarmed around its rim.

After Nicolas had spat the last contents of his stomach and wiped his mouth with the back of his hand, somebody shoved him from behind. When he turned to look, large, bloodshot eyes bulged at him.

"Listen up," the prisoner said. "I'm in charge of the *kin* around here. You want to use it, you ask me for permission."

The large man's name was Sonson, Nicolas later learned from Boss.

"But we call the old shit-minder 'Major.' He's ex-Macoute, arrested for firearm contraband. Apparently, the government has no tolerance for people stealing if it's from them. Who knew?" The old man chuckled, pulling on a clump of matted beard.

Nicolas couldn't respond.

Prisoners slept in organized shifts. It was a system that had been developed for the benefit of all, since the cells were packed far over capacity.

Cells in the fortress, Nicolas was told, often held up to forty men. Nicolas's cellmates had been reduced to eighteen before he arrived. The numbers kept growing as more prisoners arrived; this made it impossible for all the bodies to lie down at the same time. In four- to six-hour shifts, they balanced their lives between sleeping, standing, sitting, and taking small steps between each other's feet to keep the circulation going. Nicolas found this impossible at first and often remained wide-awake, learning to tune out the shrieks and bellows of torture victims down the hall. After a while, though, he would rest against the wall and succumb to fatigue.

When he was awake, Nicolas heard everything: a centipede crawling on a mat, rats scurrying in the corners, snoring, prisoners passing gas in their sleep or shitting in the bucket, and the lament of those who never gave up praying. Bedbugs and roaches infested every corner, and on the hottest afternoons, he could hear men squashing the body lice they picked off their skin. Now that Nicolas had been there a few days, his nose could distinguish good urine from bad, and he could smell blood from a cell away, where a young man lay comatose after a torture session had cracked his skull. He could smell the body odor, the infected wounds, the stale breath of fellow prisoners; the grease and food particles caked on the walls. All of it coated the insides of his nostrils and burned his eyes.

Feeble rays of light and gusts of air streamed in from the small window above their door. It was too high for anyone to reach, so the inmates had developed a ladder system. They called it "climbing the tree," gripping the wall with hands and feet to hoist themselves up. This had to be timed when the guards weren't pacing the halls, and once they had an all clear, they'd reach the opening, hoping to communicate with the cell opposite. Because the window was so close to the ceiling, the climbers often found themselves in an awkward position with their head cocked to the side, ear pressed against their shoulder, twisting their neck to catch a glimpse of the hall.

Once his body had begun to paste itself back together, Nicolas attempted to "climb the tree" and see through a second window in the cell that opened onto the courtyard.

"Are you trying to get shot?" Boss hissed after him. "If they see you, you're dead."

The risk and effort were for nothing. Nicolas couldn't see a thing. There were no trees, no pastel layers of sky, no sunlight. Only the sound of boots approaching.

"Climbing the tree is strictly forbidden," Boss said. "If the guards in the hall catch you, they beat you. And the guards in the courtyard will just shoot the minute they spot you."

"There's no hope of seeing outside?" Nicolas fell to his knees.

"The only time we get to see the light of day is when foreign delegations demand to visit," Boss said. "They've gone so far as to move us so they can clean the whole prison. If we stink up the hallways too much, they might allow us out for water at the fountain, and they make us empty out the *kin*."

Nicolas would never again see trees, leaves, roots, rivers, cattle and pigs randomly strolling through traffic. He'd never see children running barefoot on the asphalt of Port-au-Prince, chasing him down and begging for *de gouden* change, their grimy fingers digging into the sleeves of his pressed suit. He now regretted all those times he pushed those kids away and gave them nasty looks.

Nicolas shut his eyes. He wasn't proud of the past. But what good would it do now to remember moments when he'd been insensitive or condescending? In doing his research for the book, he'd presumed he was above it all. Untouchable. Somehow, he had managed to imagine himself and his life a safe, scholarly distance from the miserable souls whose torture and disappearances he'd so carefully documented. The irony was that the guards were as dismissive of him—if only more brutal—as he himself had been toward others.

Now, Nicolas paid attention to the people around him, to the stories relayed from one prisoner to the next, about how they were betrayed or denounced as traitors by people they never suspected: a shoeshine boy, a shop owner, a fruit seller, a barber—all of whom had joined the Macoutes in the hope of rising to something greater, something more important, or for protection. They couldn't beat the system, so they joined it. Those were the Tonton Macoutes: men and women who had long been disenfranchised and neglected, who were filled with rage against the world. Nicolas wondered if Philippe Joseph, the student who had denounced him, was also a Macoute. He found himself clenching his fists when he thought of the student's face, those eyes that never quite met his when he talked, that playful grin on his face, and that limp. Nicolas's eyes opened wide as it struck him. *That limp, my God. Could it be?* Could it have been a result of jumping a gate and falling on the other side? Could

128 · FABIENNE JOSAPHAT

it be that Philippe Joseph was the intruder in his garden that night? Nicolas cursed himself.

How had he not seen this for what it was? How could he have been so stupid? He was going to rot in here, not because of the book, but because of one student. How could he have entertained such madness, speaking his mind so openly in the classroom? He was nothing but a speck, a grain of sand on the shore. He was powerless against the bloody mill of this government, and it was evident now that he was a failure, that his aspiration to save his country with his writing was a joke. He could not win against Papa Doc. The greatest writers of Haiti had tried, and Duvalier had gotten rid of them all, Jacques Stephen Alexis at the top of that list. Even the English author Graham Greene had fled the country two years ago with Papa Doc's spies breathing down his neck. So who was he, Nicolas L'Eveillé, to think that he could change everything?

Nicolas missed the world. He thought of Eve and Amélie every second he wasn't too distracted by his scabs, his bones that hurt at the slightest touch, the hunger pangs in his stomach, and his parched throat. The absence of his wife and child plagued him like a disease, and when he tried not to think of them, he thought of Raymond. Poor Raymond. He had been so hard on his brother, so unforgiving. Now he would never see him again. He would never see anyone again. He prayed they had escaped, made their way to Jean Faustin's relatives in the Dominican Republic. He imagined them starting fresh. He imagined Eve finding someone new.

He would go mad, he realized, if he stayed here much longer. He was already tugging on his beard like Boss did. And if madness was the result of being caged in here, he would prefer immediate execution. The warden had told him, right before he lost consciousness, that this would be his fate in less than three months.

I should have died right there, he thought. *Oscar should have killed me.*

He thought about smashing his head against the prison walls, salvaging what was left of his dignity. Instead, he continued pulling on the beard that had begun to crawl over his face. He ached for a good shave, tugging at the wiry curls, assessing the growth with disgust.

"Get used to it," Boss said abruptly, scrawling on his wall calendar and muttering things Nicolas couldn't understand.

The guards patrolled the hallways at odd times, joking around with each other, tapping on the walls with their clubs to mess with the prisoners. Once, Nicolas woke up and found himself looking into the brown face of a young man, a guard, staring directly at him from the slit under the cell door. Nicolas's eyes widened in terror. He didn't know why the guard was there, watching. They made eye contact, and without a word, the guard's face pulled away. He saw boots, and the man was gone.

The regular business of the day, and of the night, was taking prisoners out of cells for interrogation and torture. Nicolas, like everybody else, held his breath when he heard the sound of boots approaching. The chief supervisor sometimes came with the guards if an official was coming to visit, or if delegates from America or the United Nations demanded a report on the condition of the prison system and the "observation of human rights." He would show up in a crisp uniform and shout orders before disappearing again. If there was a string of executions, he was always present to oversee the proceedings.

More than anything, Nicolas dreaded the banging on the metal doors.

"*Kin la! Kin la!*"

Nicolas felt an elbow in his ribs. He turned around and saw Major, the shamed ex-Macoute, leering.

"Your turn!"

Nicolas looked into his eyes. Major was not a learned man. He was from the working class, but he had a thirst for power. He looked like a Macoute, carried himself like one, spoke arrogantly like one, even here, behind bars. Nicolas hadn't liked him from the minute they'd met.

"*Pardon?*" Nicolas said.

"Empty out the shit," Major retorted, raising his voice. "Go on!"

Nicolas knew there was no sense in arguing. He glanced at Boss, who kept his eyes shut with his head against the wall. He knew the old man was listening. Nicolas got up and tried to pick up the bucket with both hands. He was immediately assaulted with the stink of floating feces. Nicolas turned away, nearly dropping it. The men gasped and shifted aside.

"Hey! Careful!"

Nicolas held his breath and tried to keep his face turned away from the bucket as he followed the guard through the door. The maneuver was nearly impossible. He was forced to hunch over in order to keep both hands on the handle that dug into his fingers. The bucket was spilling, and inevitably, he felt a viscous liquid dripping onto his toes. He coughed. He didn't want to throw up. Not here, not like this, in the hallway. It would make everything worse.

He walked past the break room where two guards were drinking cold fruit sodas. The door was wide open, and Nicolas caught a glimpse of the carbonated gold drinks fizzing inside sweaty glass bottles. He couldn't see the radio as he shuffled past, but he heard snatches of a broadcast the guards were listening to.

"Dominican Republic...U.S. Marines...Operation Power Pack."

Nicolas wanted to hear more, but he had to keep moving. The room was falling away behind him, and all he heard was Duvalier's fading voice yelling the words *"kamoken"* and "communism." What was happening in the outside world? How were the Haitian rebels faring? Were they on the right side of the war? Were the Constitutionalists winning? If they were, then there was hope for them to return to Haiti, hope that they might someday overthrow Papa Doc.

Nicolas grew accustomed to the changing light in the hallway, taking in every turn of the corner, every door they passed. Soon he saw a spot of light at the end of the tunnel. It stung his eyes. The light surrounded the guard's frame like a halo, and as they neared the door, Nicolas wanted to raise one hand to shield his eyes from the sun. How many days had it been since he'd seen sunlight? He couldn't remember, but his head spun and he clung to the bucket, desperate to safeguard its contents.

"Move it!" The guards shoved the prisoners forward. Nicolas blinked repeatedly and followed the others with his head down. Behind him, a prisoner collapsed, but the line kept moving. Nicolas squinted and saw nothing but yellow, sunlit mortar and dust. He was outside. Above him, the sun blazed in a cloudless sky. There was so much to see, and yet he felt blind.

"Faster!" another guard shouted behind him.

Nicolas did as he was told.

Soon his eyes had adjusted enough that he could keep them open. There wasn't much time to let his sight wander around the grounds, to take in the geography of the place. For the first time, through the padlocked gates and the spirals of barbed wire, Nicolas saw the desolation of the savanna, and beyond it, he pictured the blue stretch of the bay. He found himself yearning for the life of the poor men and women and children who roamed Port-au-Prince, hungry, scraping, but not rotting in here. The idea of escaping was more than tempting. But his fellow cellmates had already discouraged it in the first days of his arrival.

"No one escapes from here," Boss had said. "It's been tried before. That's how we know. Poor devils got shot on the spot."

"It doesn't matter how fast you run or how far ahead you get," another prisoner said. "They'll launch Jeeps and guards after you, and they'll kill you. And that's if you make it past the gates and the barbed wire."

Nicolas picked up his pace and followed the other bucket-toting prisoners. They walked with their heads down, staring at their dusty feet. The sun felt warm on Nicolas's back and bare shoulders. Sun was a healing remedy for ailments of the body and the soul, his mother always said.

The ground burned his feet, and he noticed that the others did not seem to mind, the soles of their feet hardened from years of incarceration. Nicolas had the sudden revelation, as his stomach churned, that there was a reason for stripping prisoners of clothes and shoes and for starving them. It wasn't just to humiliate them. It was to allow for exposure to slowly kill them, and if that didn't work, at least it meant they couldn't escape. Not without shoes, and not without food in their bellies. *Sak vid pa kanpe*, the proverb said. It was devious, evil, and Nicolas shivered at the realization that his incarcerators were so calculating.

Behind the barracks was a wide expanse of arid desert land. Nothing grew out of the earth aside from sparse bush trees in the distance. The earth was cracked and dry, and the wind blew up tiny dust storms around their bony black bodies. Swarms of flies dove toward the buckets, buzzing around their ears, landing on their hands. Nicolas's nose started to itch. The sulfuric smell of salt and human waste wafted through the air.

"Halt!"

They came to the edge of a ditch and stopped as instructed. Nicolas set his bucket down on the ground, right between his legs. He buried his face in the hollow of his arm, gasping for air. His eyes welled up. The ditch, approximately twenty feet across and another fifteen long, was a giant septic tank. Nicolas had never seen nor smelled anything like it.

Nicolas turned his head away from the hole and caught a glimpse of movement in the corner of his eye. A gesture. Someone was waving at him. Nicolas shielded his eyes from the sun. His mouth fell open. Was he hallucinating?

"Psst! Nicolas!"

"Jean-Jean?"

Jean-Jean stood four prisoners behind him, his long, thin legs bare like yellowed celery stalks, his belly spilling over his briefs. He looked old and pale, like a scrap of torn parchment. Nicolas's heart broke at the sight of the old man with saggy skin and bags under his eyes. It was like seeing his own father naked, and Nicolas trembled under the weight of his guilt. What was his old friend doing here? The two men locked eyes, and without a word, he read the story on Jean-Jean's face. The government spies and the Macoutes had gotten to him too. Sorrow and shame crashed upon Nicolas.

"You gave me up," Jean-Jean whispered.

Nicolas shook his head weakly, less in denial than ignorance. The other men in line dumped the foul waste into the ditch. There was a chorus of coughing and retching.

"When did you get here, Jean-Jean?" he hissed.

"A few days ago," Jean-Jean said, pausing to think. "I'm already losing track. They came for me at work and—"

"Jean-Jean, there was nothing to say about you. I didn't give you up," Nicolas said, without much conviction.

Jean-Jean shrugged. It didn't matter. After all, even if Nicolas hadn't said anything about his friends during the warden's torture, they were guilty by association. Jean-Jean's voice broke, and he looked down at his bare feet and swollen ankles.

"Here I am," he said. "Cell two."

The men between Nicolas and Jean-Jean were listening, but said nothing. They shot nervous glances around as a guard came forward, cradling his weapon against his chest.

"You are not permitted to talk here."

Others who were standing in line lowered their eyes. Nicolas looked straight ahead and so did Jean-Jean. But they did not dare look back at the guard. The gaze, Nicolas had realized, was everything in prison.

"Problem?" the guard asked, stepping closer to Nicolas.

Nicolas shook his head. He didn't want to antagonize the officer, but he refused to cower like the others. Sure, they were going to beat him senseless if they wanted to. But he could not give them the satisfaction of defeat—not in front of his mentor. The guard pointed the rifle at his face, pressing it against his jaw.

"This is no fucking recess," the guard continued. He spat every word through clenched teeth, and Nicolas felt the rage there.

Nicolas, instead of replying, picked up his bucket and dumped its contents into the ditch.

"You're nothing but a piece of shit," the guard said. "Shut your big mouth or I'll throw you in that ditch."

Around them, prisoners still gagged reflexively at the foulness of emptied buckets coated in fecal matter. Their palms and nails were soiled. Nicolas wiped his own hands against the grimy fabric of his briefs. One prisoner urinated on another's hands to wash up. Nicolas swallowed both his disgust and his rage. Instead of screaming at the guard, he watched him walk away, shooting the inmates one last look, his finger on the trigger.

Nicolas looked at Jean-Jean, saw his chest rising and falling in an irregular pattern.

"Are you all right?" Nicolas whispered.

Jean-Jean looked back at him, leaning in closer.

"I told them about my diabetes," he said, his voice sounding like the strident hiss of the wind blowing through cracked windows. "They won't give me any insulin. I'm..." He blinked. "I'm tired."

"I'm so sorry," he said.

Jean-Jean gave a weak smile. Nicolas wanted to kick himself for saying those words. What did "sorry" even mean now? What good could those words do? His actions had landed him and his friend in here, and there was no forgiveness for that. He swallowed his shame.

"They want to break us," Nicolas whispered, looking around for signs of patrolling guards.

"I think," Jean-Jean said, "that has already been accomplished."

Something in his eyes seemed to flicker out. He blinked again.

"I told Eve I couldn't help," he murmured. "I told her I was being followed. They parked in front of my house, my office. They got Georges too. But he's not here. They arrested him at the airport. Rumor is he went straight to the Devil at the Palais. Double trouble for a member of any ministry, you see."

"How is my family?" Nicolas asked.

He felt ashamed for asking, but his heart leapt at the mention of his wife's name. Jean-Jean had stopped talking. His eyes seemed to roll back for a moment.

"Are you all right?" Nicolas asked.

The guard had returned. Nicolas shut his mouth, but it was too late. The guard raised his rifle above his head and brought it down violently, striking Jean-Jean across the shoulder. The old man collapsed on his knees, nearly falling into the ditch. The guard kicked him and Jean-Jean fell out of line. The other prisoners stood in the same spot, frozen. Some of them looked straight ahead; others looked away, stared at their feet. The guard kicked again, stomping the old man's face with his boot.

Nicolas reacted by instinct. He ran to Jean-Jean to help him up, but before he could reach the body, the guard aimed his rifle at him and cocked it. The prisoners gasped. A young inmate covered his ears with both hands, sobbing. The guard stared at Nicolas, eyes wide with rage. He was a scrawny man beneath his khakis, but any man wearing military fatigues and carrying a gun could incite terror. Nicolas could tell he was itching for an opportunity to blow a prisoner away.

Nicolas dropped to his knees and surrendered, his arms in the air. He didn't look up at the guard. Instead, he kept his eyes on Jean-Jean, who was writhing on the ground.

"Back in line, now, or I'll shoot you!" the guard shouted.

Nicolas stuttered as his lips formed words he hadn't intended to speak. "M-mercy, please. Mercy for this old man."

He felt the dirt against his knees, but didn't think much about it. He was taking a risk, and he knew it. But it was the right thing to do, because everyone here was too broken, too frightened to stand up for themselves or others. It was the least he could do for his mentor.

"He—he needs help. He's very ill," he stammered.

"I don't give a shit what he is. Back in line, right now!"

The guard stepped closer and shoved Nicolas in the chest with the gun barrel. Nicolas felt the cold metal against his flesh. He got up and took a few steps back, but his eyes remained on Jean-Jean.

"Back inside, now! All of you!"

The huddled prisoners regained their composure, separated,

grabbed their buckets, and once more formed a line. They walked back toward the building, mute as dead carps.

Nicolas glanced over his shoulder. He caught a last glimpse of his friend still curled on the ground, surrounded by the other prisoners, and wondered if someone would have the courage to help him up, to help him down the hallway, help him to his mat, help him demand a doctor, medicine, mercy. There was a guard standing near Jean-Jean, cradling a rifle. He was tall, thin, his face shadowed by his hat. But inside that brown face, Nicolas thought he saw two eyes staring right at him, free of the usual hatred and rage most of the guards used to keep other, more difficult emotions in check. Nicolas shuddered. It was almost worse to see those steady eyes witnessing everything without evident judgment. And then another soldier struck Nicolas just above the kneecap, and he crumbled, the pain making everything go dark.

TWELVE

"Your brother is alive," Sauveur said in a whisper. He pulled Raymond out of earshot. "But in bad, bad shape."

Dawn was breaking on the beach, and the motorboat was ready. Raymond took a breath to let the news settle in.

"You talked to your contact?" he asked.

"There's a date set for his execution..." Sauveur's voice wavered when Raymond lowered his head. "August twenty-seventh."

Raymond inhaled sea salt.

"How do you know?"

"We have a guy"—Sauveur grinned—"a man inside."

Raymond nodded. First, he had to get Eve and Amélie out of Haiti. He silently inspected the boat while the captain approached them and spoke with Sauveur. He noticed a few rust stains on the hull and the outlines of a patch-up job on the floor.

"You sank this boat before?" he asked, pointing at the marks.

The captain chuckled silently, shook his head. He was a quiet man with wavy gray sideburns and a mustache so thick Raymond could barely see his lips. His eyes were a rare ambergris. His name was Manolo, Manno for short. Raymond understood what Sauveur meant now about "trusting him." This captain had an easy time getting into the Dominican Republic because of his mixed heritage: half Dominican, half Haitian. He looked like what many expected a Dominican to look like, Indio, with a bronze complexion and an unmistakable Spanish accent.

He'd arrived at Sauveur's before daybreak, and Raymond had gotten up at the sound of the motor. They'd gathered on the beach and made introductions, their voices caught in gentle gusts of wind. The darkness was fading, and everything came into focus. Eve wrapped Amélie in a makeshift sling and secured her on her chest. On her shoulder, she strapped a canvas bag that Claudette had prepared for her. Sauveur took her hand and Raymond took the other.

The water was warm as it rose to their knees, and the sand shifted under their heels as they made their way to the boat where her other bag was already waiting. Eve squeezed Raymond's hand. He was grateful for the ability to see her face in the early light.

"I don't know about this, Raymond."

She'd been quiet all morning, and by the way she looked at the boat and the ocean, he knew she was terrified. But she was too strong to admit it.

"Don't worry," Raymond said. "He's done this many times. Just do as he says and you'll be there in no time." His feet sank a little and his toenails gathered sand particles.

"I'm just not good on water," Eve muttered. "But we'll be fine. It's Nicolas I'm worried about..."

They stopped at the boat where the captain was waiting. Raymond looked in her eyes this time because it was important that she knew he was not giving up. He was staying to get Nicolas back. He told her about Sauveur's contact at Fort Dimanche. But he said nothing about the execution date.

"I want to give you something." Eve grabbed the bag Claudette had gifted her with.

What now? Just this morning, she'd slipped jewelry in his pocket, insisting, despite his protests, that he pawn her gold chains and earrings.

Raymond saw her hand move to the bottom of the sack, and he heard the rustle of plastic. Claudette had stuffed the bag with saltine crackers, bread, and some fruit. Raymond also knew that

Eve had taken Nicolas's notebook with her. Finally, she pulled out a bundle wrapped in familiar-looking fabric and held it out with both hands.

"Take it," she whispered.

He grabbed the corners of the cloth and pulled them apart. He couldn't imagine what gift Eve would have for him. When he saw the contents of the package, he understood. There was a moment of silence between them. Eve pressed forward, the body of the revolver reflecting the first specks of golden light.

"It belonged to Nicolas," she said firmly. Her eyes were still glued on her brother-in-law. "Take it. It's yours now."

Sauveur stood behind them, looking at the gun over Eve's shoulder. His eyes shifted from the weapon to Raymond, then back to the gun. The captain said nothing, but he too was watching them, his hands clasped on the wheel. Raymond remembered where he'd seen the fabric now: in the box with the notebook.

He took the gun from her and held it up to have a better look. It was heavy, and he kept his finger well away from the trigger. The handle was smooth and the body was cold. He had no idea how to use it. Eve stepped closer and wrapped her arms around him. He hugged her back, carefully holding the gun away. He wished, for a brief moment, that she would stay. Eve and Amélie were his family. Once they were gone, he would be truly alone.

Raymond kissed his niece's forehead. Sadness tore through him like a bad wind.

"Don't forget me," he whispered, running his fingers through her curls.

But he knew better. She was too young for his face to automatically imprint in her memory, and besides, the faces of his own children were already blurring, becoming indistinct. He and Sauveur watched the motorboat turn and head out into the open water. Then, before the sun rose above the horizon, they disappeared like ants swept off the edge of the earth.

Sauveur stood in the water just a step behind. He sighed. Raymond searched for words to cut through the awkward silence, to avoid the obvious wound this separation had inflicted on him. But there were none. There was nothing but silence between them until the sun broke into the sky. Raymond saw the horizon, the infinity of the water, and the absence of Eve and Amélie in the clarity of morning. It was as if a veil had been lifted.

"My wife and kids left me too," Raymond said. "On a *kanntè* to Miami."

Behind him, Sauveur shook his head.

"Everybody's leaving," the journalist said gravely. After a pause, he glanced at Raymond. "Did they make it?"

"I don't know."

"Something else for you to find out."

Raymond looked down at the water. He couldn't see his feet, but he wiggled his toes and sank deeper into the sand.

"Will Eve be all right out there?"

"I trust Manno," Sauveur said. "He's fluent in Spanish, and he's got family over the border. They'll get in, no problem."

Still facing the ocean, Raymond took a few steps backward and then turned around to walk toward shore. Sauveur followed. They sat on the beach.

"About your brother..." Sauveur scratched his throat.

"You said he was alive, right?"

Sauveur nodded. "But that doesn't necessarily help us. We can't have our man inside simply just break him out of prison, Raymond. No one gets out of Fort Dimanche. There are guards, and they are trained to shoot anything that moves. That's *if* you can make it past the barbed wire, or survive the torture, the starvation."

Raymond steeled himself. "So what good is he? Your man inside?"

"I'm sorry, but he'd be risking too much. He has his own grudges against the warden, but there are certain things he won't do. Let's rule that out right now."

Raymond felt short of breath as he spoke. "But he'll help us?"

"As much as he possibly can, yes."

"Then I'll have to get in somehow."

"Get in?" Sauveur said. "Why? Don't be stupid."

"Do you have a brother?"

Sauveur shook his head. Then he couldn't know what it meant, Raymond thought. Raymond remembered how, when they were little, his brother would tremble in a corner in fear of their father. He was the one to wipe the blood away from their welts at night, in their room. Raymond would not give up on Nicolas, even with so much resentment between them. He was his only family in Haiti now, and he would do whatever it took.

Sauveur shook his head again. "It's suicide. Getting into Fort Dimanche isn't tough, but how the hell do you expect to break out, the two of you? No man has ever escaped from there."

"I can't do it alone, that's for sure." He gazed steadily at his friend.

Sauveur looked into Raymond's eyes for a long moment and sighed. "We'll need time."

"That's one thing we don't have much of," Raymond said. "August twenty-seventh is just over two months away."

Sauveur sucked his teeth and shook his head furiously. "This is madness. You realize that?"

"We're all mad," Raymond said. "You ran away from the Tonton Macoutes in broad daylight and you're still here pushing the news from underground. I'm not the only one who's crazy here, trust me."

Sauveur paused and rubbed his hands together slowly, to the rhythm of the waves. When he stopped, his face brightened. Raymond saw him grin. The journalist stroked the hair on his chin. Fishermen floated by in pairs, carrying canoes on their heads. Some of them interrupted their singing to greet the two men with the common politeness of country folk. Sauveur returned their greeting with more assurance than Raymond. They waited for the men to disappear before speaking again.

"Are you absolutely sure you want to do this?" Sauveur stared at him. A dark storm was brewing in his eyes. "Absolutely certain?"

"I have nothing to go back to," Raymond said. "I've got nothing left."

Sauveur smiled. "I knew you were a different kind of man," he said, "taking me into your cab like that, driving away like you did. You're a—"

"A lunatic, I know. You've said."

"No, I was going to say 'a saint.'" Sauveur's large hand squeezed Raymond's shoulder with reassurance. "Come, let's have coffee. And then possibly a drink! I think we're going to need it ..."

THIRTEEN

Major awakened Nicolas with a shove a few days later. Nicolas sat up on his mat with his hands against his eyelids. He'd been dreaming again, but the images of Eve were already fading. All he had to hold on to was her voice.

He looked around the cell and felt his body stiffen with a savage ache. He couldn't have described it to anyone if he tried, but it was worse than anything he'd ever felt. It was more than soreness. It was dread. It was the agonizing routine of waking up between these four walls every day, waiting for death to lick his bones clean.

Nicolas thought, once more, of the only alternative: an escape that afforded him control. If he could kill himself, if he could get out of this place...

"Get up!" Major's voice bounced against the walls.

Nicolas opened his eyes. "What? What is it?" he muttered, half asleep.

Were the guards coming for him? Major towered over him in the dark. The whites of his eyes had turned yellow recently, and he'd complained of fevers. Now, staring at him, Nicolas saw it clearly. Everyone saw it. Major's arrogance was dwindling in the shadow of a growing illness.

"Get up!" he spat. "Empty the *kin*!"

"Again?" Nicolas retorted. "We're supposed to take turns."

"You'll keep on doing it until I tell you! Get off your ass!"

Major expected compliance. He'd been muttering under his breath, but for everyone to hear, that he was going to have to work hard at "breaking this nigger, teaching him his place." No one said anything. No one fought back. But Nicolas was growing weary of this game. Major hadn't been as lucky in life as Nicolas—but then Nicolas had worked hard for everything he'd achieved. This dungeon offered Major the chance to keep a chokehold on the bourgeoisie. Nicolas decided he wouldn't take it lying down.

"We take turns," Nicolas spat. "That's the rule, and it's someone else's turn."

Nicolas wanted to go back to sleep. He barely had the strength to stand up anymore. He was weakening, just like everyone else in here, unable to glean enough nutrition from the putrid meals they were given. His kidneys were starting to feel the effects of dehydration, and pissing in the bucket had started to burn. He wouldn't even make it to his own execution if things went on like this. But then again, neither would Major.

Major folded over, suddenly, overwhelmed with a cough. Nicolas heard mucus rattling in his lungs each time he caught his breath. Tuberculosis was rampant in Fort Dimanche, and Nicolas's fear was that soon enough, it would come knocking in cell six and reap them, one by one. It had already killed two men in nearby cells since Nicolas had arrived. He'd heard them scream in the hallway about a dead body, then another one. He'd heard the coughs, seen the blood in the corners of mouths of those who emptied the buckets outside. It was only a matter of time.

Major cleared his throat. "Maybe I'm not making myself clear. Get that thing out of here, or I'll let the guards and the warden know you're not cooperating."

He watched Major curl up in his corner for his sleep shift and wondered how long it would take for him to expire. He remembered reading case studies of inmate suicide. It was easy to see how that option could become increasingly attractive.

He shook his head to chase those thoughts away. No. He was not committing suicide. Not that it would have been easy to find a way, packed into this cell with all these other miserable human beings. There wasn't enough space for such a personal act. No, he had to stay alive at least a few days longer now that his friend was in the same condition. Jean-Jean—he had thought of his friend since they last talked three days ago, and had tried climbing the tree to ask the prisoners across the hall if they knew anything. But he hadn't been able to make contact. Frustration swept over him.

Nicolas grabbed the bucket. He was tempted to dump the contents on Major, but decided against it. Instead, like a good little prisoner, he waited for the guards to come and let him out. When he made it to the yard, he looked around for Jean-Jean, searched the lines with his eyes. But Jean-Jean was not there. Perhaps it wasn't his turn. Likely, he had been too badly hurt by the blows in the yard. When Nicolas returned to his cell, he dropped the bucket in the far corner where Major was sleeping. Major woke up and opened his eyes, startled.

"Say what you want to the warden," Nicolas said. "I don't give a damn. Next time, someone else does this. I'm done."

Major did not answer, but he watched carefully as Nicolas paced the cell and counted his steps, throwing a few punches, even attempting jumping jacks and push-ups like when he played soccer with his brother and their friends as a kid. Though he was still bruised, Nicolas knew that exercise would be vital in keeping him alive. The urine on his wounds seemed like some kind of miracle cure—they'd started to scab and close up.

He wanted to remain as sharp as he could, as alert as he could. If he was going to die, to be executed, and if he wasn't going to know the date, he wanted to know he could be strong when the moment came. He did not want to give the warden nor the government the satisfaction of killing him when he was already broken, weakened, reduced to less than a man. He wanted to be lucid, to stand tall when they pulled the trigger—he wanted to look his killers in the eye. He was not going to die a coward, not if he could help it. Maybe one day, when Amélie asked how her father had died, her mother, or her uncle, or someone else could say he'd been a *gason vanyan*, a great man. Valorous. Brave. But of course, how could anyone outside ever know that?

"Planning to go a few rounds?" Boss asked.

Boss, like many of the prisoners, had found a hobby. He sat around molding paint chips and fibers from his mat into a paste mixed with his own urine. When it dried enough to become something close to papier-mâché, he shaped it into small playing cards or chess pieces, or squares of toilet paper to use at the *kin*. He was rolling a rook between his fingers as he watched Nicolas jog in place.

"I suppose we all need something to keep us occupied," Nicolas said.

"I suppose we do." Boss nodded thoughtfully. He set his final piece down next to the other pawns and chuckled.

"We should call you Muhammad. Like Muhammad Ali, the boxer."

"If only I was that strong," Nicolas muttered.

He was bending over to touch his toes when voices suddenly came rolling down the hallway. It started in the first cell, and soon the voices traveled past the other doors.

"*La mort!* Death! Death!"

Nicolas stood still and listened. Here it was again, that cry. Someone had passed away. What was it this time? Tuberculosis again? Or death by torture? Sometimes, the bodies lay there for hours, days even, before any of the guards cared enough to remove them. The last time they ignored the call, and the body had begun to decompose. Prisoners got sick, guards vomited on their own shoes, and for fear of retaliation from the spirit of the dead, a rule was instituted that prisoners would carry the body out, accompanied by prayer and hymns. Because that was the proper way to leave a place. Because otherwise the spirit of the dead might stay behind and torment the living. Nicolas found it odd that these monsters who killed so callously were terrified of the afterlife, of hauntings, of spirits who might seek revenge.

Nicolas heard boots stomping down the hallway. The guards were in motion.

"Who is it?"

Nicolas shivered at the presence of death so close by. It could have been any one of them.

"Cell two! Death! Death!"

"Step away from the door!"

Everyone in Nicolas's cell listened. Dread worked its way through his stomach and crawled up his spine. He heard the familiar clicking of a padlock, keys chiming, and a cell door swinging open down the hall. The inmates' voices rose instantly, loud and clear, as if they were right there.

"This one, Faustin! The old man! He's dead!"

Nicolas gasped. No. He must have misheard.

He eyed the rectangular window above the door. Could he make it? He spread his legs and hands and tried climbing. His palms pressed against the wall, and he applied weight on his legs for support, hoisting himself up toward the opening, only to slide back down. He was too weak today. Still, he tried again.

"Jean Faustin! Jean Faustin is dead!"

Once more, Nicolas's hands and feet slid down against the surface of the filthy wall. He couldn't latch on. He looked up at the small window, powerless.

"Let me out!" he cried, banging on the door. The other prisoners behind him stirred in the dark. Some of them cursed him.

"Stop it!" Boss hissed.

"That's my friend!" Nicolas shouted, oblivious to his cellmates.

A familiar murmur rose up in the hallway. The "Hymn to Death."

"*Au revoir*," they sang. "It's only a brief good-bye, we'll see each other again on the other side."

Nicolas slammed his hands against the door. It was hopeless. He pictured his mentor in the prison yard, frail, struggling to keep his eyes open. This wasn't how he wanted to remember Jean Faustin. Horror shot through him. It had to be the diabetes. Jean-Jean had died for lack of insulin—a pointless death. He could hear Jean-Jean's voice as if he were there next to him, talking about his sugar, his sugar that was never any good.

"Jean-Jean," Nicolas cried.

"Shut the fuck up, L'Eveillé!" Major said, sitting up on his mat.

Nicolas heard a commotion out in the hallway. He pressed his ear against the cold metal door, his eyes full of tears.

"What happened?" a guard asked.

Nicolas couldn't hear what the prisoners were saying, and it didn't matter anymore. Nicolas tried to climb the wall again. This time, a hand yanked at his ankle and he fell to the ground, his knees crashing into the barren concrete. The hallways resounded with voices saluting Jean Faustin's departure, and now the men in cell six, the men around Nicolas, were singing too. Boss leaned in and shoved his finger in Nicolas's face.

"Stay down and shut your mouth!" Boss said. "I've told you: if they catch you up there, all of us get beaten." His eyes grew bigger, wider, filled with a sort of rage Nicolas hadn't seen in him before. "I'm warning you!"

Nicolas paused and tried to swallow the despair tunneling through the back of his throat. "He was a good man. He deserves better."

Boss's lip quivered. Nicolas saw a little foam in the corner of his mouth.

"Shut up and sing then!" someone yelled at him. "Sing the hymn for your friend, if he was such a good one."

Nicolas kept his back pressed against the door. Accept Jean-Jean's death? Impossible. He didn't have it in him.

"You think you're the only one to lose friends here? Or family? You think you're special?" Boss's hand wrapped around Nicolas's throat and squeezed firmly enough to constrict his airways.

Nicolas, panicked, coughed and tried to catch his breath.

"You're not!" Boss grumbled. "I can tell you about loss. I lost my son. I lost my flesh and blood here, in this hole, this rotten hole God has forgotten."

Nicolas couldn't breathe. Suddenly, his vision grew blurry.

He thought he heard the other prisoners shout for Boss to stop. He saw a hand swatting at the air over his face, or maybe he imagined it.

"I didn't mean to. I didn't. All I did was answer questions, but they twist your words..." Boss's grip eased a little and Nicolas gasped. "I didn't know what I was saying. I was just trying to cooperate. I told them where he went, who he was friends with. It's all my fault."

The old man released his grip and Nicolas fell to his knees. The old man stood there, rocking back and forth, his lips silently mouthing the words: *I didn't mean to.*

Nicolas backed away, dissolving into the mix of naked bodies, disappearing among the ghosts. He felt tears burning his eyes. What was he now? Was he like Boss? Was he going to be? He was losing his mind, becoming the old man in prison plucking lice out of his beard, trying to remember whether Jean-Jean was right. Maybe he did say something during his interrogation. How could he not remember?

The self-doubt crippled him. He stayed on the ground while the men kept singing until a voice in the hallway, louder than the others, rose with a prayer. Psalm 23. Someone across the hall shouted for them to turn the body so they'd take him out the door headfirst, to keep Jean Faustin's spirit from lingering in the cell. It was useless, to ask for things from a God who was not listening, a God who let Jean Faustin die alone in a cold cell. He'd been dead since breakfast, a few doors down, and Nicolas hadn't been able to help. Who was this God, really, and why hadn't He intervened?

Nicolas stared straight ahead, listening as Jean's cellmates carried the body down the hall. Then he buried his face in his knees. It was dark there, and safe, and in that space he could grip his hair and pull it away from the scalp where madness had begun to crawl. He allowed himself to fall apart and listened for the cackle running under the prayers, the laughter of a trickster god lurking in the corners of Fort Dimanche: Death, adjusting his hat, blowing smoke from a cigar, gyrating his hips, dancing around their cells, arms thrown wide in welcome. Death was laughing at him.

FOURTEEN

E ight stories of imposing white concrete, Hôtel Castel Haiti loomed at the top of a hill, lights blazing from every balcony and window. As Raymond's Datsun ascended the narrow road lined with banyan trees, he could hear the music from the hotel. His hands tightened around the wheel. He exhaled deeply, but he couldn't shake the fear inside him. He had to maintain his composure, even in the face of what he was about to do. He had a chance to turn around, a chance to flee back to Marigot. But he focused on the thought of seeing his brother again, no matter where that was.

A guard in a gray uniform conducted inspections at the hotel gates, and Raymond's car idled as he waited to be let through. The guard carried a pistol in an oversized holster. He leaned forward to look through the window of the cab. A cool breeze filtered into the car, carrying the scent of pine trees and jasmine from the hotel grounds. The guard eyed Raymond without much interest and glanced at the red ribbon dangling from the rear-view mirror.

"Taxi?"

Raymond nodded and the guard shrugged.

"Good luck with business tonight," he said. "Everyone's busy dancing at the Awards Ball. I can't imagine why they'd need you. Not with all the chauffeurs here."

Raymond thanked God for his taxi ribbon. Cabbies didn't make much these days, but they still had access. It had been Milot Sauveur's very first question: What access do you have as a taxi driver? After that, Sauveur did the research, made phone calls, and worked out a plan.

"This is your chance. On June twenty-second, at the Awards Ball."

It was a special night for army and government officials. The president, accompanied by the First Lady, passed out honorary medals to top men in the regime. Raymond's lips turned up a little at the thought of the corruption concentrated inside. But the word was Jules Sylvain Oscar, warden of Fort Dimanche, liked to sip on rum punches at the hotel's game tables and on the pool deck with his mistresses, and tonight, he would most certainly be in attendance.

"He wouldn't miss it," Sauveur had said. "It's one of his opportunities to be chummy with the Baron."

And Oscar was Raymond's link to Nicolas. There was no turning back.

Raymond guided the Datsun down the arced driveway. It was possible, highly probable, that he was driving to his death. Vines of banyan trees brushed against the hood of the car as if clinging to him, whispering prayers to usher him into the underworld.

Hang on, Nicolas, he thought. *I'm coming for you.*

Raymond and Sauveur had gone over the plan many times at the journalist's kitchen table, reviewing the diagrams of Fort Dimanche, poking holes in their timelines, and brainstorming contingencies, and each time, they concluded this was the best chance. Raymond noted everything, nodding, even as the plan grew riskier and Sauveur lit a fresh cigarette off the butt of his last, twitching in his chair before throwing his pencil down.

"I'm sending you to your death," he murmured. "If you survive, it is no thanks to me."

Raymond shook his head. "I asked you for help, didn't I? I trust your plan: I sacrifice myself to the lion, and then I climb back out of his mouth."

Shiny black vehicles were parked along the curb by the dozens. Men in crisp khaki uniforms strutted around, their shoulders decorated with gold boards and tassels. Men and women glided out of foreign town cars with spit-shined shoes gleaming like mirrors. Raymond had never seen this many members of high society together in one place before. The local officials wore black tuxedos and held their female companions by the waist, or offered them an arm to lead them up the stone steps. Foreign dignitaries slid out of chauffeured cars in fine suits, sequined gowns, and silk turbans—their finery undercut by the bewildered looks on their faces. They were the reason Raymond was here, the only reason he and Sauveur had designed this plan as such. Rumors abounded that Duvalier, desperate for international investments in Haiti, was on a mission to reform his image. They would not shoot Raymond in front of foreign delegates and tourists. Raymond spotted armed guards posted every few feet, holding shotguns up in the air, their eyes blank and cold.

There are too many cars, he thought.

Music from a brass ensemble and maracas tumbled out through the windows while valets huddled around, holding doors open and bowing. He sat in his car, overwhelmed. He could still leave. The whole idea was madness, certainly, and panic was setting in. Yet if he left, where would he go? He couldn't leave Nicolas behind and simply move on. His heart thudded in his chest.

There it was. He'd been looking for the car since he drove in: a navy-blue Cadillac with the license plate number Sauveur had given him. Oscar's car.

He clenched the wheel until the web of skin between his fingers ached. There was time to pray or to think, but Raymond wasted none. The more he debated, the more he felt fear's screws bite into his bones. Raymond checked his rearview mirror, carefully put the car in reverse, and backed up, getting a bit more distance between himself and the Cadillac. He could see it clearly as he fastened his seat belt. It was one of the most beautiful vehicles he'd seen in Port-au-Prince. A shame, really. Raymond stomped the gas pedal and the Datsun gave a little jolt before lunging forward. He clenched his teeth and plowed directly into the side of the Cadillac. The beautiful blue door buckled instantly and Raymond's ears began to ring. The crash was so loud that, for a brief moment, Raymond thought he'd gone deaf. When the startled valets realized what had happened, they all ran to assess the damage, gasping, *"Kolangèt!* What the hell! Is he drunk?"

Raymond unfastened his seat belt and took a deep breath. Reaching up, he pulled the picture of Yvonne, Enos, and Adeline—smiling brilliantly, as always—out of the visor and stuffed it into his breast pocket. Then, with trembling knees and sweaty hands, he staggered out of his Datsun. His head was spinning, ears still ringing, but he could see clearly as he stepped gingerly over the shattered glass of taillights. The Cadillac was totaled. The Datsun's front bumper was still lodged into its door, its hood folded like an accordion, its fuming engine exposed.

"Are you all right, brother?" asked a valet, touching his shoulder.

Raymond heard himself saying what he and Sauveur had rehearsed: "I don't know what happened. The gas pedal jammed somehow. There was nothing I could do."

As the hotel guests stared in awe at the wreckage, two armed guards approached quickly. Another valet walked around the two cars, whistling in dismay.

"Do you know what you've done? That car belongs to the warden of Fort Dimanche, Jules Sylvain Oscar. It was brand new. You are truly fucked, my friend."

"Sit on the curb over there," one of the soldiers said, taking Raymond by the arm. It wasn't an aggressive gesture, though. Everyone, even the soldiers, seemed so shocked that the only emotion they could muster was pity.

But Raymond did not budge. His body felt heavy, and his heart was pounding. He tried to take a step back, to go to his car, to sit there and wait, but the soldier held on. The Cadillac's bumper croaked, slowly detached, and fell off in the driveway. An audible gasp rose over the hotel steps.

"Did your brakes fail?" one of the valets asked.

Raymond just shook his head. "Something jammed."

The other valet muttered under his breath, "Dead man walking." Raymond heard heavy footsteps behind him and turned to discover five guns pointed at him. The men were not in Macoute uniform, but it was clear what they were.

"*Men li,*" someone said. "There he is."

A shiver ran up Raymond's spine as he recognized Jules Oscar. He looked just like his photos in the newspaper: repulsive, with a long scar slicing down his face and bloodshot eyes.

"What happened here?" the warden said.

Next to Oscar stood a man with thin black hair and pink ears. He wore a beige suit and pink tie, with a little gold pin in his lapel that caught the light. The man's blue eyes shifted curiously from Oscar to Raymond and back to Oscar again. He shook his head, dismayed.

"Oh dear! How unfortunate!" Raymond's ear picked up the accent. He was a Frenchman, a dignitary. "*C'est votre voiture?* Is this your car, Oscar?"

Oscar did not respond to the question, his mouth hanging open at the sight of the damage. After a long, silent pause, he looked around at the crowd, scanning their faces, until his eyes found Raymond.

"You did this? You did this to *my* car?"

Jules Oscar was dressed in white from head to toe, an unlit cigarette waiting to be sparked. His shirt was buttoned to the neck, where he'd wrapped a red silk ascot in lieu of a tie. The smell of luxury—of rum, tobacco, and strong cologne—wafted toward Raymond. Raymond didn't speak. His throat was clogged, his ears still ringing. He kept his eyes on the warden, who stared at the Cadillac in dismay. A woman in a blue dress came running up behind him, holding up the train of her gown. She stopped where the other armed men stood.

"My car! *C'est pas possible, chéri!*" Her scarlet lips scowled at the damage, and she gathered her gown to avoid shards of glass. "I can't believe it. Look what he did to my new car!"

"*Quelle veine!*" muttered the Frenchman, a stern man whose

sleek black hair reminded Raymond of carrion, of a vulture hovering over a bloodbath, surveying possibilities.

The warden walked over to Raymond and immediately everything else seemed to fade away.

"Do you have any idea how much this car costs?" he asked calmly. "I bought this car brand new just two months ago. I hope you're prepared to pay for what you've done."

Raymond swallowed and found his voice. "I'm just a taxi driver, sir. How could I possibly afford to repay you?"

"That's not my problem!" The warden raised his voice, his eyes wide. "You'll fix this mess if you know what's good for you."

"How?" Raymond replied. His tongue felt heavy. "I don't have the money—I can barely eat these days. What are you going to do? Arrest me and throw me in jail like you do all the other poor *malheureux* in this country?"

Oscar stared at Raymond as if he were a bizarre specimen in a science experiment. A hushed murmur rose from the small crowd. Raymond heard someone joke that he sure had balls. The Frenchman was asking someone to translate the remark. *"Qu'est ce qui se passe?"* Someone leaned in to explain.

Oscar cocked his head.

"There's plenty of room in prison for you: in Penitencier National, Casernes Dessalines," he said. "Somehow, you'll have to pay for this."

That didn't fit Raymond's plans. He had to get to Fort Dimanche somehow. He remembered what Sauveur had said, that making any political statement could cost him his life on the spot. But here, in front of all these dignitaries? In front of this Frenchman? Raymond couldn't see it. Still, he felt as though the sweat pouring off his forehead would blind him entirely.

"Well, go on then," Raymond uttered. "Finish us off. First you send my family to Fort Dimanche, and now you want my bones for dinner?"

It was like pushing a button: Oscar's whole body twitched at the mention of Fort Dimanche. He rested his hand on the hood of the Cadillac and his spine straightened.

The Frenchman asked for another translation: *"Il dit quoi, là? What is he saying about Fort Dimanche?"*

Oscar glanced at the Frenchman, then at Raymond. This time, they locked eyes and Raymond wanted to jump out of his own skin. This time, no one translated.

"Are you sending him to Fort Dimanche?" the Frenchman asked Oscar. "Come now. It's not that serious. It's only a car. The poor man didn't mean to—"

"Only a car?" The woman in the blue dress glared at the man. "It was my car, my gift. He totaled it."

"He's just a cabbie," the Frenchman said. "Look, let's get back to business before I give up and go home. We have much to discuss. Are we going to do this or not?"

Raymond stared hatefully at the visitor. He was not supposed to be part of this. He was going to ruin everything with good intentions. Only a car? This man had no idea what cars meant to people in this country, did he?

"You have a relative in Fort Dimanche?"

Oscar had heard Raymond's words.

"What is your name?" he asked.

Raymond held his breath. "Raymond L'Eveillé," he croaked.

"How interesting," Oscar said.

Raymond's throat ached. He was thirsty, he was hot, and yet he planted his feet firmly on the ground and waited without moving. A Tonton Macoute, dressed in an oversized tuxedo, pulled out a pistol from the folds of his ill-fitted vest and aimed it at Raymond's face. Raymond's heart fell, and he resisted the urge to shut his eyes.

"Sir, he came here on a mission to kill you," the gunman spat. "Look at what he did to your car! He's an assassin. A hired assassin!"

"I'm a simple cabbie, trying to get by. I'm no assassin. I'm unarmed. I don't even have a penny to my name to fix up your car. Something jammed."

He tried to calm the tremor in his knees. The Frenchman, meanwhile, was wiping the sweat off his brow furiously with a silk handkerchief as pink as his necktie. The warden stared back, said nothing. Then, just as Raymond felt like his eardrums would burst under the pressure of his own heartbeat, Oscar smiled.

"You could have killed me, and you would have, if I were in this car. But thankfully, no one is hurt."

Oscar scanned the crowd behind him, offering a repulsive, toothy grin that seemed to chill only Raymond. The Frenchman grinned right back, chuckling nervously.

"Things could be much worse," Oscar said. "We can settle this matter tomorrow. Report to my office at eight thirty—"

Raymond shook his head. No. That wasn't the plan. "But—"

"We'll get your car out of there," Oscar said. "My men will give you a lift home."

Oscar curled his lips and lowered his voice as he spoke those last words, as if Raymond were one of his mistresses in need of cajoling before being struck. Raymond clenched his teeth and watched the warden motion for him to disappear from his sight. With the Frenchman appeased, Oscar waved for his mistress to follow. They turned to head back inside the hotel.

"Wait," Raymond cried. "But wait, sir! What about my brother in Fort Dimanche? What about him?"

Oscar's men surrounded him. There was a scramble, orders shouted, a revving of engines. Someone had him by the arm, and he did nothing to fight back. When he landed on the seat, he looked through the window. The warden was gone. The crowd was gone. Everything was back to normal. No, he didn't want to be driven home. He wanted to be thrown into prison, to save his brother's life. He looked out the window again, his vision blurry, hoping to catch one final glimpse of his beloved Datsun, and tapped the picture of his family in his pocket. The driver got behind the wheel, and two men climbed in the backseat with Raymond. He knew their weapons could decide his fate.

The men stared straight ahead.

"Where to?" The driver glanced in the rearview mirror.

Raymond tried to see his eyes, but the man avoided his gaze. Instead, he looked at one of the henchmen seated next to Raymond. The car idled quietly.

Raymond muttered his address. If he had to wait till tomorrow to confront the warden, to get himself arrested, then that's what he'd do. He'd have to be flexible, do whatever it took to see his brother. He thought of his car again as they drove through the gates, and of his family as he passed his children's school and then the neighborhood of Turgeau, where Nicolas and Eve had lived. It wasn't until they passed his own neighborhood and kept right on going that he realized, squeezed between the heat of these two men, their skin burning with the kind of hunger that urged them to be killers, that they were not stopping. They were driving deeper into the belly of Port-au-Prince. Deeper into the snarl of marketplaces and businesses, of gingerbread houses and low-rise slums, until the car turned onto the familiar boulevard, sinking into the dusk obscuring the capital. Deeper and deeper, until he knew, with the strangest sadness he had ever known, that they were headed for Fort Dimanche.

FIFTEEN

Major was dying.

Nicolas had observed his fever and delirium during the hottest nights, had heard his unrelenting cough, how he spit up blood in the *kin*. It had to be tuberculosis. The other cellmates had implored the guards to remove him for fear of contamination, but in vain.

Now Major lay shivering in the heat, glued to his mat in the corner. Nicolas tried to stay far away from him, but he knew it was only a matter of time before they all contracted the disease, before they all died. One of the prisoners had stripped off Major's underwear and they'd forced him to use it to cover his mouth when coughing. He clutched it like a security blanket, and Nicolas saw that it was speckled with dried blood.

Major kept his eyes closed. His breathing was shallow, and it seemed for a while that he'd already drawn his last breath. He was withering away and had lost all his arrogance and his power over the other inmates. The tables had turned, and no one wanted to nurse him.

"Is he dead yet?" Boss asked.

Nicolas wished he had died. Not because of his dislike for Major, but because watching any man die a slow death was unbearable. If felt inhumane to watch someone fade away without helping.

"Not fast enough if you ask me," an inmate whispered in the dark.

The other inmates snickered, but Nicolas gritted his teeth.

"I can't rejoice in another man's suffering," he said, eyeing Major's frail body.

It was frightening to watch him twitch like a dying animal. His shriveled body curled in the fetal position, and soon he stopped moving. Nicolas would have covered him up if they'd had a blanket.

"We don't take pity on Macoutes in here," a prisoner spat.

"He was an enemy," Boss added. "You couldn't take a shit without him berating you. You can show him your high and mighty compassion if you want, Maître, but as far as we're concerned, he's as good as dead."

Nicolas looked over at the old man who'd been so kind to him when he arrived. Boss was a good man himself, but now Nicolas was seeing another side of him. In this moment, he was as cunning and heartless as any guard in this dungeon. Every man had his limits, Nicolas thought, and Fort Dimanche was the place to test them.

"That man over there, that could be you or me," Nicolas said. "Could be any one of us."

Nicolas waited for an expression of remorse, but he got no answer. The men ignored him. One of them sucked his teeth, a gesture of impatience. Nicolas sighed.

"I don't want to die like this," he muttered.

"Maybe we won't," said a man squatting in a corner. "I heard the guards talking this morning. President Johnson says he's going to continue in Kennedy's footsteps. They're looking closely at human rights violations here."

Nicolas eyed the man with pity.

"You think this President Johnson is going to save us?" Nicolas scoffed. "Why hasn't he landed troops here then, like he just did in Santo Domingo? How far does one need to look to see what is happening in this country?"

The other prisoners kept quiet, afraid the conversation was getting too political, worried there might be a spy among them ready to report their whispers to Papa Doc. But Nicolas knew they clung to hope. They imagined it in everything. If one picked up a penny outside, it meant their fortune would change. If another dreamed of a visitor, as Boss claimed to have done last night, it also meant change. Rumors about possible political change kept them alive, but Nicolas had stopped believing that America, or France, or any other country would really do anything.

We are not a priority to anyone but ourselves, he thought.

He shook his head. "Don't be foolish. No one will intervene for us when Haiti is still being chastised for claiming its freedom. Kennedy didn't have a chance to—"

Major's coughing spell interrupted him. The men held their breath, waiting for it to pass like a bad storm. When he stopped, they stared at his body as if expecting him to expire on the spot.

"Don't you see what we are?" Nicolas said. "How does this make us better than him?"

They sat in silence, after that, digesting the sight of death doing its work.

Nicolas was certain Major still had breath left in him when the guards came. Two of the prisoners were forced to carry him. There was no singing for him, but the inmates crossed themselves and said a quick prayer to will his spirit out of their cell.

When the conscripted undertakers returned, one of the men sat down quietly in a corner. He would never speak again after that. The second one vomited in the bucket.

"They made us dig a ditch," he groaned. "They made us throw him in and bury him. He was moaning the whole time. Just moaning."

"There's no room in hell for these monsters," another prisoner whispered.

Nicolas rolled up Major's mat. They couldn't clean the cell, so they prayed the tuberculosis away, hoping it wouldn't spread. He sat with the second prisoner, who was compulsively pulling at every strand of hair on his head. He knew that there was no way to comfort him, but he tried to find a magic combination of words.

"You didn't have a choice," Nicolas said. "You had to follow orders. What else could you do?" He knew his words fell on deaf ears. He wasn't sure how a person could recover from such a traumatic event.

"I did have a choice," the young man sobbed, his face hidden in his hands. "I was a coward. I could have joined him in the grave. They would have shot me, or thrown me in with him to suffocate. I'm a Catholic. How can I bury a man alive? I should have died with him."

"That would not be right," Nicolas said.

Later that day, the guards returned to the cell and ordered all the prisoners to stand up. Nicolas felt fear slice through him. No one knew what was happening. Maybe it was an execution, maybe even Nicolas's. He tried to feel grateful for a chance to exit this hell. The guards barked orders at them.

"To the showers!"

Nicolas followed the line outside the building, breathing in relief. He hadn't wanted to die after all, had he? His heart felt lighter and filled with gratitude for an opportunity to use water, to shower, to wash off the filth from his skin, and then to drink fresh water that didn't taste like porridge or cornmeal or beans in the bottom of his food plate. A shower outside was an opportunity to forget, to wash away what had just happened to Major, if that were possible.

"There must be a reason for the showers," the prisoners whispered. "Maybe they're releasing us."

Hope still burned in some, a persistent ember that would not die. Nicolas suspected the showers were simply to head off the spread of tuberculosis.

The guards led the prisoners to a courtyard behind the barracks. Nicolas hadn't noticed this place before because it was separated from the septic tank area. The prisoners were divided into four lines. They moved like an army of zombies, blinded in the sudden daylight. The clouds above were pregnant with a rain that never fell, and the air was heavy with a steamy heat.

164 • FABIENNE JOSAPHAT

Nicolas found coolness in the shade of a small tree growing against a concrete wall where four rusty faucets were aligned. This would be his first chance at bathing since getting here. As the guards shouted orders, Nicolas realized he would be allowed only three minutes to wash his face, maybe his arms, and maybe, if he got lucky, have a chance to drink.

The prisoners knelt under the faucets and cupped their hands under thin streams of water. They gulped voraciously before being pushed out of the way. Others washed their faces, scrubbed their hands. The water ran brown at their feet, and Nicolas saw a prisoner wash the pus from his wounds. He tried to remember the last time he'd had a bath, and he swallowed back his burning desire for soap.

Nicolas tried to keep his eyes open. The gray light burned until his skin felt like it was turning to ash. He rubbed his stomach with his dry hands and felt his ribs under his fingers. Soon he'd be skeletal. He was still alive, though. For how long, he didn't know, but he was still alive, and if God wasn't dead, as Oscar had said, if God was testing him, he would play along like Job. For some reason, he was overwhelmed with the promise of the sun hiding behind clouds, the stream of water, the almond tree.

The guards patrolled the ranks. If they heard talking, they lashed out at the prisoners' ribs or backs with the butts of their weapons. Nicolas tried to look through them like ghosts, but he couldn't ignore their menacing omnipresence. Then he saw him again, the young guard who was always watching him.

He seemed young, barely twenty-five. Nicolas heard the other guards call him by his first name, Elon. He was about six feet tall, and his brown skin seemed dewy in the daylight. Nicolas had never been this close to him before. He was just a child compared with the others, but his face was grave.

Elon walked toward him. Nicolas kept his eyes semi-closed, head down to deflect a possible confrontation. His knees trembled as he heard the sound of boots clicking on the ground. What did he want? Elon stopped, ground his boots into the earth, and leaned in conspiratorially.

"You! Prisoner!" he hissed.

Nicolas looked up, startled. At that moment, the clouds parted to reveal a brilliant sun against the cinder-block sky.

"Nicolas L'Eveillé?"

Nicolas hesitated.

"Do exactly as I say," the young guard said.

He had an amazing ability, Nicolas noticed, to speak without moving his lips.

"No sudden movements. Look to your right."

Why was this man talking to him? Nicolas blinked, tried to make sense of the words.

"I won't repeat myself!"

Obedience was Nicolas's safest bet, so he turned his head and saw the line of emaciated men burning in the sun. What was he supposed to look for? He decided this was one of those vicious tricks guards played on inmates, like when they pretended to release someone and picked him up again later that day, right at the doorstep of his home. Nicolas was certain he would lose his sanity if that ever happened to him. He was about to turn back to the young guard when he caught a movement in the corner of his eye.

At first, Nicolas thought it was a bird. But no. It was a black hand signaling to him. His eyes narrowed as he tried to focus, confused and desperate. Then Nicolas's face lit up, his lips stretching into a smile. Was he hallucinating? Tears sprang to his eyes. His brother was waving at him. Raymond. Nicolas blinked repeatedly, but his eyes were not deceiving him, it wasn't a mirage. He raised his arm to wave, forgetting where he was. His mouth opened to yell, yawning wide, as if he'd swallowed sunshine, but Raymond shook his head tersely and looked away.

Just as quickly as it had come, Nicolas's smile faded and he was overwhelmed with the reality of Raymond's presence here. So they had gotten everyone. Jean-Jean. Georges. And it was all his fault. His heart shattered at the thought of other names: Eve. Amélie.

"That's your brother?" the guard asked.

He had been watching Nicolas's expression shift from elation to horror, cradling his rifle and squinting under the sun. Nicolas nodded without thinking, forgetting for a moment that, in here, every question carried with it the threat of instant repercussions. He panicked. His line moved quickly, and there was only one prisoner in front of him now. The guard operating the faucets yelled at Nicolas.

"Move it!"

Elon shoved Nicolas forward and walked away. At the faucet, Nicolas gulped down as much water as he could, but he was distracted, knowing his brother was standing nearby in the sun. The prisoners were soon ordered back inside. Nicolas felt part of his soul die as he reentered his cell. He would have preferred to collapse outside than to expire in this steamy, crummy cave. But he felt hopeful now. He'd seen Raymond and he was convinced that they would find a way to speak to each other.

In the evening, the guards came knocking at the doors with their clubs. Supper arrived in a tin bucket, a watered-down porridge with a roll of stale bread. The men grabbed their plates with haste and broke into the moldy bread. Nicolas looked at Elon, who was standing on the threshold. The young guard's eyes were disconcertingly blank.

Returning Nicolas's gaze, he demanded, "Something wrong with your food?"

Nicolas shook his head. The other inmates eyed him curiously. It was a strange question for a guard from Fort Dimanche. Nicolas bit into his roll, chewing quickly. The food distributor waddled away down the hall, his bowed legs arching away from each other painfully, and Elon shut the door.

Nicolas broke off another piece of bread and felt something strange in his mouth. He spat it out immediately, hoping it wasn't a bug. In his hands was a small piece of folded paper. He looked around. The men were eating furiously, their lips making smacking sounds. No one had seen.

Once he was sure no one was watching, he unfolded the wet paper, which began to tear apart in his warm fingers. He made out a scribble, the letters smudged: *"Kin."* Nicolas frowned for a moment before understanding set in. Then, without another thought, Nicolas smiled and shoved the paper into his mouth. It wasn't hard to swallow.

SIXTEEN

A coral sky stretched over the small yard. Raymond tried to orient himself, coming to terms with the reality of life at Fort Dimanche: once here, behind these walls, the sun never again actually rose or set.

The reeking bucket in Raymond's hands stung his eyes. As the new man in his cell, he had volunteered to take it outside, and no one had objected. No one cared about him, it seemed. They wanted to know how he got here in his cell, but that was the extent of their concern. When the guards announced he was to be executed with his brother on August twenty-seventh, as requested by Warden Oscar, no one flinched. It was as if they were zombified, lobotomized, even. Only one prisoner muttered a response, avoiding eye contact with him.

"At least you know when," he said. "Not knowing is the worst part."

His brother was close by, just two prisoners away.

He glanced over his shoulder, and when nobody was looking, tapped the shoulder of the man in front of him. Raymond pointed at his brother and made a sign, and the inmate understood what he wanted. Quickly, Raymond skipped ahead, slipping into his new spot and slumping low to blend back into the line, nearly spilling the contents of his bucket in the process. His heart racing, he took a few breaths. This was the only way, he told himself. He had to push his luck, further and further, so he repeated his maneuver until he finally stood behind his brother.

Nicolas tried to turn as soon as he realized Raymond was there. "Easy," Raymond said. "Don't turn around."

"What are you doing here?" Nicolas hissed. "Why is that guard helping us?"

"We have a friend in common," he whispered back. "I came to get you out of here."

Nicolas chuckled silently. The idea was too absurd.

"I have a plan," his brother whispered into his neck. "Trust me."

"So you got yourself arrested?"

Raymond shifted the bucket to his other hand. The metal handle weighed heavily against his palm and bit into the callused flesh of his fingers.

"That reporter I saved in Cité Simone? Remember him?" Raymond murmured. "He's helping me. And we have a friend in here. An ally."

Nicolas kept his eyes glued on his bucket as the two brothers stood side by side at the ditch. Raymond took in Nicolas's frail figure and his grayish skin.

"Are you okay?" he whispered.

Nicolas checked to make sure the guards weren't looking. "How the hell did you get here, really? Did they come for you?"

"Don't worry about that right now," Raymond whispered. "Listen, Eve and Amélie are in the Dominican Republic. I put them on a boat myself. Now it's your turn. Come August twenty-seventh, we have a plan."

Nicolas shook his head. Was Raymond delusional?

"Escape?" he hissed as the men finished dumping their buckets, the flies swarming gleefully. The ground began to burn his feet, but Nicolas ignored the pain. "Are you crazy?"

"Have some faith," Raymond said as he shook his bucket and turned, gagging at the stench. "And yes, I may be a little crazy. I'm here, aren't I?"

Nicolas didn't seem to hear him and Raymond saw the darkness in his brother's eyes. It was only a matter of time until he lost all sense of himself, like the rest of these wretches around them. A guard strode forward, pointing his rifle.

"Break's over, get back inside."

The men lined up quietly. As they marched back into the fortress, Raymond leaned in again.

"I'll contact you soon," he whispered. "Keep your eyes and ears open. You'll see your family again. Trust me." They came to their cells, where two guards were waiting, weapons in hand.

"I've never let you down before, have I?"

The brothers' eyes met once more before the cell doors shut.

SEVENTEEN

T he men in Raymond's cell also kept a calendar on the wall. They used a heart-shaped stone picked up from the yard, etching lines into the cement. When the main calendar keeper died of a bladder infection, someone else took over, marking a new day each time he heard a distant humming. A small aircraft patrolled the skies around five thirty every morning. This was the prisoners' only clock: the whine of an engine at high altitude. Each time it passed, Raymond and Nicolas moved one day ever closer to August and their execution.

Raymond kept to himself and Nicolas didn't press him for further details. Elon rarely spoke a word to either of them, gave no sign of sympathy. The wait was excruciating for Raymond, and soon his nails were bitten to the quick. The reality of his situation frightened him, but just when he was about to give in to despair, just when he thought he'd made a terrible mistake in trusting Sauveur, something happened. It was July 10, and the heat was stifling.

The prisoners seemed to be asleep with their eyes open, but they perked up when they heard the key turning in the lock. Panicked, they scurried toward the shadows and clung to the walls.

"Taxi! You're coming with me!"

Raymond didn't wait to be told twice. He jumped to his feet and followed the silhouette down the black hall of the prison.

The young guard was walking quickly, his heels clicking against the hard tile. Raymond worried someone might find them there, ask why they were wandering through the fortress. Elon stopped and turned to Raymond, his hand twitching around the barrel of his rifle.

"You know Milot?" he asked.

"Yes, chief. I'm Raymond L'Eveillé, a taxi driver. I drove him out of Cité Simone—"

"Keep your voice down!"

The young guard looked around, making sure no one had seen or heard them. He looked into Raymond's eyes. "Don't call me chief," he said. "There's only one chief here, and that's the chief supervisor. Is that clear?"

"Yes, sir—"

"Quiet! I will confirm the plan with you when I can. It could be weeks."

Someone was coming down the stairs. Elon grabbed his shoulder and rushed him back toward his cell. Raymond wanted to scream. They were so close to Nicolas. They couldn't turn around now! But he kept quiet as the voices drew near. His cell door shut in his face.

"What's going on out there?" Boss asked.

Nicolas shrugged and he closed his eyes, listening to Elon's voice rise in the hall, calling out to the other guards.

When Raymond heard a voice in the hallway a week later, he immediately recognized it as Elon's.

"Lights out!"

He heard footsteps and waited patiently. The inmates loosened the lightbulb from the socket in the few cells where they worked, and darkness engulfed the prison. Raymond pressed his back against the wall. He felt light-headed.

When the footsteps reached his cell door, Raymond heard keys jingle and then the familiar scratch of a key turning inside a lock. The door opened with a creak, and through the slit, Raymond and the other prisoners who tilted their head at an angle saw Elon's head peering in.

"Taxi?"

Raymond sprang forward, his muscles twitching with excitement. "I'm here."

"Step outside."

Raymond looked back at the other inmates before stepping out into the hallway. He knew there were two or three prisoners who wondered what was happening, but most were just grateful that the guard's attention wasn't on them.

The lightbulb in the hallway flickered every five seconds. Raymond counted them off in his head, his bare toes curling against the hot concrete. He looked at Elon as the door shut behind him. The young man was visibly nervous.

"We don't have a lot of time," Elon whispered. He motioned for Raymond to follow him. "Hurry."

Raymond looked around. At the end of the empty hall, he saw a bright light under a door and he knew immediately this had to be the guards' quarters. He could make out chuckles and slams he knew could only come from a game of dominoes. He heard the clatter of bones as the guards shuffled them.

They approached the cell door. Elon waved his hand at Raymond, a gesture of impatience he took as an order to be quiet. Cell six was at the opposite end of the hall from cell two, where Raymond had been kept. They stopped at the door and Elon reached for the keys buried inside his pocket. No one was coming down the hall, but they had to be quick about it. Elon turned the key in the lock. Raymond heard movement inside and imagined the frail prisoners flattening themselves against the wall, panicked by this unexpected intrusion.

"Get in!" Elon said roughly. "You've been transferred."

Raymond held his breath as the guard called for another prisoner. "You're moving to a new cell," he told the man. "Hurry up!"

When the door closed behind him, Raymond was pressed with questions. Who was he? Why was he changing cells?

"I don't know," Raymond said. "I just do what I'm told."

His eyes slowly readjusted to the darkness. Everything was the same: the smell, the squalor, the skeletal frames of men who'd been there too long, the skin sagging from their bones. An old man named Boss pressed him for information. He avoided answering any questions.

Finally, a hand reached out and grabbed him.

Nicolas pulled his brother down onto a mat and they grasped each other's arms, staring at each other in the dim light, afraid to say anything, but thankful for this small miracle of embracing, something they hadn't done enough when they were out in the world. Despite the lice running through his hair, the scabs and sores accruing over his body, and his hands layered with filth, Nicolas was, for a moment, at peace. They sat like that until the cell was quiet and most prisoners had fallen asleep.

"Why are you here? You could get yourself killed," Nicolas whispered. He squeezed his brother's arm. "This is madness. I'm as good as dead."

"You're my brother."

They were silent again. Raymond glimpsed limbs in the shadows, legs and arms searching for space to stretch out. They reminded him of crabs tangled in a fisherman's basket.

Nicolas hung his head. "I'm sorry," he said. "When you came to the house and I yelled at you. I shouldn't have said what I did. I shouldn't have done a lot of things. That book, thinking I could change things. The way I treated you. I shouldn't have."

Raymond shook his head. "All of that is past now."

Nicolas cleared his throat. "What about Yvonne? And the children? How could you leave them?"

Raymond grew cold and lowered his head. "They're gone."

"Gone?"

Nicolas's heart sank as Raymond repeated the word. "Gone. To Miami. They took a raft about two months ago. There's been no news of them since, so..."

"Oh, Raymond." Nicolas sighed deeply and listened to Raymond pronounce the words that had been hard for him to share with Eve and Sauveur. Nicolas listened and realized how difficult it must have been for Raymond to swallow this bread of shame. His wife and children had abandoned him.

"I failed them," he whispered. "I couldn't do enough, so they left."

"No," Nicolas said, resting his hand on his brother's knee. "You did what you could. This is the world we live in. We're all churning water hoping to make butter."

"We'll get out of here," Raymond replied. "We'll get out of here and I will find them."

He leaned closer to Nicolas and whispered the tale of his own arrest. Nicolas sat in silence, astonished. Raymond felt his brother twitch as he listened to his story.

"You're right. You are crazy." Nicolas shook his head, marveling at his brother's courage. He never would have done it, put in the same position. "I'm so frightened. Jean-Jean is dead. He barely survived a week in here."

"I'm sorry," Raymond said after a pause. "But Jean-Jean turned us away when we went to him for help. And the fat one—"

"Georges?"

"Yes. He hid in his closet rather than talk to us. It was pathetic, Nicolas."

Somewhere near them in the dark, a man murmured prayers.

"I can get us out of any scrape, just like the old days. Okay? We'll get out of this. But once we are out, we'll have to run, and run hard. I need you to be prepared for that. You know Cité Simone?"

Nicolas nodded, though he'd never been there himself. Cité Simone's reputation preceded it. A slum filled with peddlers, street vendors, prostitutes, pimps, charlatans, and swindlers.

"Any other part of Port-au-Prince will be too dangerous. La Saline and Croix des Bossales will already be swarming with Tonton Macoutes. We can hide in the shanties of Cité Simone until we get a chance to get out of Port-au-Prince."

Nicolas leaned toward Raymond and asked, "But how do we get out?"

Raymond shook his head. "It's better if you don't know. We have people on our side."

"It doesn't sound like the odds are very good."

Raymond moved his lips closer to Nicolas's ear. "Either we die here or we die trying. I'm not going to let Duvalier or Oscar or any one of them kill us, you hear me?"

"What makes you think you can trust these mysterious people? If my friends, people with connections, turned tail and ran, how can these people possibly accomplish the impossible?"

"There is some good left in this world," he said.

Someone screamed outside the cell door, down the hallway, and the shriek caromed off the walls. Raymond caught his breath and shifted away from Nicolas. More prisoners began to wake.

A crash shuddered through the cell. The prisoners froze, their skin blue black in the faint light. Then a white flash came through the tiny window. Lightning. And more thunder, as loud as if the storm was sitting right on the roof of Fort Dimanche. Then the rain began in earnest. The prisoners shouted in happiness at first, applauding the heavens and running to the small window to see if they could catch a glimpse, but only gusts of petrichor infiltrated the fortress.

Soon, the cell began to steam, and Raymond and Nicolas were soaked as if they'd plunged in a hot bath. Breathing became difficult, and Raymond tried to remain calm as his brother gasped for air. This torrent of rain was speaking to them, Raymond assured him. August was coming. Freedom was near. And Nicolas, in response, coughed the blood out of his lungs.

EIGHTEEN

When he saw Elon the following day, Raymond whispered to him about medicine.

"I think it's TB, and he says he might have an infection. It burns when he pisses."

"The doctor won't come unless it's payday," Elon said quickly. "He never sees the prisoners unless the orders come from the warden, and that's not going to happen."

Raymond looked at him with imploring eyes.

"I'll see what I can do," Elon said.

For three days, Elon managed to remain inconspicuous as he visited Raymond and Nicolas in their cell.

"The doctor sends you these," Elon said, dropping tiny bags of medicine in the palms of their hands. "It's what he's got on-site."

"But..." Nicolas looked at the pills. "I thought the doctors—"

"The warden knows you're ill," Elon replied. "I told him. It was the only way to get you any meds."

Nicolas and Raymond stared at the guard, dumbfounded.

"He wants you alive," Elon said, looking down. "Anyway, this is just a stopgap. If you have tuberculosis, these pills won't help. I'm told what you really need is to be hospitalized and quarantined. That could take months."

"It'll have to do for now," Nicolas said. "Thank you. Thank you so much."

Elon would sometimes bring extra cornmeal and rolls of bread and pass them to Nicolas when the cook came to the door. Boss would stare in dismay, and Nicolas would avoid his gaze. The old man was speaking to him less and less these days. He tried to avoid starting a quarrel. The men in here were already arguing about who would become the next "Major." Nicolas recoiled at man's apparent need, even in the face of such horror, to create hierarchies. Some of them were already kissing up to the guards. No matter how sneakily delivered, the medicine and extra food made him unlikable, so he kept to himself.

Nicolas's coughing diminished within two weeks. He could feel a difference in his body, and he'd started exercising again, following the lead of other inmates in his cell. He found the strength for push-ups and sit-ups, and more often than was wise, Nicolas climbed the tree. But always, the old adage came back to him: *What God has in store for you, nothing can take away.*

The morning of August twenty-six, Raymond's eyes scrolled through the list Elon presented him at the door of the cell. It was written in French, so it took him a few minutes to decipher. *Autorisation de liquidation des conspirateurs, 27 Aout 1965.* The letter was authorizing Jules Sylvain Oscar to "rid the Republic" of the named plotters by any means necessary. And there, in the mix of all those wretched souls the Macoutes were to slaughter, were their names: *Raymond L'Eveillé. Nicolas L'Eveillé.* The letter was concluded, in fresh blue ink, with the familiar ornate signature that read *Président Duvalier.*

Raymond drew a deep breath. He and Nicolas had prepared for this. It was time.

Elon fidgeted with his keys, and he swallowed before looking into Raymond's eyes.

"It'll be at midnight. Be ready."

Elon's voice cracked, but Raymond pretended not to notice. He tried to swallow, but his throat was parched. They heard a creak at the other end of the hall. Elon quickly shut the cell door and locked it. Once he was left in the dark, Raymond turned to his brother.

"*Lè a rive.*"

But the time came sooner than expected. Long before night had even fallen, the door swung open again to reveal the chief supervisor.

"Brothers L'Eveillé, come with me."

Nicolas shot his brother a terrified glance, but Raymond only stared at the imposing figure in the door. This was not part of the plan.

The brothers were led to Jules Oscar's office. The door was open. A man was standing there in a guard's uniform, facing the warden's empty desk. Something moved in the corner of the room and Oscar emerged from the shadows, nostrils flaring.

"Step forward," he ordered. "I won't bite."

They shuffled closer and Oscar told the uniformed man to face them. Raymond's jaw flexed in anguish. Elon gazed at them, his eyes vacant as he swallowed hard. Raymond felt the earth opening beneath him as Oscar stepped closer.

"Do you know this man?" Oscar growled.

Raymond flinched. "I— He's a guard."

"*How* do you know him? You've met him before?"

"No, sir," Raymond said.

"You're a liar! You're lying, like you lied that day when you plowed into my car. You're some sort of vermin spy sent to destroy me."

Raymond was silent. Oscar walked around them, these three men huddled in the middle of the room in a pitiful triangle. Nicolas kept his head down. Raymond wanted to reach out for him but didn't. He didn't dare move. Oscar's rage permeated everything.

"You don't think I know what's going on here?" Oscar stopped next to Elon. "Who authorized you to put them in the same cell?"

"Sir, I got soft," Elon said. "I wanted to help two brothers. That's all."

"Don't speak!"

The door was still open, and Oscar glanced toward the men

standing there, rifles in hand. With a quick motion of his head, he signaled for them to come closer.

"You're up to something here. It isn't entirely clear what, but I want you to know something very, very important: it doesn't matter."

Raymond was the only one who looked at the warden as he spoke.

"S-sir, you have to believe me," Elon stammered. "I just thought—"

"You do not think here," Oscar yelled. "You follow orders. Anything else is insubordination." He glanced at the men. "Take him."

Elon opened his mouth, but no sound came out. The men grabbed him by the arms. He shot a final glance at Raymond, who wanted, more than anything, to say thank you. To say he was sorry. To say anything that might help. But nothing could. Without a struggle, Elon let the men drag him away through the open door, his face suddenly calm. Standing stock-still, Oscar watched his guards disappear. Stupefied, Raymond and Nicolas stood with him. Finally, Raymond managed to speak.

"Where are you taking him?"

Oscar's eyebrows arched in amazement at Raymond for having spoken.

"He's innocent," Raymond pressed. "All I did was beg to be with my brother."

"After all this, you believe you still have a voice?" Oscar spat. He was done listening. Head bowed, shoulders hunched, he inched closer to the brothers like a dog sniffing fear on a stranger's ankles.

"To be sure, you are responsible for that young man's corruption." Oscar's eyes flicked back and forth between them. "You're going to die tomorrow with that on your conscience. Both of you. Together."

They were ordered back to their cell. Raymond marched alongside Nicolas, pacing his steps to the beating of his own heart, the rhythm of its rage. In that moment, he realized he would never hate anyone more than he hated Jules Oscar.

In their cell, the ceiling seemed lower than usual and the walls like they were closing in. The lump in Raymond's throat would not dissolve no matter how hard he swallowed. His hands felt cold, and he held them together to conceal his tremor. He wasn't brave enough for this. The hour of execution was fast approaching and everything in the cell spun. Sometime later, his brother's lips touched his ear in the darkness. A hot, terrified breath.

"Is it all off? Are we ruined?"

Raymond shook his head. He turned and brought his lips to Nicolas's ear. "Just remember where we are going. Cité Simone. Be prepared. Nothing has changed."

But that wasn't true. Everything had changed. Raymond had no idea if the signal that would trigger their escape was supposed to come from Elon or someone else. If their escape was dependent on Elon, all was lost.

Huddled next to Raymond, Nicolas caught himself praying. His entire life had been spent doubting the existence of a higher being. But he was praying now, wanting to believe that God was real, that He was alive and listening, that He was a benevolent and loving God. If He was, one thing was certain: they would succeed or they would die. Either way, Nicolas resolved hazily, at least neither he nor his brother would be coming back to the hell of Fort Dimanche.

When dinner was distributed, neither of the brothers had any appetite. The fear tied knots in their stomachs. Still, they forced the horrid food into their mouths, needing all the strength they could muster. As night began to fall and the prayers wore thin, Raymond found himself vomiting in the *kin*.

Nicolas didn't want to be a coward. When the boots came, Nicolas heard his name called and he stood up immediately, knees knocking under him. The heat, the pressure, and the fear were crushing. Raymond reached for Nicolas's wrist and grabbed it. Nicolas felt a warm assurance in his grasp. A few other names were called, and finally, at the end, Raymond's.

"*En avant!*" the chief shouted. "March, you dogs! Quickly. I have a football game to catch."

Over his shoulder, Nicolas saw Boss staring in silence at the ground. They didn't wave good-bye. In that moment, Nicolas was disgusted by his own suspicion that somehow Boss had given Elon up. The prisoners followed orders, marching out of the building and into the warm belly of night where everything was still and quiet.

NINETEEN

The night air was pregnant with the smell of salt and mud. The prisoners' feet sank into small puddles.

Raymond climbed into the truck first and Nicolas, standing behind him, took one more look at the fortress glowing under the jaundiced moon like a yellow-eyed beast. He didn't know whether to wave good-bye to Fort Dimanche or spit his contempt for it on the ground as he left. He followed the others into the back of the waiting vehicle.

There were two women and ten other men in the truck with them, and they were forced to squeeze in, elbow to elbow, on the small benches. Nicolas and Raymond sat side by side in the dark. There were no windows except for an opening to the front cabin. Not being able to see where they were was as terrifying as the knowledge that they were headed to their deaths. Raymond felt a thigh against his. A foot stepped on his toes as the other prisoners held on in the dark. The engine roared and he closed his eyes. Sauveur. Where was Sauveur? He'd said to expect a diversion, and Raymond was on edge.

Soon the truck turned down a bumpy road. Stones bounced off the bottom of the vehicle, startling the prisoners, who were whispering prayers with their eyes closed. Nicolas wrapped his fingers around Raymond's arm and felt how moist it was. They were both sweating.

"Thank you for being my brother," Nicolas said. He'd never said this before, and Raymond was grateful.

They waited for that dreadful moment when the truck would finally stop. But it seemed to drive on and on, rattling its passengers' bodies and nerves.

Raymond turned to Nicolas and whispered something. Nicolas shook his head.

"What?"

They could barely hear each other over the noise of the road, the driver's garrulous chatter, and the guards' laughter. The chief made a comment about the football game that was playing on the radio. There were fewer guards than usual at the prison. They'd gone to the Stade Sylvio Cator to watch the game, leaving the chief and just a handful of shooters from the firing squad.

Raymond sat still, feeling for changes of pattern in the road. He scrunched his nose. Someone had lost control, poor soul, and soiled himself.

The vehicle continued its sinister dance, and soon a worse odor pervaded the air. Raymond knew they must be approaching the swampy execution fields, stagnant and black. As the truck slowed, the chief shouted something.

"*Sak gen la?* What the hell is going on?"

The front cabin fell suddenly quiet.

The driver stepped on the brakes and the truck came to an abrupt halt. The prisoners froze and listened.

Raymond felt for his brother's hand in the dark and squeezed it. It sounded like they'd run into an obstacle in the road. Raymond raised his eyebrows and held them in suspense, his blood rushing. This was it.

"Son of a bitch! What the hell do they think they're doing?"

Raymond recognized the chief's voice, then a guard responding.

"I don't know, Chief!"

The sound of doors opening. Raymond sat up and stretched his neck. If he tried hard enough, he was sure he could see through the little window into the cabin. He leaned forward and nearly fell onto another passenger. The prisoners pulled away as Raymond inched closer to the window.

In the front of the truck, he spied the driver clenching the wheel while the chief climbed out the passenger door. Ahead of them, in the glow of the truck's headlights, Raymond saw a vehicle broken down in the middle of the road: a white four-door sedan, its doors wide open. It looked like a Peugeot. It was parked transversally, blocking the road to the fields, and he saw a silhouette run around the car before hiding in the shadows. Someone was there. The darkness was thick, the window was small, but he knew what he saw. The driver glanced in the mirror and saw Raymond's face, his eyes wide through the opening.

"Sit your *bounda* down, prisoner!" the driver ordered. "Now!"

Raymond squatted, pretending to obey, but he remained in the same spot, observing the chief.

"Hey! You there! This is government property. What the hell are you doing? Move that *bogota* away from here before we blow you away!"

One of the men from the sedan shouted something back, but Raymond couldn't tell what. They were too far away. The driver was nervous. He gripped the wheel like he was going to tear it out of the dashboard. Raymond felt his chest swell with adrenaline. He glanced back in the direction of his brother.

"Are you ready?"

Nicolas was trembling. The moment had arrived. His tongue felt like a stone inside his mouth. Outside, the chief stood his ground, but did not venture closer to the car, his hand readied around the revolver in his holster. Raymond saw him cock the hammer back before yelling toward the Peugeot.

"This is a private road! I repeat: you're on government property. This is your last warning."

Raymond saw everything happen quickly. A door swung forward and a man jumped out of the Peugeot. Gunshots erupted in quick flashes of fire. Raymond dropped to the ground and the other prisoners followed suit. Outside, shots and screams sliced through the night. The chief yelled orders. His voice grew closer as he retreated back into the truck.

"Get down! Ambush! Ambush!"

Raymond felt the bodies of the other prisoners all around him. He crawled across the floor on his hands and knees. Nicolas stayed close behind him, breathing on his ankles. Raymond stopped at the metal doors. He turned around and pressed his back against them, the cold metal digging into his bare flesh. The doors were bolted shut from the outside.

"Nicolas! Help me break the door down!" Raymond called.

He knew it was a long shot, but what other choice did they have? He started to slam his shoulder against one of the doors, and soon someone else started to kick. All the men joined in. One prisoner flung his entire body against the doors. Nicolas punched against the metal with all his might, until the bones in his arm felt like they'd snap. Outside, bullets whistled past the truck, and the women screamed, ducking for cover.

"*A l'aide!*" they cried. "Help us!"

"We have to get out of here!" someone shouted.

Just as Raymond started to think the metal would never give way, he heard a shot fired on the other side of the doors and felt them vacillate under his weight. His heart skipped a beat. Someone out there had fired a bullet into the bolt. Raymond shoved one more time, a roar rumbling out of his chest.

The doors flew open.

Prisoners who'd been pushing against the doors spilled out of the truck, landing in mud and gravel that cut their skin. Air! They were out in the world, the rocks shining milky white, the black desert bushes around them, and the marshes reflecting the glow of the moon.

On the horizon, there were lights. Raymond recognized them as Terminal Varreux, the gas storage facility between Fort Dimanche and Cité Simone.

"Quick! Nicolas!"

The last inmates jumped out of the truck under the gleam of the stars. They ran in all different directions. They seemed to be surrounded by nothingness, but in the distance, Raymond saw the swamps and the wall beyond them. That was where they would have lined up the prisoners to shoot them. It was the first obstacle between them and freedom. It was the dividing line between Fort Dimanche's land and Terminal Varreux.

"Come on!" he shouted to Nicolas.

They ran together toward the swamps, Raymond holding his brother by the wrist. Gunshots peppered the night and sent chills down Raymond's spine. He'd never been so close to gunfire before. It sounded as if a whip was lashing through the air, as if the Devil himself was breathing down his back. Nicolas ran beside him, trying to keep up. The gravel felt like needles under their bare feet, but soon they reached damp earth, and their feet sank into the thick muck of brackish water. Nicolas slowed and held his breath as he caught a whiff of putrefaction. Raymond had to pull his brother forward.

"Move, Nicolas! Move!"

The muddy water rose higher, but they couldn't stop now. Behind them, they heard the guards screaming in the night.

"Shoot them! They're escaping."

Raymond did not look back. The plan was now over. Raymond knew to expect a diversion, but he wasn't expecting a group of armed rebels to survive this ambush and whisk them away. Once they'd broken free, they were to run for their lives toward the slums. The rebels had risked their lives for a cause, no matter the consequences.

Raymond pushed Nicolas to keep moving. The water was now waist high. They would swim through it if they had to, no matter how much detritus floated in the darkness, no matter what critter or foreign body came their way. At least there probably wouldn't be bullets. The guards were too busy defending themselves for now.

"Shoot them!" Raymond heard the chief shriek, but his voice was growing faint. Raymond knew he needed to put some more distance between them and the commotion. Nicolas was out of breath next to him.

"Don't stop!" Raymond hissed. "We have to reach the wall."

Raymond faltered in the water. Something brushed against his arm, and he jerked away violently. He thought he recognized, in the moonlight, the shape of a human head, the flesh rotting around the empty eye sockets. There was no time to be sure. They had to half swim, the water now shoulder high. His chest burned with fear. He turned when he realized his brother was stopping. What happened? He reached to grab his brother's arm. If Nicolas got shot, he wouldn't forgive himself.

"Come on, Nicolas! Come on!"

Nicolas had come face-to-face with a dead body, probably another inmate. The man's eyes were still wide open. His skin was milky and glossy, his body swollen, and the flesh had started to disintegrate. Nicolas was paralyzed, his mouth open, nearly filling with brown water.

Raymond yanked harder. "Don't get us caught, damn it! Come on!"

Each bullet sounded as if it were coming straight at them. Raymond swam, frantic, stroking the water away from him, his brother at his side. Soon they felt firmer land beneath their feet, the wall finally within reach. Raymond spotted a tree growing against its cement bricks.

"There!" he shouted.

He crawled out of the swamp, his underwear soaked and falling off his emaciated waist. He held it up with his left hand, and with his right, he reached for his brother, pulling him out of the mud. A bullet whirred past, grazing the ground next to Nicolas.

"Alert! Alert! Prisoners escaping!"

On the other side of the swamp, the guards were still shouting and scrambling, cursing as their heavy boots sank in the mud. Nature was on their side. Others were crouching behind the doors of their truck, shooting at the escapees who'd scattered everywhere in the night, shooting at the rebels' sedan.

They heard screaming, shouting as prisoners fumbled about in the dark. Some of them fell on the ground as bullets hit them. Then they heard the rumble of an engine. Raymond squinted, but he couldn't catch much more than the outline of the white sedan, sitting low on the ground, its tires deflated. Then, suddenly, there were headlights aiming straight at them. The truck had now regained control, and it was backing up. Were the guards giving up? Leaving? The truck's engine roared again, hiccupped in the dark, and suddenly charged forward. It was coming right at them.

The truck veered left, looking for a solid path around the swamp. Raymond felt a cold rush under his skin. They were being chased. The ambush had failed—the guards had survived. They had to get out of there.

"Run, Nicolas! Run!"

Raymond reached the tree first. Bending at the knees, he offered his hands to Nicolas as a ladder, interlacing his fingers together.

"Go on!" he said.

Nicolas set his right foot into his brother's cupped hands and used the boost to hoist himself up onto a branch. Raymond followed. The truck was catching up, its tires crushing the tall grass, churning up mud. Raymond and Nicolas scaled the tree as if they'd been doing it their whole lives. Nicolas's lungs ached when he tried to breathe, but he had to try his best. He was not going back to prison.

After what felt like an eternity, they were finally level with the top of the wall. Raymond's heart was pounding, and he felt sweat beading on his forehead. When he looked down, he saw that the truck had stopped. One of the guards popped out of the passenger window, gun in hand, aiming at the tree branches.

The first shot missed them and grazed a branch Raymond had just released. He moved faster, helping Nicolas when he could. Beyond the wall, they saw the massive shape of containers and turbines rumbling in the dark, smelled diesel in the night. Raymond's feet rested on a branch as he inched toward the wall, his brother on his tail. Another shot came toward them. Raymond groaned, but managed to keep his balance as he clasped his foot. He felt the blood ooze, warm and thick.

"Raymond, are you hit?"

Nicolas reached for his brother and touched his back, but Raymond shouted back at him.

"Jump, Nicolas! Now!"

Before Nicolas could argue, Raymond extended his arms like a bird, leapt forward, and fell into the abyss behind the wall. Nicolas followed right as the guard fired a third time into the foliage.

TWENTY

T he brothers fell on the dusty terrain of Terminal Varreux S.A. Raymond rolled away from the wall and called to Nicolas. The drop hadn't been as steep as they'd expected. Still, the shock of landing had hurt their feet and knees. Raymond was bleeding profusely from where the bullet had grazed him. Still, he found the strength to stand.

"Nicolas! Keep moving! We must keep moving!"

Nicolas crawled toward him and struggled to his feet. They ran toward the turbines. They heard the roar of the truck die down behind the wall, but the guards' voices were still close. Behind them, more gunshots.

Terminal Varreux had been quartered off the wharf, away from the cruise port, and had been designated to hold shipments of tanker fuel. It was deserted at this time of night, but there were guards on the grounds and possibly dogs, and the Macoutes would alert one another soon enough. They would be caught if they stopped. But Raymond and Sauveur had planned for this, calculating that it was only two miles to Cité Simone.

So they kept moving alongside the enormous containers stacked under the black sky. Soon the grass turned into gravel again, and Raymond felt the pain in his leg intensify. He was leaving a trail of blood, but he could do nothing about it. He had to reach Cité Simone.

Nicolas kept quiet, staying in Raymond's shadow. They stopped behind a cluster of drum containers and crouched in the shadows.

"Easy," Raymond whispered.

They'd come to an open driveway, and the darkness of the path was illuminated every few minutes by a beam of light spinning in the terminal's watchtower. Nicolas saw his brother's lips moving. Counting. *One. Two. Three.* Raymond was measuring the timing of the light. *Six. Seven. Eight.* The darkness was back.

Nicolas started forward, but Raymond held him again, firmly, his hand squeezing the bones in his wrist. Voices. Two guards were coming. They were dressed in olive green, their boots laced all the way up under their calves, and they each toted a shotgun. One of them stopped and lit a cigarette. Raymond stared intently at the man, the flame of the match illuminating his brown face and his broad nose as he sucked on the butt. Nicolas's eyes rested on a sign pasted against the container: "*Défense de Fumer.* No Smoking." The guard blew a plume of smoke in the air.

"Hey! Did you hear that?"

The other guard stopped and listened to the distant rumble of engines and what sounded like people shouting over the wall.

"Who knows?" the other mumbled. "Fort Dimanche is over there. Could be anything." He too lit a cigarette and started smoking.

"An execution, you think?"

"Could be..."

The men smoked their cigarettes, their eyes glued to the wall. The tower light spun incessantly, flooding the driveway, bathing the guards in bright white light every few seconds. Raymond held his breath and felt his brother forcing himself to breathe through his nose.

"I'll go back to port, see if I can find out what's going on," the second guard said. "I've never heard this much racket before. Doesn't seem right."

The first guard drew on his cigarette again. "I'll take the front gate," he said.

Once they were alone, Nicolas sighed heavily. His legs felt like lead and he was racked with exhaustion. They needed another wave of adrenaline if they were going to make it, or else fear would destroy them both.

Raymond motioned ahead. Under the moonlight, they could see the outline of Cité Simone. Nicolas glanced at it and nodded. Yes, he could do it. He had to do it. And then there was no more time to think, because Raymond had counted to eight. A shadow flashed past him. Nicolas gasped in surprise. Raymond had already bolted forward. Nicolas ran across the driveway, following his brother. The gravel crunched under their feet as they sprinted toward the slum.

Raymond felt Nicolas's presence behind him and thought this was it: now they were safe as long as they were together. A voice rang out.

"Freeze! Trespassers on grounds! I'll shoot!"

Behind them, a guard was standing in the driveway, the bright light of the tower now steadily aimed at him. At his feet, the gravel was speckled with Raymond's blood.

"Freeze, I said!"

But they didn't freeze. They charged forward, reaching the dividing line between the terminal and the slum. Raymond knew what was there: the Canal Saint-Georges. But seeing it sprawl now before his eyes, his heart skipped a beat.

"Shit!" Nicolas clenched his fists.

The guard took aim, fired three times, and missed three times. The bullets whistled past.

"Jump!"

Canal Saint-Georges's water flow had slowed over the years as the trash had piled up. Then, as poverty and famine struck the masses, the people of Cité Simone, which was named after Papa Doc's wife, began to dump their waste into the now stagnant water. Cité Simone had attempted to have it cleaned up, but the city management never sent sanitation crews. Now, Canal Saint-Georges was the local dumpster where the children came to search through rubble, hoping to find a small puddle of water for a bath, and where stray dogs and goats and pigs and rats came to scavenge. It was one of the ugliest secrets of Port-au-Prince, the blemish that the haute society pretended not to know about.

The brothers' heads surfaced from the cesspool of feces and soap scum. Raymond gasped for air as if to swallow the stars. He paddled across mud, cups, scraps of fabric, and decomposed foods with his brother on his tail.

Nicolas felt his knee stiffen, so he pushed against the debris with his arms more, hoping to alleviate the pain. Both brothers tried to cover their mouths against the burning fumes.

The canal was only about fifty feet wide, but they crossed it slowly, so as not to attract attention. Raymond reached the other side first and remained on his knees for a moment, his muscles spasming. Nicolas crashed next to him, grunting with pain. His leg was oozing blood.

"Is it bad?"

Raymond inched closer. The wound was open and the flesh exposed, red and wet.

Raymond felt a jolt as if his muscles were reigniting yet again. He wanted to take a moment to revel in amazement at the divine hand that had given him the courage to run, to jump, to pull Nicolas out of hell. But the infernal staccato of gunshots had resumed. On the other side of the canal, over the wall, Terminal Varreux was buzzing. The spine-crackling howl of a siren followed and Cité Simone awoke before their eyes.

Windows blinked with flickering orange candlelight. Raymond saw flames twitching on the naked wicks of *tèt gridap* lamps set on windowsills. He imagined the rattle inside dark homes, husbands and wives bumping against corrugated metal or thatched rooftops and shutters, stubbing toes against table legs, or rolling off their beds in surprise. The entire slum, the surrounding townships of La Saline, of Croix des Bossales, and neighborhoods all the way to the Champ de Mars and the Palais National were being alerted. Prisoners had escaped, and squads of Tonton Macoutes were undoubtedly on the move.

It dawned on Raymond that they'd actually succeeded. They

were the first prisoners to escape. This was real. But the guards and their reinforcements would be in Cité Simone soon if they weren't there already.

TWENTY ONE

When Raymond opened his eyes, the sky was flushed pink with dawn. Where was he? For a moment, he thought he'd died. Then he thought he'd awakened in an open field back in his home village, except the smell was different. Unpleasant. Someone was burning rubber. He sat up, wide-awake, and remembered: they were free. He was in the heart of a trash field in Cité Simone. He didn't know how long they'd slept. He was still covered in the cardboard sheets he'd piled up on his brother and himself. Nicolas was at his side, wrapped in layers of newspaper.

Raymond sat up and smelled the air again. Definitely burning tires. The guards of Fort Dimanche, the police force, and the Tonton Macoutes must have set up roadblocks while they canvassed the neighborhood. Unfortunately, that meant that innocent people might pay the price.

Aching all over, Raymond crawled to the nearest puddle. At least he could wash his face. He dipped his fingers in the water, ignoring the grime at the bottom. His hands were red and raw, the wounds on them still fresh and open. The blood on his foot had coagulated, thick and black, like the sap from a bleeding mango tree, and it still hurt when he touched it.

When Nicolas woke, he found Raymond scavenging for scraps of fabric. He seemed confused at first and stared at the sky for a long time. The streaky clouds in the blushing sky were the most magnificent sight they'd seen in a long time. This was freedom: the sky.

Raymond made his way back to his brother, carrying torn scraps. He had wrapped his foot, and he was limping a little, but he still managed to move quickly. He wrapped Nicolas's leg and wiped his hands. Nicolas tried to speak, but his throat was parched.

"I'm not sure how much time we've lost," Raymond whispered, tying the fabric into a square knot. "We slept a few hours. We have to move."

The dawn streets were swarming with Tonton Macoutes. Raymond and Nicolas hid behind boxes and sheds, trying to assess the situation. Women and children screamed while men were pulled out of their homes, furniture tossed onto the sidewalk, as Macoutes searched for signs of fugitives. The busiest crossroads of Cité Simone were blocked with piles of burning tires. The Macoutes doused shanties with gasoline and set them on fire. They walked around, pistols in hand, shooting at anyone who stumbled into their path. Trucks drove past with megaphones, Macoutes shouting orders from the moving vehicles.

"Anyone aiding and abetting the fugitives will have to answer to His Excellency himself. If you have information on where these criminals could be hiding, you will be duly compensated."

"Who would believe that?" Nicolas sputtered.

But Raymond could only shake his head. He knew how many people—regular people—would do anything for a chance at a better life, whether they trusted the president or not.

Raymond found an empty shack with clothes hung on a line out back. He made sure the coast was clear before snatching pants and shirts. Behind the small house, they found drums of water and helped themselves to a drink and a quick washing of face and hands, overlooking the mosquito larvae and dust floating on the surface. They wiggled their legs into the too-large pants and put on the shirts. Raymond sat Nicolas down on a small chair among roosting chickens and proceeded to shave his brother's head with a large shard of glass he'd found in the dust. Nicolas winced.

"Hold still," Raymond whispered. "I know what I'm doing. I've done it for Enos plenty of times."

He said his son's name, but fought off the wave of sadness it brought. In the distance, they heard shots. Screams. Nicolas's heart started to pound in his chest.

"They're coming this way," he whispered.

Raymond didn't stop. When he was done, Nicolas's bald head was ashy and dry. Raymond took a closer look at his brother and nodded.

"You look like a new man," he said.

Nicolas's heart swelled with gratitude, but Raymond was already on the move. Cité Simone was radiant in the morning light. The metal roofs mirrored the sun, and a thin stream of soapy water rushed down the *rigòl*. They were still barefoot, but moving around was easier now that they weren't naked. Raymond stopped once to unwrap his foot. It hurt, but it was no longer bleeding, and the rag he'd used as a bandage had become a nuisance.

A girl turned the corner ahead and came running toward them, haggard and out of breath. Her hands balanced a basket of bread on her head. Raymond stopped her.

"*Sak gen nan zònn nan la a?* What's all the ruckus about?"

"Prisoners from Fort Dimanche escaped last night," the girl replied in a rapid, breathless Creole. "Tonton Macoutes have blocked all entrances to Cité Simone. They're searching everywhere."

She quickened her steps and walked away. Raymond glanced at his brother but showed no sign of alarm. He had to be hopeful and optimistic to keep Nicolas going. Through open windows and doors of shacks, Raymond smelled coffee and the pungent aroma of smoked fish. They were hungry. Starving. They hadn't eaten in a day and a half, and their stomachs growled as they walked among the locals who now flooded the streets. They couldn't stop for food, however. It was too risky.

Once they'd reached the busiest artery of Cité Simone, they stopped at the intersection and Raymond took a deep breath. His heart raced so fast, he rested a hand on his chest to keep it quiet. He knew this place well. It was where the taxi drivers stationed their vehicles along the sidewalk, where Raymond always came, at the end of his day, to count his money, drink a cola with his friends, and dream. There they were, his fellow taxi men, sharing bread and cups of coffee, eating spaghetti sandwiches in the early morning, leaning on their cars. This used to be his life, here on Rue Carton. Chez Madame Fils was still there on the same block, the snack bar open for breakfast.

Raymond searched the crowd for a familiar face. He saw men he recognized, but not the one he was looking for.

"Stay behind me," Raymond said.

Nicolas felt his muscles stiffen with panic. In the corner of his eye, he caught a glimpse of men in blue, recognized their red bandannas, their soft hats. The sight paralyzed him all over again. Macoutes...

"Psst!" Raymond was calling him, and Nicolas realized he was supposed to follow his brother into the street.

"Come on!" Raymond gestured impatiently.

He looked at his brother and his lip quivered, but he moved forward anyway. There was no point in letting fear win. He joined Raymond and they melted into the crowd. The masses seemed to swallow Nicolas whole, and he took deep breaths to stay alert when all he wanted to do was collapse. Somehow, the world felt different now, like a giant, humming, monstrous vacuum sucking the breath out of his lungs. He didn't know it anymore. Granted, he'd never set foot in this slum before. He'd driven past but never through it. And yet to his brother, this was familiar territory. Raymond glided through the crowd easily, twisting his body to avoid bumping into the *machann* and peddlers carrying loads of merchandise.

Around the corner, a white van was being loaded up, the engine running. Raymond recognized the lettering on the doors.

Tannerie Nationale S.A. Raymond spotted Faton instantly: his bell-bottom pants, his striped shirt, his thick Afro, the comb sticking out of his back pocket, always at the ready.

"Faton!"

For the first time, Raymond found comfort in the strong, familiar smell of cowhide. Faton stepped away from his van, and his eyebrows arched in surprise. His jaw dropped, and the color drained from his brown face.

"Raymond?"

"It's me."

"Raymond! Jesus, Mary, and Joseph..."

Faton glanced at haggard, shorn Nicolas, then threw nervous glances over his shoulder. He wiped his hands on his pants. His gold chain sparkled.

"Raymond, I didn't think it was true. I heard your name on the radio, but I thought—"

"No time," Raymond said, cutting him off. "Please, we need you."

Faton nodded toward his truck.

"I was just leaving for work. *La ri a cho!* The streets are burning with chaos."

Raymond looked at him. "What can we do?"

"Let's get you out of here," Faton said. "They've barricaded all the entrances and exits. It's not safe."

Faton opened the doors to the back of his truck. The foul odor of hide nearly knocked them over. The truck bed was piled high with a mountain of unprocessed cow skin, an amalgam of black, brown, and white-spotted fur. Some skins were folded in two and some hung from the ceiling, dangling like grotesque curtains. Raymond covered his mouth as Faton helped them inside.

"Hurry," he told them.

They had no other choice. Nicolas curled up in a corner, and Faton started to pile cowhides over his legs and arms.

"What are you doing?" Nicolas asked.

"Quiet! Stay still."

Raymond squatted low next to Nicolas, signaling to be quiet, to do what Faton said. Raymond trusted his friend to save them.

Faton covered Raymond next, hiding him under mounds and mounds of skin. Then he backed away to assess his handiwork and shut the doors before bolting them. The engine started and Raymond felt the van driving through the slums. He knew they'd turn left, knew what street they were on when Faton veered right two blocks later. He followed every step, Cité Simone etched in his cabdriver mind.

He knew Faton was doing his best to avoid barricaded streets. From where they hid, under the cowhide, Raymond smelled another tire fire. He imagined the scene like the other ones he'd witnessed before when the Macoutes set up roadblocks: chairs and baskets overturned, charred by red flames, along with smoking truck tires. Both brothers hid their mouths and noses inside the opening of their shirts to keep the stench from overpowering them.

"We'll suffocate in here," Nicolas grunted.

"It won't be long," Raymond replied. "Stay quiet."

Without warning, the van came to a full stop, the engine still running. Had they made it to Boulevard La Saline already? Maybe they were stuck in traffic. Raymond heard the rumble of vehicles behind them, waiting.

"Driver's license? Registration?"

A checkpoint. Nicolas curled tighter under the hides and squeezed his eyes shut. The heat in the back of the van was stifling. Raymond felt as if he were being cooked alive. He listened, and between the words exchanged outside of the vehicle, he heard a click. What was that sound? He glanced over to where his brother was, but couldn't see anything under the skins. He imagined Nicolas coiled like a discarded fetus, clenched his jaw to stop his teeth from chattering the way he did when they were young and their father searched for him in a fit of anger.

"Shh," Raymond whispered.

It sounded like Faton was still seated at the wheel.

"Do you know why I stopped you?"

It was a Macoute. Raymond was certain of it. The voice was stern, authoritative.

"You're looking for those two fugitives, right?" Faton asked. He sounded impressively calm.

"Seen anything?" the Macoute asked.

"Nothing but rats and rodents in this piece-of-shit town, Chief!" Faton retorted. "Haven't seen anything."

Silence. Then a tap on the door. Raymond gave a little start.

"Open the back!" the Macoute ordered. "Hurry up! If you do anything stupid, I'll shoot!"

Raymond wondered if Nicolas was shaking like he was. They heard a door slam and Raymond heard Faton's keys jingling as his hands trembled. Raymond's heart broke for his friend.

"Is this really necessary?" he heard Faton ask.

"Hurry up!" the Macoute shouted.

Faton's keys rattled as he inserted one into the lock. As the back doors swung open, he heard the Macoute begin to cough uncontrollably.

"What the—"

Light flooded the back of the van. The vapors were suffocating. The brothers needed to come up for air, and soon. But they had to wait just a little while longer.

"What the hell is that smell? Jesus!"

Faton apologized profusely, explaining to the gasping Macoute that this was his job. He was a tanner and those hides were being delivered. The Macoute was welcome to search the truck, but Faton was afraid of what it would do to the man's uniform.

"I can't seem to wash the smell off my clothes," Faton said. "So sorry. I must warn you, the smell will follow you everywhere..."

The brothers heard what sounded like a smack. Something landed in the trunk and the van bounced on its wheels. The brothers felt the sway and held on.

"Get out of here! Get away from me with that shit!"

"Yes, sir! Yes."

The van swayed again. Something shifted. Faton shut the doors, encasing them once more in darkness.

"Yes, Chief!"

They heard him running.

The engine started again and they pulled away. Soon they'd left Cité Simone. Raymond knew it. The smells were changing; the sound and the flow of traffic were different. They'd made it out. But Raymond stayed still and urged his brother to do the same.

Faton dropped them off steps away from Portail Léogâne. Nicolas could barely move his legs when they got out of the vehicle. He stepped away and vomited in a jasmine bush. Raymond clenched his teeth to repress his own nausea. How Faton did this for a living, he didn't know. But he was thankful.

Faton pulled some money out of his pocket.

"That's all I have," he said, counting two hundred gourdes. "I wish I had more."

Raymond shook Faton's hand and held it. His friend smelled less like hide than he did now.

"I won't forget this," he said. "I don't know how to thank you."

"Get out of here," Faton said, grinning as he wiped the sweat from his brow. "Hurry. If you get caught, all of my hard work will have been in vain."

The pavement was searing hot under their bare feet. They tried to stay in the shade as they entered the bus station. Raymond shouted at Nicolas to stay close. It would be all too easy to lose each other in the crowd of travelers, bags, boxes, and clusters of chickens hung upside down, their feet bound with tight rope. Raymond caught sight of a school bus converted into public transportation, its hood and body painted blue and red. The stenciled letters on the back read "La Belle Cayenne." It was headed southbound and so were they.

TWENTY TWO

Raymond and Nicolas got off the bus on the main road. The gravel crunched underfoot as they staggered, groggy, pebbles lodging between their toes. Half a mile later, Raymond spotted the house, as beautiful as the first time he'd seen it, there against a backdrop of turquoise ocean and green palms, its shutters wide open. The gravel changed to sand. Sauveur came out to greet them, alerted by the kids who'd come running to his window. He stopped just a few steps away from them, shaking his head in wonder.

"I'll be damned," he whispered. "L'Eveillé. You're alive. Both of you."

Sauveur was grinning with joy, a tear in the corner of his eye. He took Nicolas's arm with care, looking to make sure no one had followed them. Shouted to the kids to fetch the captain right away.

"Let's get you inside," Sauveur said.

Claudette brought water and bread, bits of food saved in the *garde-manger* that she served with bitter, freshly brewed coffee.

"Drink," she urged them. "For your nerves."

Nicolas ate slowly, ponderously, tearing off small bits of bread and chewing carefully. His hands trembled.

Claudette smiled with pity.

"And to think I was going to warn you about eating too quickly."

She glanced at their torn-up hands, turning them at the wrist to evaluate the damage.

"Let's get you cleaned up."

Nicolas barely spoke, his desire to thank them stifled by the overwhelming gratitude he felt for these people he'd never met. He never dreamed he'd find himself sitting in such a small, modest house, eating from enamel plates, drinking coffee brewed in *grèp* cheesecloths his mother had used back in their village. He had thought the rural life was behind him, but now he'd come full circle. The unfamiliar faces of this woman and this man who doted on Raymond and on him, the sight of their smiles, filled him with joy.

Claudette led Nicolas to a bath while Raymond sat sipping coffee. He gazed at the ocean and listened to the furious roar of waves. The tide was high and the sea frothed like a rabid monster. It was not a good day to be on the water. He knew no fishermen would attempt it. Their canoes sat on the beach, painted hulls fading in the afternoon sun. The wind blew a fishing basket out of a canoe and a boy chased it into the forest of leaning palms.

"The captain is on his way."

Raymond heard Sauveur behind him. His host joined him on the steps with his own cup of coffee. He shook his head in disbelief.

"Raymond, I have to tell you, I really didn't believe you would make it," he said. "This is unprecedented."

"You set up the ambush," Raymond replied. "Why are you so surprised?"

His throat was raspy and he felt his body at last capitulating to exhaustion, but he continued to drink, hoping the coffee would keep him awake a few more minutes.

"Yes, but it was such a long shot," Sauveur said. "The men in that mission all must have died, you know. None of them have contacted us since yesterday, not even Elon."

Raymond looked at his hands.

"He didn't survive."

He explained what had happened. Sauveur stayed silent for a moment, then cleared his throat.

"He was a good man. All of them were good men, insurgents from the southern hills. Men who'd been building their own small militia to fight this government. I'd heard of their work through the grapevine, and when I put out the call, they volunteered to help. There are more like them out there. Duvalier knows that, and it terrifies him.

"Right now Port-au-Prince is a time bomb," Sauveur continued. "All they're talking about is your escape. They've set up roadblocks everywhere. You and your brother should get out of Haiti as soon as possible. So should I. Once we get you out of here, Claudette and I are packing our bags."

Sauveur reached for a box of matches in his pocket, lit his cigarette between cupped hands, and the crisp marine winds carried wafts of tobacco away from them. Raymond gazed at the ocean. It was vast, like the desert, and in the distance he saw a sailboat swaying on the waves. He squinted, but couldn't see it distinctively. He imagined the men on board struggling with the sails, fighting against the wrath of the wind. Sauveur blew more smoke.

"Don't worry," he said with calm. "Everyone here is a child of the sea, including Manno. They know what they're doing."

Raymond's stomach knotted at the sight of the captain. Spanish flowed between him and Sauveur far faster than the brothers could follow.

"We're ready," Sauveur said, and grinned. "You are following your wife and child."

The wind had dropped, and the waves were less agitated now. Sauveur spoke to the captain and folded some gourdes before shoving them into his hand. He'd pay him the rest upon return. The captain nodded toward Raymond and Nicolas.

"I know what I'm doing," the captain said. "No need to be afraid."

The boys who roamed the beach gathered to help, pulling the boat closer to shore. Then the captain motioned for Nicolas and Raymond to climb aboard. Nicolas tossed in his bag, an old rice sack that held a change of clothes and his ID card, which Eve had left with Sauveur. He got in and waited for his brother. Raymond motioned for the captain to get in, and along with Sauveur and the boys standing onshore, he pushed the boat onto the waves.

Nicolas stared back at Raymond, confused, then started to stand as his brother pushed. He gripped the gunwales to keep steady. Raymond let go of the boat and let the waves lick the keel. The water was up to his knees as he stood there, staring at Nicolas, who stammered, his hands now extended toward his brother.

"Raymond, get in. Now!"

Raymond stepped forward and gave another push. He didn't answer. He stepped where the boys stepped. They knew where to place their feet, to stop as soon as the water hit them at the thighs. The ocean floor was sometimes like quicksand underfoot, and the undertow could be deadly. Raymond looked up and met his brother's eyes. Something hurt in his chest. Instead of seeing Nicolas as he was now, he saw the face of a confused child terrified at the thought of being alone.

"What are you doing?" Nicolas shouted.

"Go on, Nicolas!" he shouted into the wind. "I'm not coming with you."

Nicolas tried to reach for Raymond and tripped over the thwart. He gripped the edges of the boat again to steady himself.

"What? What do you mean? Get in, now! Don't be ridiculous."

Raymond stopped one step ahead of the boys. The sand shifted between his toes. He looked at Nicolas and felt his ears burn with shame for not having spoken honestly about his plan. He should have told Nicolas everything. But it was better this way. Nicolas never would have understood and they would've wasted time arguing.

"We should go separately," he shouted back. "They're looking for two fugitives. We can't be seen together from now on, in case we get caught by the Macoutes. Understand? Go! Go on your own."

"No!" Nicolas shouted, his eyes bulging.

Raymond continued to wave as the captain revved the engine.

"What are you doing?" Nicolas yelled. His voice was already fading. "I'm not leaving without you. That wasn't the plan, goddamn you! Get in! Get in, Raymond."

Raymond waved again, feigning a grin, but he couldn't really smile. There went his brother, floating away toward the infinite turquoise of water. There went Nicolas, whom he felt so close to now. He knew there was another world waiting for Nicolas. A family, a book to be published, a life to be rebuilt. For him, there was nothing.

"I'll see you very soon, brother," Raymond shouted as the boat glided toward the horizon. "Go to your family. Kiss Amélie for me, and Eve."

"Raymond! Don't leave me."

"You go ahead," Raymond continued. "I have to wrap some things up here. I'll see you soon."

Nicolas clutched the boat, watching his brother disappear. The captain tapped him on the shoulder, motioned for him to sit. The waves smacked the hull of the boat like a hungry beast, and Nicolas felt the motor kick in as the captain revved it. He fell into the stern seat and looked back toward Raymond, anger searing through him. How could Raymond desert him like this, after all they'd been through? He wanted to yell at him, but it was useless. He wanted to embrace his brother once more, but it was too late. The motorboat sliced the surface of the ocean, soaring and falling back into the blue waters violently. His stomach began to churn.

"Stay low," the captain shouted.

Nicolas tried to catch his breath as a wave of nausea overwhelmed him. He watched as the bay swiftly vanished before his eyes.

He closed his eyes and held on tightly, fighting another wave of sickness. He held fast the last image of his brother waving, feet deep in the water. He was now alone with the captain. Alone with the sea. "I have to wrap some things up here," Raymond had said. What things? Why did Raymond insist on separating? What would happen to him now? If they didn't have each other to hold on to, life would push them apart again. Nicolas had found new love for Raymond. He hadn't expected to lose him again. The weight of that loss crushed him against the floor of the boat, and he curled up in the hull, his eyes burning with tears.

TWENTY THREE

Nicolas found the house at the exact address, half an hour into his walk. He realized he'd been afraid, the whole time, that it wouldn't be. That the lot would be empty. But his chest swelled when he spotted it. It was a rental, a small house painted carnation pink with white wooden doors and shutters on the windows, protected by iron bars. Jean Faustin's sister Mariette's house.

A small forest of banyan and fig trees served as a backdrop, and a patch of burned grass sprawled out front.

Nicolas caught a glimpse of a familiar silhouette out in the front yard and froze. He thought he felt his heart crack.

Eve was too far to see him. He stared right at her as she crouched in the garden below the windows. It was her. Her hips were wide, her body strong, but she looked smaller at the waist. Nicolas took a few steps forward. A few more. Was this really happening?

She did not see him, her eyes fixed on the weeds. She was stabbing at the dry earth with an old kitchen knife, uprooting a row of dandelions. Her sandals were coated in dust, and she wiped sweat from her brow with her forearm. She crouched low to the ground, skirt tucked between her legs, thighs wide apart. It was an image the old Nicolas would not have been pleased with, a scene he would have deemed undignified. But now, he simply appreciated his wife's curves, her strength as she pushed the blade into the cracked soil, the contours of her face beneath the black locks he loved to bury his face in. She was not a dream. She was real. She was here.

Nicolas swallowed hard. He willed himself to cross the street. He took in the windows and doors of the house, the clothes dangling on the line in the sunshine, the old shutters falling off their hinges. On the patio sat a tiny white chair next to a larger one. His heart melted when he noticed the details painted on its wooden spindles: little red flowers with green leaves. It was a child's chair. Amélie's chair. He was sure of it.

Nicolas stopped on the sidewalk in front of the house. Eve was just a few steps away from him. He could call her. Better yet, he could go to her, touch her shoulder or caress her hair, let her scream with joy and hold him. But instead, he stood there, trying to catch his breath. What if they didn't want him back? What if Eve was angry with him for putting them in such danger? What if she wasn't okay with being married to a fugitive? He was uncertain how to proceed, so he waited, his eyes glued on his wife.

A dog barked down the street. Nicolas, startled, dropped his sack with a thud, prompting Eve to look over. She squinted in the sun. Nicolas held his breath. God, she was beautiful! He found himself tongue-tied. All the speeches he'd rehearsed in his prison cell had now evaporated.

"Yes? Can I help you?" she asked.

Nicolas stared back, speechless. Was he that unrecognizable? He'd shaved. He'd bathed. Sure, he'd lost a few pounds and he was sweaty and tired after his trip. But this was the woman who knew him intimately. He waited for her to speak again.

Instead, she shielded her face from the sun with her hand and took another look at him. His eyes began to well up as he began walking up the path to the house. Eve sprang to her feet and gasped, dropping the knife in the bed of weeds. From the open window, Nicolas heard a soft female voice humming a familiar Haitian lullaby.

"*Dodo titit*, go to sleep, so the big bad crab won't eat you."

Her eyes were wet with tears. Slowly, she took a step forward, and another.

"Nicolas," she said. She repeated his name as she stepped toward him. "Is that you... ?" Her voice trailed off.

She flung herself at him, and, wrapping her arms around his neck, she buried her face against the protruding bones of his chest. He let his arms wrap around Eve's waist. Could she feel the difference in him? Could she tell he was not the same man? That it hurt? That he'd shed the excess and the ego, and that he had come to her, used and finished and reborn?

She was not entirely the same either. Her ribs felt hard against his arms as he squeezed. He felt her hot tears roll against his skin, soaking his shirt. Her body rippled in his arms like a broken instrument. Nicolas buried his face in her hair and breathed in love.

TWENTY FOUR

R aymond had managed to do what the government could not. He'd found out where Jules Oscar was hiding, and when the warden stepped onto the sunny sidewalk outside his mistress's house at ten o'clock in the morning, Raymond was there, waiting.

"You called for a car?"

Raymond didn't make eye contact. Before hopping out of the black Peugeot he'd borrowed, he pushed his hat low over his face and kept his eyes glued to the ground. Oscar thought nothing of it. In fact, he was too busy smoothing the wrinkles away from his gray suit. His jacket and pants had been pressed, as usual, by La Providence Dry Cleaning on Chemin des Dalles. His exorbitant tab had always been waived by the fearful owners. Raymond knew this the same way he'd learned about the warden's hiding places: cabbies.

The taxi drivers of Port-au-Prince had access everywhere and knew everything, and when Raymond had started contacting one trusted cabdriver after another, they'd kept their eyes open and driven around the neighborhoods Oscar was reputed to frequent. They made themselves available to chauffeur the help at this mistress's house, or to chitchat with the gardener at that one's.

Raymond learned what had happened: there was no absolution for Warden Jules Oscar so long as he remained in Haiti. The government was determined to hunt him down like an animal. Duvalier had announced that Oscar was personally involved in the Fort Dimanche ambush that night, that he had helped the L'Eveillé brothers communicate with rebels on the outside and escape. The way Papa Doc saw it, this was all a plot to overthrow him. A failed plot, but one facilitated by Jules Oscar.

Since then, the warden had been on the move. After being turned down for asylum by various embassies, he'd packed his belongings and fled his three-story home. He hadn't bothered to inform his wife, who'd already left months ago, tired of his humiliating infidelities. His own cars would be too easily recognizable, so he'd been using taxis to stay out of sight.

Raymond held the Peugeot's back door open and Oscar jumped in, wiping his brow with a handkerchief. Raymond shut the door. He had him.

"Where to, *patron*?" He took his place behind the wheel and avoided the warden's gaze in the rearview mirror. But Oscar was too preoccupied to bother looking. He was leafing through a passport. Raymond caught a glimpse of green American dollars in his briefcase.

"*Aéroport!* Hurry, I have a plane to catch."

Raymond took off, swerving around other cars. His hands were sweating against the steering wheel. He'd lured the animal like he wanted, and now he was not turning back. He had a plan for this son of a bitch. Raymond watched the orange-and-red flower petals, the bright pink buildings, the banners and painted signs, and the dome of the cathedral all dissolve into a blur against his windshield.

"No luggage, sir?" Raymond asked.

"Just get me there, and mind your own business!"

Raymond caught a brief glimpse of that nasty scar. His mouth filled with spit and he swallowed back the rage. He sped down narrow streets through the town of Nazon. Oscar grabbed the empty passenger seat in front of him for support. Pedestrians and bicycles swerved out of the way of the honking taxi. They merged onto the major vein of Delmas before pulling down smaller corridors, zooming past residential neighborhoods. Then Raymond veered right and drove toward a wide expanse of green—a sugarcane plantation. The rooftops of shacks and slums mushroomed on distant hills.

"What the hell are you doing?" Oscar asked. "This isn't the way to the airport."

"Don't worry," Raymond said. "I know my way."

"Turn around right now," Oscar shouted. Sweat pearled on his scarred cheek. He pulled out his handkerchief—white linen with his initials embroidered in the corner—and wiped his brow. His eyes were bloodshot, and Raymond knew he was angry.

Raymond accelerated, throwing Oscar forward.

"What are you doing? Stop the goddamn car!"

The Peugeot entered the fields at full speed. Raymond caught flashes of green as the sharp edges of leaves scraped against the vehicle's window. In the rearview mirror, he saw Oscar shut his eyes and hold his breath, as if afraid that the thick foliage would close in on him, swallow him up.

Finally, the car came to a stop in a clearing among the cane fields. Oscar opened his eyes, panting like a rabid dog.

He looked around nervously. "Where the hell are we?"

Out the window, Raymond caught a glimpse of black birds, crows, swirling above the field. He could hear their caws in the distance as they flew in formation.

"What are we doing here... ?" Oscar's voice trailed off, and he tried to maintain his composure. Raymond smirked at his wide eyes, his lips wet with fear. He had him cornered. Oscar was realizing this was no average taxi ride.

"Who are you? Have you been sent to kill me?"

Raymond killed the engine. Oscar leapt toward the door and grabbed the handle, pulled it toward him in a rage. Nothing. He slammed his fist against the door, but it wouldn't budge. He pushed against the handle for the window, then pulled up, but the glass did not move. *Now he's looking for a way out, like a real animal would*, Raymond thought. Like a rat cornered in a drain, and he was about to pour the hot water to scald the life out of him. It was only right, after all Oscar had done. He didn't deserve to live.

Oscar sat up and tried to adjust his suit. Raymond felt his blood boil as he watched in the mirror, eager for the moment of recognition.

"I don't know who you are or what they're paying you, but—" Oscar stopped and licked his lips. "Listen, I have money. I can double it. Tell me your price."

Raymond spun around and removed his hat. The warden froze in his seat.

"You?"

Oscar's eyes grew wider, and his lip curled to reveal the gold rim on his tooth. Raymond stared back, his eyes glued on the disfiguring scar. Warden and prisoner, torturer and victim, sitting in a car together face-to-face. Raymond could smell the terror seeping through Oscar's pores.

"You remember me, don't you?" Raymond said.

Oscar tried to grin, but his face distorted into a grimace. Raymond's upper lip curled in contempt. Oscar tried to open the door again to flee, but the handle came off in his hand. Raymond leaned over to the glove compartment. He turned and revealed Nicolas's revolver, the barrel aimed right between Oscar's eyes.

"Say you recognize me. Raymond L'Eveillé. Say it."

Raymond's arm trembled as he aimed at the warden's face. He'd practiced holding the Colt before. Sauveur had shown him how to use it. Yet it still felt like the first time he was touching it.

"You have some fucking nerve, you know that?" Oscar's lip quivered before speaking.

Raymond noticed. He recognized the stench of cologne coming from the backseat, the way the white shirt Jules Oscar wore now stuck to his skin. He knew fear because he'd seen it in the prisoners, in the way Nicolas's face changed every time someone was pulled out of their cell for interrogation. He knew fear because Oscar had taught him all about it. Now it was Oscar's turn.

Raymond felt his jaw twitch and his finger wrapped around the trigger.

"Who do you think you are, *hein*?" Oscar hissed, still pressing against the back door. "How dare you? You think you can just shoot me and get away with it? *Hein?* You fool! The entire country is hunting you down. They will find you, and they will kill you. You and your brother are dead men!"

"I don't care," Raymond snapped back. "You said it: We're dead men. We're already dead. So why would I let you live after what you did to my brother? To all of those people!"

Raymond adjusted himself behind the wheel, turning his body entirely to face the warden. He steadied his shaking hand with the other, gripping the revolver the way Sauveur had shown him. Men like Oscar or like the Tonton Macoutes made holding a gun look so easy, like it was a toy. A revolver meant something, weighed something, felt cold to the touch.

"I'm not afraid to die," Raymond said. "Are you?"

His voice did not waver. But his heart, pulsing in his chest, felt like a balloon ready to pop. There was a rushing in his ears that deafened him, the sound of his own blood coursing in his veins. The sun beat down on the vehicle, cooking the men inside.

Crows cawed again overhead.

"Are you?" Raymond repeated.

He knew the answer by the way the warden's eyes searched the car for a way out. There were no openings. The back doors would not give. Raymond had chosen this old Peugeot because an accident had left the doors permanently locked from the inside. The driver at the car service center, an old friend of Faton's, had guaranteed it.

"Let me out!" Oscar roared. "You can't shoot me in here like a fucking coward. You can't shoot an unarmed man."

Raymond stared at him and cocked the weapon slowly. Oscar jolted at the sound of the click. His good eye filled with tears, and Raymond hoped he would cry. He wanted to see him squirm and beg. He wanted this man reduced to his basest form, to crawl like a worm. But tears did not fall.

"That's just it. You're not a man," Raymond said. "Don't you see? You are a monster, and I will make you pay for your sins!"

He wanted to pull the trigger and see Oscar's face blasted apart, see the blood splatter. He wanted Oscar to scream, to beg for his life like his victims did in that interrogation room where he tortured Nicolas and every other man who spent the night screaming and crying, keeping others awake in their cells. He wanted Jules Oscar dead. It was his right.

"My brother is a man," Raymond said. "Nicolas L'Eveillé is a man, and you tried to break him. I am a man. And you tried to break me."

"I was doing my job," Oscar said. "Understand—I was acting under orders. I was correcting you. It was my duty."

"Shut up!" Rage spewed out of Raymond's throat like a gurgling volcano. He tightened his grip on the weapon even more, biting his lower lip. "You're a murderer!" he shouted. "You tortured all these people. You killed them."

Oscar took a breath. "My brother, I have no idea what you mean. I only do what I'm—"

"Brother?" Raymond scowled, cocked his head to the side. "I'm not your brother," he said. "You and I are nothing alike."

"You won't shoot me," Oscar said. "You don't have it in you."

Raymond saw the warden's face morph, his lips stretch into a grimace, and then he understood that the warden was smiling, a wicked, ghastly smile.

"You're a good man," Oscar continued. "A cabbie, right? A poor taxi driver. You're not a killer."

For a moment, the car was silent as they tried to inhale what was left of the air. Raymond's brain seethed. Now what? Shoot him? That was the plan, and now the plan seemed sordid. He couldn't go through with it. As much as he hated this man and wanted him to pay, Oscar was right. Raymond was not a killer. He could not pull the trigger.

He didn't react quickly enough when the warden lunged forward to grab his arm. Jules Oscar was notoriously strong, and he flung Raymond's arm to the side. He held on to him and started to smash his wrist against the dashboard. The horn blared, Raymond's back pressing against it as he fought off his opponent. The crows darted upward into the indigo sky.

Raymond pushed back and shoved his elbow into Oscar's stomach. Pain surged through his arm, but he would not let go of the revolver, and he turned it, angled his wrist to aim the barrel at Oscar. The warden's face was close to his, and Raymond suddenly found it impossible to breathe in this simmering cauldron in which he'd imprisoned himself and his worst enemy. Raymond thrust his leg forward and kicked deep with his knee, pushing Oscar into the backseat. The car rocked furiously as the men struggled, and Raymond's skin crawled with panic. He sat back up and aimed again. Oscar seized his arm once more, but let go when the gunshot tore the air.

The blood splattered like wet confetti on Raymond's face. He recoiled as he saw the warden's body fall onto the backseat, mouth ajar in surprise, eyes wide and staring at him. Under his good eye, a fleshy red hole let loose a torrent of crimson blood that ran down his face and onto his suit. Blood was everywhere, on the windows, the seats, and Raymond froze in awe. He'd shot the warden. Jules Sylvain Oscar was dead.

Raymond dropped the revolver and looked down at his hands, but he didn't recognize the sweaty yellow palms, the shaking fingers. He saw the blood on his skin. Oscar's body was bent, his neck twisted at a strange angle, like a stuffed effigy tossed in a corner after the last day of Carnaval.

Raymond dry heaved and pushed his door open, a gust of hot air assaulting him. He stumbled out and fell onto his stomach in a dry patch of grass that smelled of manure. Raymond sat up and held his head in his hands. He'd killed the warden, and yet the anger was still there, eating at his entrails.

When the sun prickled his skin like angry fire ants, he stood up with care. He looked back into the car, at the monster's body, and felt nothing but emptiness. Raymond heard the crows cawing furiously, as if talking to one another. His eyes swept the fields around him and caught a glimpse of their purplish-green feathers glistening in the sun, their beady eyes peering curiously from behind the sugarcane stalks. He looked up into the endless blue sky, marveling how undisturbed the world was when he'd just taken a life. He hadn't meant to shoot, really. Or had he? He couldn't remember anymore.

Raymond climbed back into the car. The warden's briefcase was still there. As he grabbed it by the handle, he noticed something poking out of Oscar's pocket. Raymond pulled it out, as if afraid to awaken the body. It was Oscar's passport, with those crisp American bills stacked inside the pages. Money. American money. So much of it. He blinked. He could use it to pay his rent, buy food, pay his children's tuition.

Enough with the daydreams, he thought. This money would do a lot, but it couldn't bring Enos, Adeline, and Yvonne back to him. He tossed the passport onto the body and stepped away from the car, leaving the back door open.

The crows would be hungry. They would need a way in.

Raymond walked away from the car without turning back. He entered the sugarcane field and wove his way through it, ignoring the leaves scraping his skin, the call of birds. He was alone. No one was around for miles. Money in his pocket, blood on his hands, Raymond marched forward, losing himself in the foliage.

NASSAU, BAHAMAS
1972

Nicolas wiped his face with a handkerchief that still smelled of Eve. Her lavender perfume clung to the fibers of the embroidered linen and eased his nerves. The crowd he was about to address was smaller than the ones he'd grown accustomed to in Paris. Only twenty-three people were there for his book signing, but this was the Bahamas, after all.

Half the guests were Haitians, migrants who'd fled Haiti and ended up here by accident or by fate. The others were simply curious readers who wanted to see Nicolas L'Eveillé, that man whose name was barely pronounceable in English, that brave soul who'd escaped the neighboring island of nightmares. They sat in wooden chairs in the cramped bookstore, the women fanning themselves, the men listening closely to the manager's introduction.

"Nicolas L'Eveillé's first book, *The Reaping Season*, was published in Paris last year, just two months before the death of Papa Doc. It was recently translated into English, and we are so lucky to have him here in the Bahamas to speak to us about the ordeal of our neighbors."

Nicolas wasn't comfortable reading in English, but the store manager had found a French speaker to help translate, and the manager would be reading portions in English himself. Still, it was with a pounding heart that Nicolas read. Public speaking made him immensely uncomfortable now. Plus, he still struggled with cramped spaces and darkness, and the bookstore, which sat on the flank of a hill in Nassau, was so small that he felt trapped inside a matchbox. He replayed his wife's voice in his head. "Just breathe and take your time," Eve had said. "It will be over quickly. You'll see."

He looked at the brown faces around him. They looked back eagerly.

"The book is dedicated to Mr. L'Eveillé's brother, Raymond, who valiantly helped him escape and who today has yet to be found."

Whenever someone spoke of Raymond, Nicolas felt a sharp blow, as if someone were chopping down a great tree. Raymond's disappearance had left a hole in his life that he could not fill. Life abroad, away from Haiti, was hard enough. Since he'd moved to Paris, he'd spent his days trying to conquer his anxieties, souvenirs of his incarceration in Fort Dimanche. It was difficult to step inside the small elevator in his building in the arrondissement of Ménilmontant, and his sleep was punctuated by nightmares of Jules Oscar biting his flesh like a rabid beast. When he thought of Raymond, of the last time they saw each other on that beach, Nicolas felt a crushing sadness that sat on his chest.

He was desperate for a drink. They'd offered him water at his table, but he wished he had a glass of whiskey to numb the gnawing pain in his heart.

He began to read. He'd selected the passage about just how many arrests and executions Duvalier had ordered during his presidency. He looked up from time to time and saw how the guests shook their heads in contempt and outrage. What good was this reading doing? Nicolas wondered if it wasn't all a waste of time. These folks would go back home to their families, have dinner, and sleep soundly while Haiti sank deeper into quicksand. When the news of Papa Doc's death from illness was announced, he'd felt so relieved he burst into tears in the middle of a *supermarché*, a supermarket. The Haitian population in Paris had been frenzied with joy. They'd gathered at local cafés or friends' homes and poured liquor and played music and danced. *"Bawon Samedi mouri! Vive Haiti!"* The laughter had poured out of them uncontrollably. Nicolas twirled Eve in the middle of their living room to the sound of Webert Sicot, while their friends, Haitian immigrants from neighboring apartments, clapped their hands and sang along, engaging in dances of their own, everything bumping against the furniture.

But the celebration was cut short when the news broke the next morning. The Duvalier reign had not ended. Papa Doc's nineteen-year-old son, Jean-Claude, was proclaimed his successor. Nicolas's blood ran cold. Then a neighbor in their building, another migrant from Port-au-Prince, blasted *"Duvalier Pou Tout Tan"* on the radio. *Duvalier for life.* Nicolas felt ill and confused by the absurdity of it all and stopped talking to the man.

"Maybe we shouldn't worry," Eve said. "He's young, he's not his father. Maybe things will be different now. Maybe we can go back..."

But Nicolas would not consent to returning to Haiti. It was too dangerous.

"Piti tig se tig," he said. "Tigers only birth tigers. We can't risk going back."

Nicolas looked around him now, in this bookstore, and knew that these Haitians were here for similar reasons. There was no salvation for them. They knew it was unwise to return too quickly. He read to them because he wanted to share his story, but really, this could have been their story. They were all here to escape brutal oppression.

After the applause had died down, the manager invited the audience to ask questions. Nicolas poured himself more water. He couldn't wait to get out. He needed to return to his hotel, to have a drink, to call Eve in Paris and tell her he missed her. Book tours in the Caribbean wore him down, and plus there was the fear, the persistent paranoia that one day, as he spoke, someone would walk in and shoot him in the head, or take him away, abduct him and kill him in an unknown place where they would dispose of his body. Who knew what young Duvalier's henchmen could do? That very thing had happened to Jules Oscar, after all. He'd heard the news, that the man was found dead in a field, his face half eaten by crows, blood everywhere. Nicolas had felt overwhelming relief at the news, but also a tinge of jealousy. He'd fantasized often about being the one to kill Jules Sylvain Oscar himself.

The questions they asked him at these signings were always the same. How did he do his research for his book? How did he manage to hide the manuscript for so long? Could he speak more about the efforts of others to topple Duvalier? What had happened to the other prisoners in Fort Dimanche? And mostly, what they really wanted to know: What about Raymond? What had happened to him? Nicolas wished he knew.

Raymond had disappeared off the face of the earth. Nicolas spent his nights wondering where his brother was, whether he'd been caught by the Tonton Macoutes. Maybe he'd been killed and thrown into a ditch. Sometimes he grew angry—at Raymond for lying to him and at himself for not doing more.

"I should have insisted he get on that boat with me," he said to Eve on nights when she tried to console him. "I should have put my foot down. I can't close my eyes without seeing his face, but I'm so afraid I'm going to forget him."

Nicolas looked into the audience tonight and surprised himself by saying those very words in French. The Haitians in the audience held perfectly still, while the other attendees nodded with assumed empathy, as if it made sense to them.

"My greatest fear is that one day I will wake up and forget," Nicolas said. "Forget my brother's face, forget his stature. And I fear for my daughter who will grow up not knowing or remembering her uncle, how brave a man he was."

Nicolas stopped himself. He'd said enough to an audience of strangers. What he didn't say was how often he looked at that photograph from his old office, of him and his brother at his

First Communion. Eve had saved him when she'd grabbed it, along with the research notebook full of clippings. He couldn't have rewritten his book without both of them.

Nicolas signed copies of the book and made small talk. He was tired and his collar was damp with sweat.

"It's very brave of you to write this book," said a Haitian woman, holding her book open for him to autograph. "I hear Papa Doc was furious when he heard about it."

Nicolas shrugged.

"My brother was brave," he said. "All I did was write."

When the last guests trickled out of the bookstore, Nicolas wiped his forehead and swallowed his last sip of water. The manager said he would call a car to drive him back to his hotel.

"Thank you," Nicolas said. "I'm much obliged."

He gave a few copies of the English version to the manager and kept a few for himself. He stacked them on the table and gathered his briefcase, paying no mind to the man who'd approached. He thought longingly of his hotel room, of the hot shower and soft bed.

"Taxi pour monsieur?"

Nicolas recognized the accent. Haitian. He could smell the man from across the table. He exuded a familiar, warm scent of sweat and leather. Nicolas looked up.

It took him a moment to focus, then another to recognize who it was. Nicolas's knees nearly gave out. A brown face was staring at him, lit with a mischievous smile. The eyebrows and temples were peppered with gray. The frame seemed smaller. But he was the same, he was alive. He was here.

"Raymond!" Nicolas's voice broke and he stepped back, knocking over the chair behind him. This was not possible. Nicolas wondered if he was having a heart attack.

Raymond's eyes were veiled with tears. Words eluded them both as they took each other in, hearts pounding.

"Raymond?" Nicolas repeated. "Brother, *apa se ou vre*? You're really here?"

Nicolas reached forward, squeezing Raymond's warm, dewy flesh in disbelief. This was not a dream. This was not another false alarm, like all those times he thought he'd seen a man who looked like Raymond in odd places, like the subway or in front of Amélie's school. How many times had Nicolas stopped in his tracks and called out his brother's name?

Today, it was really him. Raymond grabbed Nicolas by the wrists and the brothers locked in an embrace. Nicolas dug his fingers into Raymond's shoulders and sobbed without reserve.

Finally, Raymond stepped back and smiled. Nicolas's skin rippled with goose bumps. He watched the tears stream down Raymond's cheeks and began to nod. Now that they'd found each other, he wouldn't let go. Never again.

Raymond's eyes were red and his lashes wet. He wiped his nose with the back of his hand and looked over his brother from head to toe.

"Little brother? Is that you? Where have you been?"

Nicolas coughed and tried to swallow the knot in his throat. His head ached with a powerful, joyful migraine. He let Raymond squeeze his biceps and examine him, just like he used to do when they were younger, to make sure Nicolas was unharmed, intact, still strong.

"It's me," Nicolas managed, wiping his tears away.

"Yes, of course. Of course."

"I thought..." Nicolas found his voice. "I thought you were dead."

There was so much to say, but where to begin? He'd been so angry at Raymond for so long, and he had questions. Raymond must as well.

"All these years, and I never heard from you," Nicolas said.

Raymond nodded. "It's been a long journey, brother."

He launched into his tale quickly, scrambling to get an explanation out at once.

Life, Raymond told him, had been more than merciful. After losing his family, after Fort Dimanche, after saying good-bye to Nicolas, and after what had happened in the sugarcane fields that day, he knew life was speaking to him, screaming in his ear: "Live, Raymond. Live." So he willed himself to live.

He pocketed the warden's money and crossed over the border to find his brother, but Nicolas was long gone. It seemed the Dominican Civil War had frightened off him and Eve, and Raymond thought he'd lost them for good. When the newly elected Dominican president Joaquín Balaguer promised to send Haitian refugees back to Duvalier, and the panicked rebels vanished into thin air, he had to think quickly. What could he do? Return to Haiti? Or go elsewhere?

"I would rather die than risk ever going back to Fort Dimanche," Raymond said.

So he made the decision he'd never wanted to make: he jumped aboard a tugboat filled with refugees and made it to the Bahamas, where the captain helped him doctor papers and find work. Raymond got a driver's license and a taxi permit. He was now living in Nassau, staying well under the radar of the authorities.

"You're driving taxis," Nicolas said. Of course.

Raymond nodded. Nicolas sensed the hesitation there. This had always been a point of contention between them, this job that Raymond had done all his life. Nicolas felt his lips part and stretch into a smile.

"You are amazing," he said.

Raymond asked about his niece and about Eve. It was evening now, and outside the bookstore window, the streets filled with people headed to clubs and restaurants. Nicolas told the manager he didn't need to call a car.

"I have a ride," Nicolas said.

Nicolas grabbed his briefcase with one hand and his brother's arm with the other.

"I'm very thirsty," Nicolas said. "We could both use a drink."

"I know a place," Raymond replied.

Out on the curb, the air was spiced with sea salt, wild flowers, and notes of perfume from the hair and scarves of tourists strolling by. The brothers walked past blocks of colorful shops and boutiques like crayons in the dying sunlight.

"Look at this country," Nicolas muttered. "It's so much like home. The sun, the people. How I miss Haiti."

Raymond glanced at him. "We can't go back."

"I know," Nicolas said. "But sometimes I feel like I'm dying a slow death, dying of a broken heart. Like I've been forbidden to see an old lover."

"Always the poet," Raymond said.

Nicolas chuckled at first, then heard himself laugh. Raymond squeezed his shoulder.

"We can only move forward now," Raymond said. "I'm saving money I confiscated from that swine Oscar, to go to Miami."

"Miami?"

"My kids are there."

Nicolas gave a start, and his lips trembled in disbelief.

Raymond smiled. "I found them."

He'd never stopped calling Madame Simeus, his old landlord. And eventually Yvonne had contacted her to say they were safe.

"The U.S. Coast Guard rescued them and now they are political refugees," he said.

Raymond paused for a moment, and Nicolas imagined he was pondering the perils of their journey.

"They're with her uncle," he said.

Nicolas nearly laughed again with relief. Raymond said he was going to get to Miami to see them, maybe find a way to persuade Yvonne to come to the Bahamas. She wasn't convinced yet.

"Places have a way of changing people," Raymond said. "She's found where she wants to be. I just want to see my kids."

"Maybe I can help," Nicolas said. "We'll talk about it over drinks."

They came to a stop in front of a small car, a powder-blue Nissan.

"Is this you?" Nicolas turned to Raymond. His brother's chest was puffed outward, eyes glinting with pride.

"This is me," Raymond said. "My taxi."

They looked at the car, how clean it was, the leather seats like new, the body waxed and shiny. Nicolas looked at the reflection of his brother's face in the glass. That was what he'd missed for so long.

"Can we go for a drive?" Nicolas asked.

Raymond stared at him. Nicolas had never driven with his brother before.

"Now? Are you sure?"

"I'd like to go for a drive."

Raymond nodded. He tried to open the back door but Nicolas was already climbing in the passenger seat. Raymond, stunned, wiped away a tear before shutting the door. As he came around the vehicle and sat behind the wheel, Nicolas glanced at him but said nothing. He waited for Raymond to smile back.

The brothers relished the silence between them, and Nicolas rested his head against the seat. Raymond expertly pushed down on the clutch, put the car into gear, and began to drive.

ACKNOWLEDGEMENTS

T his book would not be possible without so many people:
My agent Charlotte Gusay, for believing in me and in this story, and for fighting tirelessly on my behalf. I'm thankful for her encouragement and that of her team at the Charlotte Gusay Agency. I'm grateful for her emails and phone calls that always light a fire under me. She is amazing at what she does.

My brilliant editor, C.P. Heiser, for helping me see the light at the end of dark tunnels when editing, and shaping the novel into what it is today with intensive labor; thank you to Olivia Taylor Smith and Amanda Armstrong, and the wonderful team at Unnamed Press for publishing and designing such a perfect cover for this book.

The MFA program at Florida International University, and the professors who taught me everything I know about writing, specifically my mentor on this project, Dr. Les Standiford, who taught me to "get the duck out of the bottle."

Professor Lynne Barrett, who taught me what plot really is, and whose advice was truly helpful after the writing process.

The voices that helped me hash out minute details about Fort Dimanche: the indomitable Jean Mapou, for patiently talking to me and sharing his personal experiences as a survivor of Fort Dimanche, and reading through the early draft process; historian Anthony Georges-Pierre; the writings of Fort Dimanche survivor Patrick Lemoine, the writings of journalist Bernard Diederich, the writings of Elizabeth Abbott, and the writings of

Gérard Pierre-Charles. Their works are a goldmine of historical events during this infamous era.

My writing hero Edwidge Danticat, for her support of this novel, and Katia D. Ulysse, who spoke prophetic, hopeful words still toll in my head.

To my solid workshop team lead by my dear friend and writer extraordinaire Corey Ginsberg, for offering honest and crucial feedback and helping me through the agony of editing. I am so lucky to be in the midst of such genius.

And thank you to the one person who is certainly fatigued by now with this story but never tells me he is (not to my face, anyways): my husband, Gordon K. Merritt.

ABOUT THE AUTHOR

Fabienne Josaphat received her M.F.A. in creative
writing from Florida International University.
Dancing in the Baron's Shadow is her first novel. She
lives in Miami.